HALO®
BATTLE BORN

HALO®
BATTLE BORN

CASSANDRA ROSE CLARKE

SCHOLASTIC INC.

© 2019 Microsoft Corporation. All Rights Reserved. Microsoft, Halo, the Halo logo, and 343 Industries are trademarks of the Microsoft group of companies.

All rights reserved. Published by Scholastic Inc., *Publishers since 1920.* SCHOLASTIC and associated logos are trademarks and/or registered trademarks of Scholastic Inc.

The publisher does not have any control over and does not assume any responsibility for author or third-party websites or their content.

No part of this publication may be reproduced, stored in a retrieval system, or transmitted in any form or by any means, electronic, mechanical, photocopying, recording, or otherwise, without written permission of the publisher. For information regarding permission, write to Scholastic Inc., Attention: Permissions Department, 557 Broadway, New York, NY 10012.

This book is a work of fiction. Names, characters, places, and incidents are either the product of the author's imagination or are used fictitiously, and any resemblance to actual persons, living or dead, business establishments, events, or locales is entirely coincidental.

Library of Congress Cataloging-in-Publication Data available

ISBN 978-1-338-25364-1

10 9 8 7 6 5 4 3 2 1   19 20 21 22 23

Printed in the U.S.A.   23

First printing 2019

Cover illustration by Antonio Javier Caparo

Book design by Betsy Peterschmidt

CHAPTER ONE

EVIE

Evie waited until her father was grading student projects before she approached his door. He always said that he hated to be interrupted during grading, but over the years, Evie had learned the opposite was true, that really he was grateful for the break. It meant he was more likely to say yes to whatever it was she wanted to do.

This discovery was a tactical maneuver Evie was careful not to overuse. But she suspected she would need it for the concert.

She knocked lightly on his office door. "Yes?" he called out tersely—grading did that to him. Evie slid the door open.

"I know you said not to interrupt you while you're grading . . ." Evie leaned up against the wall and pulled her hands into the sleeves of her sweater. The room was dim, the overhead lights turned down low so that her dad could see the hologram projections more clearly.

"It's fine." He darkened the projector, flipped on a desk lamp, and then leaned back in his chair, like she was one of his students showing up for office hours. "What's up?"

"I was wondering . . ." She took a deep breath, then spilled the rest out in a rush. "IwaswonderingifIcouldgotoaconcerttonightwithVictor."

Her dad frowned, scrunching his forehead up. "Did I just hear you ask to go to a concert? Tonight?"

Evie nodded. "Everyone's going," she said, a little breathlessly. "This guy from school, his band is playing, plus some other bands from Port Moyne."

Her dad's frown deepened.

"I'll be there with Victor," Evie said. "Please? Nothing cool like this ever happens here." *And it's not like you ever let me go to Port Moyne with you.* Port Moyne wasn't much, but it was the biggest town next to their little seaside village of Brume-sur-Mer, big enough that it had a University of Meridian campus.

Where her dad taught.

Where his students lived.

Maybe she shouldn't have mentioned the Port Moyne bands.

"Shouldn't you be studying?" her dad asked.

"I did my homework already." This, she was prepared for. "Including the extra credit for Mr. Garbett's computer science class."

Her dad smiled, the worry vanishing out of his features. "Good. That Mr. Garbett doesn't challenge you enough. Was the extra credit difficult?"

Not really, but Evie figured a white lie might help her case. It was very important to her father that she be Challenged. "Totally," she said. "Definitely harder than the usual work."

"That's good." Her father rubbed at the few days' growth of salt-and-pepper stubble on his chin. "Victor will be with you?"

She nodded.

"His parents are okay with this?"

"Of course."

Usually the approval of the Gallardos was enough to swing her father, but tonight he just kept rubbing at his chin. The frown had come back too. Evie tugged at her sweater's sleeves. The rain had picked up again and was pattering softly against the windows of her father's office, its soft, constant rhythm hinting at the impending rainy season.

"I don't know," her dad said. "I'm not sure a *concert* is a good place for someone like you."

Evie resisted the urge to roll her eyes. Hope fluttered inside her chest, though, since her dad had just given her an opening to use her best weapon in the war of father-daughter negotiations. She took a deep breath.

"I think Mom would want me to go."

Her dad sighed, the universal sign of parental defeat. Evie didn't want to take her chances, though.

"I mean, every time I talk to her, she tells me I need to do something besides studying. That I need to go out and experience the world."

Her dad shook his head. "Your mother is too adventurous for her own good." He paused. "But I suppose you going to a concert for one night won't hurt anything."

Evie shrieked with delight and threw her arms around her father's neck. "Oh, thank you, thank you! Victor's going to be so excited—he didn't want to go by himself. You're the best, Dad." She kissed him on the cheek.

"Yeah, yeah. Now get out of here so I can finish my grading. And remember that your curfew is still in place!"

"I know!" Evie bounded over to the door and gave her dad a little wave. He flicked the holo-projector back on in response.

Evie stepped out into the hallway and let the door ease shut behind her. The house was quiet except for the rain falling across the roof. Maybe it wasn't *entirely* fair to bring her mom into it, but it was true—Evie's mom was always telling her to go out and rebel. "Just a little," she'd say, smiling through the transmission's interference. "Evie, you're almost eighteen. Don't let your dad keep you locked up like his little scholarly princess." And Evie's dad would scoff at that, shake his head, and her mom, every time, would say, "My rebellious streak is why your father married me," with a sly little smile that made Evie's dad blush.

Evie's mom was a soldier, which was weird for Evie to think about. She hadn't always been a soldier. But five years ago she had enlisted in the United Nations Space Command and disappeared into the starry night sky to fight aliens. Sometimes when Evie thought about it, her chest would get hard and tight, like a fist was squeezing around her heart. Her father told her she should be proud, and she was. But her mom being gone meant the house always felt empty and echoing, like it couldn't make sense of the blank space where Evie's mother should be.

Evie shook her head—her mom wouldn't want her getting morose like this. In fact, her mom was going to be thrilled during the next transmission, when Evie told her all about the concert. Her first concert! Excitement arced down Evie's spine—excitement and anxiety. She needed to get ready. She had to figure out what someone would wear to a concert, especially this concert, which was happening down in the old town bomb shelter. At least her dad hadn't asked about *that*. Probably he assumed it would be at the meeting hall downtown.

Evie scurried up to her bedroom, heart pounding, her thoughts flipping through the latest VR concert she'd watched of her favorite bands. VR was fun—but now she was going out, *really* going out. And for the moment, at least, the house seemed a lot less empty.

Victor was waiting for her in the usual spot, beneath the big banyan tree that grew at the entrance to her neighborhood. He lived across the highway, down on the beach, where his parents owned a seaside motel. He also had a car, which idled beside the tree, the headlights shining on the thick, draping vines and on Victor, who stood out in the rain with his comm pad focused on something up in the tree.

"What are you doing?" Evie called out.

"Shhh." Victor tilted the comm pad up. Evie crept over to him and held the umbrella over his head—not that he noticed. Too involved in his art.

Evie leaned over his shoulder, peering at the image on the comm pad's view screen. The car's headlights carved the tree branches into shadows, but there was something moving in the darkness.

"A sardans cat," Victor breathed softly. "I've never seen one in the wild before."

Evie scanned the tree branches until she saw a pair of glowing yellow eyes set into a round face with tufted ears. The cat clung to the branches, its long, sleek body hunched up tight, its tail dangling like a hook.

"What's it doing so close to town?" she whispered. Sardans cats lived deep in the surrounding forests, stalking through the thick, lush overgrowth. They were terrified of humans and never came into town. Or, almost never, apparently.

"I don't know." Victor took a hesitant step forward. The cat stared at him warily with its bright eyes. The end of its tail twitched. Rain whispered around them.

There was a sudden crack of thunder, a brilliant flash of lightning. In the explosion of light, the cat dove out of the tree's branches and disappeared down the dark, rainy highway.

"Well, that was cool while it lasted." Victor stopped recording and slipped the comm pad back into his pocket.

"How'd you even see it?" Evie stared up at the now-empty tree branches in wonder. "I mean, I could barely make it out, and I was looking for it."

Victor opened his car door. "Lucky shot. It ran in front of me while I was driving. I swerved and saw it go up the tree."

Evie peered up at the tree a few seconds longer. A sardans cat showing up in town. It felt like an omen, like some secret message from the universe. Not that Evie believed in that sort of thing. But the forests were protected land. No one could build out there—what could possibly have drawn it so far away from its home?

A blare of a car horn. Evie jumped. Victor waved at her from behind the windshield. "Come on!" he shouted. "It's gone, and I'm freaking freezing."

Evie smiled. "Shouldn't have stood out in the rain," she called, before climbing into his car. She shook the rain off the umbrella as best she could and tossed it in the back seat. Victor had turned the heater on and ruffled his damp hair at the vents.

"Yeah, but it was the shot of a lifetime," he said. "Once I get that up on my comm channel, it'll be great exposure."

"People do love cat videos."

Victor snorted and gave his hair one last shake, then put the car into gear and pulled out onto the freeway. "A sardans cat. Crazy."

"Yeah." Evie looked at the patterns of raindrops forming on the window. She could almost make out her reflection in the darkened glass. "I wonder what it was doing out here."

"I bet the UNSC is screwing around in the forest." Victor tapped the steering wheel. "Running training exercises and stuff. We should sneak out there and try to record them."

"Are you kidding me?" Evie laughed, "What would your sisters say about that?"

Victor glanced at her sideways. "They would say it was totally bad-ass."

"They would not." Victor's sisters had both joined up with the

UNSC when they finished high school. His oldest sister, Camila, had actually served under Evie's mother at some point, although they didn't see each other much now. Once when Camila came back to visit, she showed Victor and Evie how to fire her rifle, and they went out to the beach and shot at the sand dunes, the sand glittering as it exploded in the sun. Evie's mom, in contrast, refused to talk about the fighting when she was home. "Just let me pretend things are normal for a weekend," she always said, stretched out on the hammock in their backyard.

"Anyway," Evie said, "I doubt it's UNSC. The forests around here are protected, remember? And they wouldn't train so close to civilians anyway."

Victor shrugged. "There are, like, five hundred people in this town. We barely count as civilization."

Well, that was true enough. It only took ten minutes to drive from the banyan tree to the other edge of town, where the main entrance to the shelter was located. Evie suspected other concertgoers would trickle in from the other entrances closer to the center of town, winding their way through the maze of tunnels to the concert space. Outside the entrance, the houses were big and sprawling, designed to look like chateaus from old Earth. They were also empty and overgrown these days. Before Evie was born, rich people from all over the galaxy used to come vacation in Brume-sur-Mer, but the war put an end to that. Now rich Meridians didn't want to travel here. And so the beautiful stone palaces where they used to stay had started to crumble and fall back to the forest.

"Where is this thing again?" Victor grumbled.

"The entrance? I thought you knew."

"I know the general *area*—oh. Never mind, I found it."

They had turned a corner, and the entrance was impossible to miss—lit up with a couple of blue spotlights, cars parked haphazardly on the street around it, clumps of unfamiliar people spilling out into the overgrown yard of one of the vacation homes. Everyone had long, glossy hair, their eyes painted with luminescent makeup. Evie knew, seeing them, that her own makeup was all wrong. Too understated, too subtle.

Victor drove up to the curb in front of the vacation home and killed the engine. Then he pulled out his comm pad.

"Are you really going to film this whole thing?" she asked.

"Yeah." Victor made a show of rolling his eyes. "I told Dorian I would."

"Since when do you talk to Dorian Nguyen?"

Victor scowled. "We're in calculus together. He saw me screwing around with my channel and asked if I could film the show tonight."

Evie shrugged, more surprised that someone like Dorian was taking calculus.

They both climbed out of the car, and Victor stumbled around with his comm pad, taking in shots of the crowd and the dilapidated houses. Evie ambled over to the entrance to the shelter, where a tall man with a scraggly beard was scanning people's IDs and collecting the ten-credit entrance fee.

"You coming in or not?" he barked at her.

Evie jumped and glanced over at Victor, who was lurking next to a streetlamp, trying to film a pair of particularly gruesome-looking concert-goers, their faces streaked with purple and white makeup and their hair twisted up into vicious spikes. They hadn't seemed to notice Victor yet.

"Just a second," she said, and she marched over to him and grabbed his forearm.

"Hey!"

"Don't film people without permission," Evie said. "Plus, you said you'd buy my ticket. Since I got lunch the other day."

"How do you know I didn't have their permission?" Victor grumbled, although he was fumbling around in his pocket for his credit chips.

"Like you would have the guts to talk to those two guys. They look like they're part of the Covenant."

Victor grinned. "Yeah, that's the whole thing with these bands! It's for the shock value."

Easy enough to do something like that out on Meridian, Evie thought, irritated. They were far enough from the fighting that the Covenant felt distant. As distant as her mother.

As promised, Victor paid for Evie's ticket, and the bouncer activated something in their ID chips to note that they were both underage. Then he let them into the narrow, dank stairwell that led down the shelter. Music clanked off the walls—a shriek of a guitar, some disconsolate banging of drums—but mostly the stairs were filled with excited, echoing voices. Probably the most people who had been down here since the things were built. That was assuming, of course, you accepted the official story, that the shelter had been built at the start of the Human-Covenant War so that the rich tourists would be protected in case of an attack. But rumors floated around that the shelter was even older than that, that it had been used during the Insurrection, as protection for the rebels, the Sundered Legion. It was all ancient history these days. But still, Evie felt that quiver of the past as she clomped down the stairs in her mom's old boots. At least she'd worn the right shoes.

The stairwell opened up into a cavernous metal-clad room, mostly empty save for the people pressed around a stage that had been set up on the far side. The walls were mottled and streaked with what, for a jolted moment, Evie thought was blood—but no, it was just rust, running in thin stripes through the old metal. The floor was paved with concrete, save for a grated gap cutting through the room. Evie wandered over to it, peered down into the darkness.

"To stop flooding," Victor said.

Evie jumped. "What?"

"My dad explained it to me. They were worried about the shelter flooding during the rainy season, so they built rivers into it." He leaned over the grating, his dark hair falling across his eyes. "Not much in there yet."

"Huh." Evie poked at the grating with her toe. It wobbled in its frame. "Weird."

"Yeah, especially since it's not like we get tourists during the rainy season." Victor whipped out his comm pad and turned on the video recorder. He took a long shot of the grating. "My dad says it wasn't built for the tourists at all, you know."

Evie rolled her eyes. "Yeah, yeah, I know the stories. But it's not like the town doesn't need shelter too."

Victor shrugged and kept filming. Evie scanned the crowd, looking for anyone she knew. A couple of girls from her colonial history class were there, standing in a circle over in the corner, and she spotted a handful of people she recognized from the hallways.

"Hey, there's your boyfriend," she said, nudging Victor.

"What?" He blinked up at her. She pointed to a spot next to the speakers.

"Dorian. He's the whole reason you're here, right?"

"We talk sometimes. God's sake, Evie." Victor swung his comm pad around, taking in the crowd. Over at the speakers, Dorian lounged against the rust-streaked wall, tapping furiously on his own comm pad, holo-light shining into his face. He wasn't like any of the other boys at their school. He had the same long hair as the Port Moyne guys, and his clothes always seemed frayed at the edges, like they were on the verge of unraveling. Plus, he skipped class, like, all the time.

Evie left Victor to his filming and ambled closer to the crowd at the stage. The band was taking their places, picking up their instruments, sending a few jagged guitar chords out into the world. Dorian had slipped onstage too, behind the holographic impressions of an elaborate QJ setup. One of the guitarists gave him a head jerk of acknowledgment.

They began playing almost immediately, not bothering to announce themselves, just releasing a torrent of music that burned in Evie's ears. The crowd started jumping around, and Evie wriggled her way to the back, away from the crush of bodies. Then she stood awkwardly, unsure what to do with her hands. She caught sight of Victor with his comm pad, trying to move closer to the stage. The band thrashed around, and the lead singer howled lyrics in that half-English, half-French pidgin old people used sometimes. Evie slid farther and farther back, away from the noise and the tumult.

She bumped up against someone, and her face flushed hot with embarrassment. When she turned around to apologize, she was startled to see Saskia Nazari slouching coolly behind her.

"Oh," she said, then realized there was no way Saskia could hear her. "I'm sorry," she shouted.

Saskia shrugged in that offhand way she did everything. Her bare shoulder poked out of the drape of her fashionable silk dress. She looked even more out of place than Evie did.

Evie took a few steps away and crossed her arms over her chest. She couldn't stop herself from glancing sideways at Saskia, though, who stood with one hand on her hip, her head tilted to the side, her body bouncing slightly to the beat of the music. It was disconcerting seeing her here, in this run-down shelter, listening to a local band torment their instruments. Disconcerting still to see that she seemed to be enjoying herself.

The band finished their first song, and the lead singer screamed something into the microphone that might have been the band's name.

Saskia applauded with her hands in the air. So *weird*. She never talked to anyone during school, just sat in the middle row of her classes in her expensive, stylish clothes, always looking bored out of her mind. Afterward she vanished to that huge locked-down house set deep in the woods on a strip of private beach. Her parents did something with weapons manufacturing. Tourists who decided to become local.

Evie wondered where Victor had scurried off to; filming Saskia was exactly the sort of thing he'd want to do, especially with the way the crowd seemed to part around her, like she was carting around one of her parents' experimental weapons. Plus, Evie had seen the way Victor looked at Saskia whenever she brushed past him at school. Like she was a work of art.

Everything in the shelter cut out.

The stage lights, the music, even the safety lighting in the stairwell: All of it vanished, and the room slid from a swirl of sound and chaos into a void. But only for a split second, before everyone started shouting like little kids afraid of the dark. Comm pads came out, transformed into spheres of light that bobbed in the darkness. Evie pulled out her own comm pad and turned on the light and shone it around. She spotted Victor loping toward her, the record light on his comm pad still blinking. Of course. He was probably lapping this up.

"What happened?" she asked.

"Circuit likely blew. I'm sure the wiring in this place is complete crap."

Evie frowned. Then a hundred alarms went off at once. Everyone's comm pad lit up with blue and red lights, and the voice of Salome, the town's artificial intelligence, came spilling out of all of them, speaking in unison with itself:

"Attention, citizens of Brume-sur-Mer. A power failure has been noted—"

"It's all over town?" Evie said.

"—and I'm in the process of fixing it up again. Hold tight!"

The red and blue lights blinked out; the crowd grumbled.

"Think it was the storm?" Victor asked.

"That wasn't a storm," Evie said. "Just some rain. And it wouldn't have knocked out power to the whole—"

The lights came back on. Not just the stage lights, but the overhead lights too, flooding the room with a sallow, flickering glow. Up on stage, Dorian hit a key on the computer, releasing a wave of some distorted, sampled audio, and the band took up playing like nothing had happened.

CHAPTER TWO

DORIAN

Dorian pressed his head against the seat of his uncle Max's truck and sucked in a deep breath as they made their way down the bumpy road. Uncle Max's antique junker was a bone-rattling reminder that not everyone could afford gravity compensators. At least the light was gray and misty from the rain, so there was no blazing tropical sun beating down on him.

He'd stayed out late last night, lounging around at the party after the show. They'd broken into the old tourist house and sat in the moldering living room strumming their guitars while the rain drizzled incessantly outside. He'd snuck in a little before dawn and collapsed into bed, only to be woken a few hours later by his uncle, who'd nudged him and said, "Get up. Need your help with a job."

So here he was, bumping along some muddy back road toward the town's fusion reactor. It was one of the few things in town not managed by Salome, Brume-sur-Mer's resident AI, as it lay too far outside the city limits. Which left it to the humans to deal with problems.

"It's your fault," Uncle Max said, "staying out till all hours."

Dorian just looked out the window at the blur of wet greenery growing along the side of the road. "Lost track of time," he finally mumbled.

Uncle Max scoffed. "You're as bad as your mother was."

Dorian didn't want to talk about his mother. Didn't want to talk about either of his parents, who'd decided that fighting a war was more important than having a son.

Uncle Max pulled up to the fusion reactor station, a flat slab of gray concrete blinking with warning lights and the metal tube of the reactor itself. Even from the truck, Dorian could tell everything was fine. The reactor's activity light winked at them, bright in the gray haze of the day.

"Let's see what we can find," Uncle Max said, stepping out of the car. Dorian followed, his temple pounding. At least Uncle Max always split his wages fifty-fifty when Dorian came along. He was fair that way.

"It looks fine," Dorian said. "Probably just a fluke last night."

"It certainly didn't mess up your plans any." Uncle Max flashed a grin at him, and Dorian scowled in response.

"The power cut out in the middle of our set. Threw us off for the rest of the night."

They trudged through the calf-high grass toward the station. Dorian's boots sank into the mud. The forest pressed in around them, a tangle of green shadows. This was as far out as the town was allowed to build—something about the forest being protected wilderness. It looped like a semicircle around the town, pushing it up against the shoreline.

"Let's see what we got here." Uncle Max punched in the access code on the control panel, then waited for the facial recognition scan. A half second later, the control panel popped open.

While Uncle Max worked, Dorian walked around the edge of the cement slab, listening to the insects chittering around in the forest.

He pinched the bridge of his nose, willing the pain in his head to go away. He wasn't sure if Uncle Max had brought him out because he really needed the help, or because he was just trying to teach him a lesson.

But then Dorian noticed an imperfection on the smooth, glossy surface of the reactor. He knelt down and pressed his fingers against it, and they came back flaked with black ash. A scorch mark.

"Hey!" he shouted. "I think I figured out what caused the outage."

Uncle Max stuck his head around the generator. "What'd you find?"

Dorian motioned toward the scorch mark. His uncle knelt beside him, frowning.

"Looks like a bullet mark," Dorian said.

"How do you know what a bullet mark looks like?" Uncle Max peered at him sideways. "You better just be playing music when you're staying out till all hours."

"Everyone knows what a bullet mark looks like."

"There's no dent in the metal." Uncle Max rubbed his finger over the black mark, smearing the ash with the rainwater. "But the metal's damaged for sure. Look at that. Burned." He peered closer. "I wonder how deep it goes. Call up Salome, will you?"

Dorian pulled out his comm pad. "Salome," he said, speaking into the local Brume-sur-Mer channel. "We need you."

"What's up, Dorian Nguyen?" Salome spoke with an old-Earth-style French accent, although at some point the city council had decided to update her to sound more modern. The result was a mother trying too hard to sound cool to her teenage kids.

Uncle Max took the comm pad from Dorian. "Salome, play back the security footage from the power station last night." He looked over at Dorian. "Could you turn the holo on for me? I can never remember how to work this thing."

"Just swipe right there." Dorian showed him. A second later, the holo switched on, revealing a transparent woman with long, glowing hair and clothes twenty years out of date.

"Running the footage now," she said. "But I didn't notice anything out of the ordinary. I would have mentioned it."

"There's a scorch mark on the reactor," Uncle Max said. "You really didn't notice anything?"

Salome frowned. "You should know I can't access the reactor's systems."

Uncle Max sighed. "I know, but you had to have noticed something unusual on the security footage."

Salome tilted her head. "Perhaps. Let me run it for you."

Salome vanished in a streak of blue light, which stretched out until it became a shot of the reactor station. The surrounding trees trembled with rain. Then—

A flash of white near the reactor. A trickle of smoke. Then nothing.

"The hell was that?" Dorian asked. "Lightning?"

"No lightning appeared in the area," Salome chimed in, her disembodied voice floating out of the comm pad.

"You didn't think this was worth reporting?" Dorian said. "This—whatever? Look at the time stamp."

"Yeah. I see it," said Uncle Max. 19:48.

"Right in the middle of our set."

"Salome?" Uncle Max said. "Any suggestions?"

Salome's holographic form materialized again. She gave a jaunty shrug. "'Fraid it didn't ping any of the usual threats."

"You said there was no damage to the reactor," Uncle Max said.

"There isn't. It's working quite fine, as far as I can tell from its effects in town. Any of the damage you see is purely cosmetic." She flipped her hair; the hologram shimmered in a gust of damp wind.

Uncle Max sighed. "Fair enough. Let me run a diagnostic just to be sure. Dorian? Some help?"

"See you later, Salome," Dorian said. She waved goodbye and flipped her hair again.

Dorian switched off his comm pad and leaned up against the reactor while Uncle Max ran back to the truck to get the mapping scanner. The wind blew harder, bringing with it more rain. So something sparked against the reactor last night and shut down the power for a couple of minutes. It really did look like a gunshot. What was it the Covenant used? Plasma rifles? He'd seen images on the comm channel like everyone else, bursts of violet light that incinerated whatever they touched.

But even if the Covenant made it to Meridian, Brume-sur-Mer was a middle-of-nowhere town. Why would the Covenant even bother?

Still, Dorian squinted into the dark green of the forest, looking for monsters among the rain and ferns and tangled vines.

Uncle Max got a notification as they were driving home from the reactor. "Looks like Mr. Garzon's having some trouble down at the docks. Roof's leaking all over the dry storage again. Got some other jobs for us too."

"Fine." Dorian's headache was starting to fade.

"Didn't give you a choice." Uncle Max laughed. "Still, want to swing by the house first. Make sure Remy's doing okay."

"Wait, you left him alone?" Dorian jerked his gaze away from the window and over to his uncle. "He's only eight years old, man!"

"Left you alone when you were eight. He was all wrapped up in those comm channel games. I'll bet he hasn't moved from the living room."

Dorian crossed his arms over his chest and returned to his vigil of the overgrown road. He hated when Uncle Max left Remy alone. Little kids shouldn't be abandoned liked that.

They pulled up to the house ten minutes later, the road emerging suddenly out of the forest and dumping them unceremoniously onto the beach. White-capped waves dragged seaweed toward the shore. The sky, the water, the sand—everything was gray from the rain.

Dorian jumped out of the car and took the steps to the front door of the house two at a time. Not that it mattered—he spotted Remy through the window in the door, and just like Uncle Max said, he was sprawled out on the rug beside the couch, a headset pulled over his eyes.

Dorian slipped in quietly and crept over to where Remy was playing his game. He was still wrapped up in it when Dorian pounced, grabbing him around the shoulders. Remy shrieked and tore off his headset.

"I was just about to kill that guy!" Remy shouted. "You made me miss."

Dorian shrugged. "Just keeping you on your toes."

Remy swung a tiny fist at Dorian's shoulder, and Dorian curled up in fake pain, howling like he did when he was performing with his band. Remy giggled and kept hitting him while Dorian writhed around.

"Knock it off, you two." Uncle Max clomped into the house. "Remy, you doing okay?"

"I was," Remy said, before giving Dorian a final, decisive punch. "But then Dorian came and *ruined* my game."

"I didn't ruin anything," Dorian said. "It's a game. You'll get another chance to kill Hinfelm the Horrible."

"Remy, don't you have something more productive to do than sit around playing games all day?" Uncle Max pulled open the hall closet door and switched the light on, then fumbled around in the mess of tools and beach toys.

"No."

Dorian grinned and bumped Remy's fist.

"Now, that's just not true." Uncle Max emerged from the closet with his tattered black supply bag. "I seem to remember giving you a list of chores to get done today."

Remy shrugged.

"I want 'em done by the time me and Dorian get back," Uncle Max said. "We're going down to the docks. Should be back in a couple of hours." He jerked his head toward Dorian. "You ready?"

Dorian lounged back on the couch. "You really need me? I can stick around here—"

"Yes, I need you." Uncle Max shouldered the bag. "Somebody's got to fly that scud-rider."

Dorian felt a surge of excitement, not that he let Uncle Max see it. "I thought you said the roof was leaking."

"It is. But he also needs somebody to fly out and adjust the signal towers. Too choppy to take a boat, and it's something Salome can't fix on her own. Must need a power cell." He pushed the door open.

Dorian leaned over Remy. "Don't get too much work done," he whispered.

"I won't," Remy said.

"Stop encouraging him."

Dorian jumped off the couch and strolled across the living room. The rain was picking up again. Nice. He always did enjoy a challenge when it came to flying.

They loaded up Uncle Max's truck with some old plywood for the leaky roof and then headed on their way. Dorian's comm pad chimed—it was Xavier, the guitarist for Drowning Chromium.

"Girlfriend?" Uncle Max said.

"No."

"Boyfriend, then?"

"Wrong again." Dorian opened up the message:

HEY MAN, GREAT NEWS. TOMAS REYNÉS SAW OUR SHOW LAST NIGHT AND WANTS US FOR TONIGHT. BOAT SHOW, OUT AT SEA. YOU IN?

Dorian grinned. **HELL YEAH,** he wrote back. Then he shoved the comm pad back in his pocket and said, "Don't make any work plans for me tomorrow. We got another gig."

Uncle Max glanced at him. "Oh yeah? Well, congratulations. I mean that."

Dorian smiled a little and ducked his head to hide the blush. Uncle Max gave him a hard time, but he wasn't so bad. Better than Dorian's parents, who didn't even bother to send transmissions most of the time.

They arrived at the docks a few minutes later. The place was shut down for the season, all the boats tucked away in storage. During the dry season, Uncle Max would take tourists out on trips around the bay. He usually roped Dorian into helping him too. Not that they got many tourists these days.

Mr. Garzon was waiting for them outside, standing underneath the overhang. He lifted one hand in greeting.

"You sure you can fly that thing in this weather?" Uncle Max asked, slapping Dorian on the shoulder. "Rain's picking up."

"I've flown in worse." It was Mr. Garzon who'd taught him to fly, actually, a couple years ago, before Dorian got into music and joined up with Drowning Chromium. He'd said Dorian had the knack for it and ought to consider joining the UNSC, a suggestion that left the air bitter. Like his parents, that was the implication. Even then Dorian hadn't wanted to be like them, though he did like flying.

Dorian jumped out of the truck and ambled over to Mr. Garzon, not minding the patter of rain. Mr. Garzon nodded at him. "Still haven't cut that hair, I see."

Dorian shrugged.

"Where's the leak?" Uncle Max said.

"Left side of the structure. Let me get Dorian up to speed, and then I'll be over there to help."

Uncle Max nodded and vanished around the corner of the building.

"What's up?" Dorian asked.

Mr. Garzon nodded toward the ocean. "Having trouble with the light signals out there. Blinked out during the power outage last night and never came back on. Salome didn't see anybody messing with them either. Water's too choppy to take a boat out."

Dorian frowned, wondered if he would find scorch marks on the light signals like he did the reactor. But he didn't say anything to Mr. Garzon beyond "Sure, I can check it out."

"I'll pay you separate. Don't let Max try to claim halfsies on it." He grinned. "Use it for a haircut."

Dorian rolled his eyes. "Rider in the usual place?"

"Sure is." Mr. Garzon threw the key at Dorian, and it blinked, recognizing his fingerprints. Dorian tossed it up, caught it, then made his way over to the hangar next door. The scud-rider wasn't much—the cheap thing couldn't even leave atmosphere. But Dorian had learned to fly on it. He had a soft spot for the old pile of junk.

The key opened the warehouse doors, letting in the gray light from outside. Inside was a small, solitary aircraft—scud-riders were single-pilot puddle jumpers originally designed for monitoring coastal territories, and fitted with buoyant skids to take off and land on the water if necessary. Dorian hopped up into the rider just as the hatch creaked open. He slipped easily into the worn-out seat and shoved the key into place. The controls booted up immediately, but the engine rumbled in distress until Dorian reached out the open hatch and thumped the side of the rider hard with his free hand. Lights flickered into place on the controls and along the side of the rider's interior. His heart thudded in his chest, the same thrill he got playing in the shelter last night, seeing all those people jumping around in the dark to his music. Flying and playing both took over his whole body. They made it so he didn't have to think about anything else in the universe. Not his parents, not Uncle Max, not school, not anybody. He could just plug himself in like a machine and do something he wasn't a total screw-up at.

He eased the throttle forward, and the rider glided out of the hangar, into the gray curtain of rain. He pulled the rider over to the launchpad and slapped his palm against the glowing Ignite button. The rider jerked straight up in the air, rain spattering across the windows. Low visibility. A challenge—just the way he liked it.

Dorian punched in his course—he had the path to the light signals memorized—and then brought up the holo-map and set it over the rain-soaked windshield. He always started with the light signal that was the farthest away, the one out in the deep ocean. It was nice to get some real flying in before he had to stop every couple of minutes and run diagnostics.

He pulled back on the throttle, twisting it with the weight of his body, then took off following the holo's trajectory, heading out to sea. They'd be playing somewhere around here tonight—Tomas Reynés's boat shows were unauthorized, so you never knew the exact location until you got the message from Tomas himself. But they were always at sea, as far from the land as he could get them. No sound restrictions out there. No chance of the cops shutting you down for other reasons either.

Dorian pushed the scud-rider up to a higher altitude, plunging into the gray rain clouds. He had no real reason to go this high, not with as short a distance as he needed to cover, but he kept climbing in altitude anyway, the rider rattling around him.

Then he erupted out of the clouds. Sunlight poured through the windshield, drowning out the holo. Dorian straightened the rider and cruised forward, over the clouds. They looked like the ocean, gray and churning. He tapped the holo, adjusted for the sunlight. He'd already overshot the light signal.

So Dorian yanked back on the throttle again, pulling the rider around in a tight, thrilling loop. Bits of cloud whipped up around him. Then he pointed the rider in the right direction and killed the ignition; the rider dropped with a sickening lurch, plunging him down into the clouds again. Dorian whooped with exhilaration as the g-forces of his plummet pressed against his skin. He closed his eyes, and the pressure throbbed against his temple like music.

Then he reached down and activated the engine and pulled the rider up just as he dropped out of the clouds, swooping up, leaving a parabola of smoke in his wake. The first light signal was up ahead, close enough that he could see it through the rain-smeared windshield, a smudge of darker gray against the endless sweep of gray ocean.

Dorian glided the rider to a stop on top of the waves, then threw the stabilizers into place. He told the hatch to open and crawled out, his whole body electrified after flying through the cloud layer.

Rain and seawater sprayed against his face, bringing him back to his dreary reality. It was easy to feel like Brume-sur-Mer was a distant dream when you were up in a scud-rider. Sucked that he only really got to do this when Mr. Garzon needed help around the docks.

Time to see what was wrong with these light signals.

Dorian balanced in the hatchway, the wind whipping his hair into his face. He took a deep breath and then jumped, landing easily on the side of the light signal. The thing was dead for sure. No humming from its generator. Dorian crawled around the circumference of the signal until he found the service panel and flipped it open.

Stopped.

Blinked the water out of his eyes.

No, he'd definitely seen correctly—the wiring inside the signal was nothing but crispy black twists, already washing away in the rain. Dorian slammed the panel shut. The wiring in those things was literally fried.

He opened the panel again, trying to shield it from the rain with his body. He knew better than to stick his hands in there while it was raining, but something told him there weren't any electrical currents to zap him anyhow. He peered inside, lighting up the blackened wiring with the light from his comm pad. It wasn't just the wiring. The circuit board, the metal casing—all of it looked burned.

Dorian closed the panel and took a careful step back. There didn't seem to be any damage on the exterior of the signals. No black scorch marks. And Salome supposedly hadn't seen anyone out here when they blinked out.

Dorian crawled back into the rider and pulled the hatch down. He sat dripping in his seat, looking at the coordinates for the next signal glowing on the holo. Something told him he'd find the same thing there. A fire in the interior. A fried system. Why would someone knock out the signal lights? They were just there to help guide boats back into the docks—it wasn't like they cast enough light to see by, if you were out here screwing around. Tomas didn't even worry about them blowing his shows' cover.

This town is falling apart, Dorian thought, hitting the ignition and jerking the rider off the water. The whole place was a relic, a memorial to some long-ago time when it was just humans killing other humans and people still flew down here to lay in the hot sun during the dry season.

He wondered how long until the town crumbled back into the jungle. Wondered if he'd be out of here by then.

CHAPTER THREE

VICTOR

The rain had stopped. Victor threw open his bedroom window and stuck his head out. The air had that heavy feeling of impending rain, mixed with the salt from the beach, and there was even the faint golden glow of late afternoon sun coming around the clouds.

He whipped out his comm pad and checked the precipitation report—it looked like they had a good three hours or so of clear weather before the rain would pick up again. Perfect.

He pulled up Evie's name and sent her a message: **MEET ME AT THE TREE. I NEED YOUR HELP WITH THE FILM.** Then he dragged his equipment out of his closet—the spotlights, the high-quality holo-camera his parents had bought him for his birthday last year, the little model of the town he'd built out of wood, and, of course, the monster.

The monster was the star of his film, a glittering aluminum dragon he and Evie had made at her house after school. He'd designed the hardware and she'd done the software, programming the dragon so that it could fly, roar, shoot fire out of its mouth (which reminded him, he needed to grab a power cell before he left), and generally destroy his model village and terrorize his characters as needed.

Victor's comm pad chimed. It was Evie, and she was, unfortunately, being a drag.

I DON'T KNOW IF I CAN COME, she wrote. **DAD USUALLY DOESN'T LET ME GO OUT TWO NIGHTS IN A ROW . . .**

Victor sighed with frustration. **BUT YOU'RE THE ONLY ONE WHO CAN FIX THE DRAGON IF ANYTHING GOES WRONG! TELL YOUR DAD IT'S PROGRAMMING STUFF!**

In Victor's opinion, Evie's dad was pretty unreasonable about letting Evie be normal. Not that Victor's parents were much better, always fussing over him since his two sisters had both joined up with UNSC, like they were more afraid he'd get killed here in the middle of nowhere than they were of his sisters getting killed fighting the Covenant. Fortunately, his parents were both at the motel tonight, which meant he had some freedom, assuming he made it back before ten o'clock.

Another chime on his comm pad. Evie: **FINE. I'LL BE THERE. DAD'S GOT A MEETING TONIGHT, SO I HAVE TO BE HOME BEFORE HE IS.**

Victor laughed. He couldn't believe she was actually sneaking out.

YOU WILL!!! Victor wrote back. Then he tossed all the supplies into a box and headed down to his car. It was only a five-minute drive to the banyan tree, and sure enough, Evie was waiting for him, leaning up against one of the draping vines, the strange, cloud-filtered sunset blurring the colors of everything. *Perfect light,* Victor thought. Although they would need to hurry.

He didn't bother getting out of the car, just pulled up to her and waited for her to crawl in.

"Rebel, rebel," he said. "Actually sneaking out this time?"

Evie glared at him. "Just promise me we'll be home by nine."

"I promise. Your dad'll never know you slipped out."

Evie sighed and gazed out the window. "I was hoping I'd see another sardans cat while I was waiting."

Victor grinned. "Yeah, that was a once-in-a-lifetime shot, I think."

"Have you put it on your channel yet?"

Victor shook his head. "I decided to work it into the footage of the concert. Pretty cool, huh?"

"Is that what *Dorian* would want?" Evie lowered her voice and batted her eyes when she said Dorian's name.

"Stop it." Victor swatted at her. "I don't know where you got this crazy idea that I'm into Dorian Nguyen."

Evie laughed. "It's just weird, you two talking."

"He likes my channel!" Victor shook his head. "Anyway, I'm tired of talking about this. We need to focus on the film. Honestly, filming that concert was kind of a distraction."

Evie let up then, thank god, and Victor pulled out into the road, heading toward the beach at the edge of town. He'd scoped it out a few weeks ago, for reasons that had nothing to do with Dorian Nguyen and everything to do with Saskia Nazari, not that he was going to tell Evie about *that*. She would never let him live it down if she knew that he'd actually gone driving around the woods on the edge of town trying to run into Saskia. He knew she hung out here—he'd seen her once or twice lounging by the rocky shoreline or winding her way through the forest. She probably lived nearby, but he wasn't sure.

It definitely hadn't been one of his prouder moments. It was just that he'd failed a chemistry test and his parents had gotten after him about it, and then he'd received word that his oldest sister, Camila, had been hurt in the fighting—she was okay now, but it had been like a punch to the side of his head. And he'd been lying in his room, listening to music and feeling sorry about himself, and he just thought, *Maybe I could see her*, and decided to be a creep for an evening.

It worked out, though, because while he'd been driving on those narrow, ancient forest roads, he'd stumbled across a secluded little cove, too rocky for swimming but filled with shimmering tide pools that would make a perfect location to set up his little seaside village.

"Where are we going?" Evie asked, peering out the window. "I thought the film was supposed to take place on the beach."

"You'll see." Victor turned down another narrow road. Vines and ferns scraped against the side of his car.

"Are we even supposed to be driving out here?" Evie asked.

"There's a road!" Actually, Victor wasn't so sure of that himself, given how overgrown and crumbling the road was. "Besides, we're here."

The cove looked even more spectacular in the sunset than it had the night he discovered it. Even Evie sat up and took a sharp breath, leaning against the car's dash with wide eyes. The tide pools all glowed orange and pink, and the sky above the water was a swirl of gray clouds and brilliant light.

"We've got an hour till this light runs out," Victor said. "We better make the most of it."

"No kidding!"

They climbed out of the car. The wind blowing in from the sea was cool and damp and felt like a rain cloud. Victor pulled his box of supplies out of the car's trunk, and the two of them traipsed down to the shoreline. Victor set the box next to the largest tide pool he could find.

"This one," he said. "Okay, I'm going to set up the village, and you set up the dragon."

Evie nodded and lifted the dragon out of the box of supplies. Then she carted it over to a clear spot on the rocks and pulled out her comm pad. Victor left her to work on it while he set up the village. He tipped the box and dumped its contents out on the sand: a cornucopia of miniature wooden buildings, hand painted and installed with tiny electrical lights that were controlled by the same program Evie had designed for the dragon. The film—still currently untitled—was set on Earth, back during the pre-space-exploration era. He wanted to capture that era's tone as best he could, from the practical effects all the way to the design of the buildings: flat and angular, with no metal reinforcements squatting on the roofs. Victor had designed the houses after spending hours on the school's library channel, looking up old 2-D photographs of Earth housing. So much of this work could be faked with bootleg rendering software, but Victor wanted to channel his favorite indie directors by using real 3-D printed models.

He arranged the model buildings around the edge of the tide pool, flicking bits of seaweed and rock out of the way, making sure that everything looked exactly right. He'd set the village up so many times he was able to get it done in just a few minutes, right as Evie came trotting back over with the dragon cradled in her arms, its eyes glowing bright red.

"Got him working!" she announced. "Where do you want him?"

"In the water, there." Victor reached over and adjusted one last building before straightening up and surveying the whole scene. In the eerie orange light, all the pieces seemed to glow. He grabbed his holo-camera out of the box and steadied it on his shoulder. He wasn't going to bother with the stand—he wanted that jittery look for the dragon attack.

"Did you remember to pop in the dragon's power cell?"

"Sure did."

"Okay. Let's do this."

Evie scurried over to his side, comm pad at the ready. He counted down with his fingers, hit Record, and then pointed at Evie. Immediately, her fingers flew over the comm pad. Out in the tide pool, the dragon unfolded the thin, gossamer wings Victor had made out of synthetic silk. They caught in the sea breeze and shimmered, throwing static shadows across the sunset-filled tide pool. A glow grew up from the dragon's belly, red-hot and molten, and the wings pumped once, sending tiny ripples across the water.

"Looks fantastic," he breathed.

Evie grinned at him.

"He needs to swim toward the village."

Evie attacked the comm pad again, switching up the dragon's programming.

"Make them bigger too," Victor called out. "Like sails."

Evie hit a few more keys. A sudden strong wind blew in from the ocean, bringing with it the metallic scent of rain. Victor's muscles tightened with anxiety—the rain was supposed to hold off for a couple more hours. But then, rain always did come in fast and unexpected this time of year. They would just have to work faster.

"How's that?" Evie hit one final key.

The dragon's wings stretched to their full size, round and pale. Another warm blast of wind pushed across the beach, and the dragon jerked forward in the tide pool, wings furling and unfurling as it glided slowly toward the blinking village. Victor zoomed in on it with the camera, following its movement across the glassy, bright water. Evie had programmed it to move slowly, ominously, a threat drifting inexorably toward the village—

A sudden sharp *crack* sliced across the beach. Victor yelped and the holo-camera slipped out of his fingers for a few horrifying seconds before his instincts kicked in and he plucked it out of the air.

"What was *that*?" Evie squeaked.

Victor pressed the camera to his chest and looked up at the sky. The sun had dropped lower toward the horizon, leaving bloody streaks in its wake. Hestia V, the gas giant around which Meridian orbited, loomed off in the west, a pale imprint of itself stamped into the heavens.

"It was probably just thunder." Not that he saw a single sign of a storm. But what else could it be?

Evie smacked him hard on the shoulder. "It didn't sound a thing like thunder. It was like something—*ripping*. Besides, there aren't any clouds."

"What else could it be?"

Evie fixed him with a steady, dark stare. "You know what else it could be."

For a moment, Victor could only breathe, his heart hammering against his chest. He thought suddenly of Camila teaching him how to fight on the beach in front of the hotel: how to throw a punch, how to handle a knife, how to shoot a gun. His other sister, Maria, had done the same when she came home. They were never on leave at the same time. But somehow they had both shown him how to handle himself if the Covenant ever showed up on Meridian.

"*When* the Covenant show up," Camila had said, the last time she was home, and he had pretended not to notice the change.

Another crack shattered the twilight. Victor whirled around, away from the sea, toward the jungle, which loomed thick and dark and impenetrable in the twilight. No sign of Covenant ships descending through the painted sky.

"We should go back," Evie said.

"It's nothing," Victor said, drawing up his chest. "Probably just Salome dealing with whatever caused the power failure last night. Or thunder."

"It's not thunder."

"Fine. But it's not—" Victor waved his hand around rather than say *the Covenant*. "You know. C'mon, let's finish this scene. I'm on a deadline."

Evie frowned, then squinted up at the sky, as if she could see something he didn't. But there was nothing there. Just the quickly evaporating natural light and the toxic spill of the sunset.

They had nothing to worry about.

CHAPTER FOUR

DORIAN

orian pulled the curtain aside and peered out at the deck of Tomas's boat. Lights swam across the faces of the audience. At least two hundred people, all crammed in tight together. They bounced in time to the music throbbing out of the speakers, half a thousand bright eyes bobbing in the darkness. It was the biggest audience Drowning Chromium had ever played for.

"Good crowd tonight."

Dorian jerked his head back, turned, and found Tomas Reynés himself, standing with his arms crossed over his chest, his long brown hair hanging like a curtain around his face.

"Yeah," Dorian muttered.

"Your band's looking for you." Tomas jerked his head toward the dark corridor leading away from the stage. "And you shouldn't be looking past the curtain like that. The audience can see you."

Dorian shrugged. "Nobody was paying attention to me."

Tomas laughed, although there was a knife's edge to it. "They will be. Assuming you're as good as you were the other day."

Dorian's cheeks burned hot. "We will be," he snapped, and pushed past Tomas, who grinned at him, eyes glittering. Out on the stage,

Scintilla and Charybdis released a torrent of music that made Dorian's stomach coil up with anxiety. It was just the two of them, a guy and a girl. The girl was hunched over the computer, fingers flying, and the guy howled in a throaty, angry voice. They were good. Better than Drowning Chromium? Dorian didn't want to think about it.

He shuffled down the corridor until he found the rest of the guys, Xavier and Alex and Hugo, who were lurking around a table stacked with bottles of water.

"Where were you?" Xavier asked.

"Checking out the crowd. You needed me?"

"Just wanted to make sure you hadn't lost your nerve." Hugo grinned at him. He'd smeared purple makeup across his eyes for the show, and it glowed phosphorescent in the dim light.

"Hell no."

Scintilla and Charybdis reached a crescendo, and the roar of the audience filtered backstage. All the guys shifted uncomfortably and tried not to look at one another.

"Almost time," Xavier said, picking up his guitar.

Tomas materialized in the corridor. Scintilla and Charybdis's crescendo had decayed into a low, dissonant hum. "I want you set up as quickly as possible," he said. "No downtime. Like we talked about."

The stage went silent. Dorian could hear his blood pumping fast though his body.

Then: a thunder of applause, screams of appreciation. Dorian was suddenly aware of the motion of the boat bobbing on the waves. His stomach lurched. He'd never thrown up before a show, but he guessed there was a first time for everything.

Tomas had vanished down the corridor. The members of Scintilla and Charybdis shuffled around, gathering up their instruments. Dorian picked up his computer and the QJ kit, nodded at the others.

"Give it up for Scintilla and Charybdis!" Tomas shouted from the stage, and the applause thundered up again. Dorian's stomach flipped around. He didn't look at the others—they were all nervous, and there was no reason to invade their headspace in the moments before they trundled onstage and performed for the biggest audience of their (admittedly short) career.

Dorian and the rest of Drowning Chromium stopped in the wings of the stage, just as Scintilla and Charybdis came stomping past them, their skin gleaming with sweat, their faces flushed with heat. The girl nodded at Dorian, gave him a manic grin. "Good luck," she said, and Dorian smiled back at her. Two percussion engineers meeting on the road to a show.

The stage lights shifted, turned a kind of sickly green, and Tomas flipped his hair back and shouted out to the screaming audience.

"We've got some newcomers for you tonight," Tomas yelled. "One of the best rising talents I've seen in a while—"

The audience didn't care about this, but Dorian's chest squeezed up in a brief fit of pride, which he quickly shunted aside.

"I had the pleasure of seeing them perform live just yesterday and knew I had to add them to the lineup immediately. Let's welcome Drowning Chromium!"

The crowd screamed, pumped up from Scintilla and Charybdis's performance. For a moment, the whole world seemed to spin around, blurring into nothing but noise and light. Then Dorian caught sight of Tomas again, gesturing with one hand for Drowning Chromium to come out on the stage. Dorian glanced at the others, and then he was moving, dragged as if by a string onto the stage. Everything went white, like the explosion of a nuclear bomb—the stage lights, shining straight into Dorian's eyes. He turned away from the audience, found the stand where he could set up his computer and his QJ kit, and he flung himself into his work, moving as quickly as he could, connecting wires, pulling up his music program. The others strummed on their guitars, tapped against the microphones. The sound of the audience and the sound of the ocean bled together into a staticked roar that may have just been the blood in Dorian's ears.

He looked up, saw Hugo and Xavier and Alex in silhouette against the lights, standing in the same formation they always did when they practiced. And finally, for the first time since he'd set foot on Tomas's boat, Dorian felt like he knew what the hell he was doing. The music he'd written months ago appeared inside his head like an abstract painting.

Tomas had left the stage. It was just Drowning Chromium now.

Hugo turned around and said something. Dorian couldn't hear him, but he recognized the shape of the words on his lips. *Ready?*

Dorian nodded. He swept his gaze back out toward the audience. The white lights burned his retinas and then cooled, revealing the first few rows of faces and the dark glittering expanse all around them. He couldn't tell where the audience ended and the ocean began.

Dorian picked up the microphone waiting for him in its stand. He pressed it close to his mouth.

"Ready?" he screamed.

Hugo grinned at him and threw a fist in the air. The audience roared. Dorian activated the holo and immediately the stage lights blinked out, and there was only the thin, ghostly projection of an empty field of stars. It shone out past the rest of Drowning Chromium and transformed the audience into dapples of light and shadow. Dorian leaned into the keys of his computer, jump-starting the sample of a UNSC ship engine he'd pulled off one of his mom's rare transmissions. Then, slowly, he dragged it out until it became music, long and haunting. He lifted his head, stared not at the audience but at a place beyond, a single bright star burning in the distance.

The band began to play: guitars wailing, Hugo growling, Dorian's preprogrammed drum line thudding against the stage. Dorian flung projections out over the audience, blazing white lights streaked with gunmetal gray, static flashes dappling over the audience as they lifted their fists and screamed into the wild tumult of Drowning Chromium's music. Dorian was already sweating, beads of moisture sliding in a long, sticky trail down his spine. He flung his head back and felt a coolness brush against his forehead and then vanish. Heat seemed to radiate off the stage—from the band, from their performance, all that untamed noise streaming out over the dark, silent ocean.

The song was almost over. Dorian's fingers flew wild over the computer display, pulling the last shimmering notes out of Xavier's and Alex's guitars and amplifying them into a shatter of metallic shrieking.

Silence.

Dorian's ears buzzed. For the first time since the start of the song, he looked up at the audience, murky in the stage lights. Why were they being so quiet? Drowning Chromium had just killed it, and they were just standing there, not even looking at them—

Hugo twisted around, looked confusedly at Dorian, then at Xavier and Alex, and they shrugged, looking as perplexed and irritated as Dorian felt.

But then he realized the audience wasn't looking at the stage because they were looking up at the sky. Dorian lifted his gaze just as a white streak, an inverse shadow, sailed overhead, lighting everything up bright as day. Then it vanished, and they were plunged into a gloomy purple twilight.

"What was that?" Xavier bumped into Dorian, who jumped, blinking. "Where's that light coming from?"

Dorian shook his head. He realized the buzzing in his ears was the audience chattering in anxious voices.

"Are we playing another song or what?" Hugo turned around, his sweat-streaked makeup suddenly absurd.

"What's going on?" said Alex.

Someone in the audience screamed. Dorian immediately jerked his head up, and he caught sight of something moving—a flare of purple arcing against the eerie dark of the sky.

The audience erupted into panicked shouting. Dorian thought he heard someone say *Covenant*.

The purple light grew brighter, larger, closer. Dorian wandered away from his setup, over to Xavier, who stood with his head thrown back, his mouth hanging open. The crowd surged toward the side of the boat, shouting and pointing up at the sky.

"You really think it's the Covenant?" Xavier asked.

Dorian didn't answer. The purple light was coalescing into a shape. A kind of half ring with a knot on its back.

"It's not a human ship," Alex said, suddenly at Dorian's side. Hugo was with him. "Look at that light."

Dorian trembled. Purple light shimmered between the dark arms of the ship. No human technology would use light like that.

Screams rippled down the boat. The audience swirled in a panicked frenzy. Not an audience anymore. A mob.

Where was Tomas?

"Covenant!" someone screamed, and this time the word was crystalline in its clarity as it rose above the dark noise of the crowd's terror. "It's the Covenant!"

The ship was close enough that Dorian felt the blast of heat from its engines.

"It's headed toward shore," Hugo said. "Toward Brume-sur-Mer."

Dorian glared at him. "Why would it go there?"

"Where's Tomas?" Hugo said. "Why isn't he hightailing this thing back to la—"

A sharp, strange *zip* rang out. A sudden, inexplicable *thud*. A chorus of screams.

A smell like something burning.

"Get down!" Dorian screamed. He shoved hard on Hugo and then slammed against the stage, dragging Alex with him. Plasma fire scorched the air above his head. The far side of the stage erupted in a flare of white-tinged flames, the heat sudden and overwhelming. Dorian peered over at Alex and found him staring back at him with his hands pressed against his head.

"They just fired on us!" Alex shouted.

"Stay low," Dorian hissed. He lifted his gaze, found Hugo and Xavier both cowering against the computer stand.

"You okay?" Dorian shouted at them.

"No!" Xavier shouted back.

Dorian scowled. "I meant, are you hurt, dumbass."

Xavier shook his head. Dorian glanced at Hugo, who jerked his head once, enough that Dorian took it for a no. Somewhere below the deck the boat began to groan, canting slightly to the side. Whatever had been fired down on them had shot clean through.

Dorian craned his neck back. The Covenant ship was rumbling away from them, but it had left something in its wake. Shadows that buzzed in the air like insects.

There weren't many, maybe five or six. But they were all coming toward the boat.

Plasma fire erupted across the deck, bathing everything in

brilliant purple-tinged light. Bodies crumpled into the crowd. "Get backstage!" Dorian shouted at his bandmates. "Find Tomas!"

Alex started to stand, but the plasma fire started up again. Dorian jerked him down. "Crawl," he hissed. "Go."

"What about you?"

"I've got a plan." This was a lie. But Dorian didn't think the others would be able to handle themselves, and he wasn't about to watch his friends die. "Now get the hell out of here."

Alex nodded and crawled toward the curtains on the right side of the stage—still unharmed, the fire having burned itself out. Dorian jerked his head at Hugo and Xavier. "Go, both of you! I'll be right there."

Hugo and Xavier didn't have to be told twice, no shock to Dorian. They scrambled across the stage, vanishing behind the curtain just as the first of the Covenant soldiers landed on deck.

It was an insect, a bipedal creature vaguely the size of a human, with transparent, veined wings that shimmered once and then snapped to its back as it opened fire, plasma bolts streaming into the crowd. The rest of the soldiers swarmed closer, their weaponry shredding the boat into splinters. Dark water bubbled up over the boat's sides, sizzling when it hit the fires burning on deck. The boat tilted; everyone was tossed casually aside except for the Covenant soldiers, who hovered with a low thrum from their buzzing wings. What the hell were those things called? They'd learned it in school, but Dorian couldn't remember.

Whatever they were called, they were preoccupied with the crowd, not the burning stage. Not Dorian. He pressed his belly against the stage and crawled over to where Xavier's guitar lay discarded. Dorian grabbed it by the neck and dragged it over to him, wincing at the sound of it scraping against the wood. Not that the Covenant heard it, not with that horrible, constant screaming, not with the punctuated whine of plasma pistols.

Dorian stood up, shaking, all his muscles tense. He wrapped his hands tight around the neck of the guitar. A Covenant soldier was facing away from him, still hovering in midair, so that the two of them were level. Dorian glanced at the rest of the Covenant—they were preoccupied with the crowd.

Dorian lunged forward, swinging the guitar with all his strength. It connected with the side of the Covenant soldier's body, crumpling the wings and sending the soldier slamming over the side of the boat. Strings popped off the guitar.

If they survived this, Xavier was going to kill him.

Immediately, plasma bolts exploded around him. Dorian leapt off the stage and slammed hard against the deck, wet with a few centimeters of water. The soldiers chittered at one another, and it was then that Dorian realized the screaming on the boat had died down. His skin prickled with understanding of what silence meant here, now, the boat burning around them.

He hoped his friends had found Tomas, and he hoped Tomas had a lifeboat tucked away somewhere, and he hoped all of them were shredding through the water toward Brume-sur-Mer. He hoped, he hoped, he hoped. Because he didn't think he could go back for them. He didn't think he could do anything but get off this sinking ship.

Dorian crawled through the murk on the boat, keeping himself low. The plasma fire had shifted away from him, but he wasn't going to risk drawing attention to himself again. He couldn't jump over the left side of the boat—that was where the Covenant were coming from. But the right side might still be safe. He still had Xavier's guitar. Would a guitar float? He'd find out.

Heat and light erupted beside him, and he felt a stinging along his side. Exploding embers from the stage. He crawled more quickly, then scrambled to his feet, running as hard as he could. The cracked railing waited like a ghost in the firelight.

He heard the Covenant shrieking. Heard the scream of plasma fire.

Then he jumped, barely clearing the railing. For a moment, he was suspended in an inky darkness, lit only with streaks of orange from the fire.

Then he slammed into the cold crush of the ocean. The salt water stung where the embers had burned him. He opened his eyes and looked through the gloom at nothing.

When he broke the surface, gasping, it was like being born. He didn't give himself a moment to rest. Only kicked his legs with a ferocious panic, propelling himself away from the fire. The guitar was a deadweight, worthless. He dropped it and dived beneath the sea, swimming with the easy strokes he had learned from Uncle Max as a child.

He hoped this was the direction home.

CHAPTER FIVE

EVIE

o you smell something burning?" Evie asked.

"What? Hey, don't move the spotlight."

Evie jerked the spotlight back into place, shining it on Victor's homemade village. He was hunched over one of the buildings, trying to repair it. Their mechanical dragon had smashed into it. They'd spent a good thirty minutes arguing over whose fault it was—Victor said Evie had programmed it to be too strong, Evie said the hardware was too heavy—until they both realized how dark it had gotten.

"Let me get out the lights," Victor had grumbled.

Now, an hour later, Evie had to hold the spotlight steady while Victor fumbled with his village, cursing constantly under his breath.

"I smell something burning." Evie squinted out at the water. The sky seemed a little lighter than it should, a sickly violet-orange color, like light pollution in the cities. It made the ocean black. "Don't you smell it?"

"Probably just the lights," Victor muttered. Then he sat up, looked over at her. "Hold on, it's not the dragon, is it?"

Evie shook her head, pointed at the place near her feet where the dragon was stretched out, still and silent, waiting for his next shot. "Dragon's fine."

"It's probably nothing, then. I'm almost done."

He pressed the roof of the broken house into place and held it there, squinting in concentration. Evie scanned the horizon again. The sky seemed hazy and thick. Smoke? But she couldn't see a fire.

"Okay, ready."

Evie looked back over at him. Victor and the village both cast long shadows over the tide pool, the harsh glare of the spotlights carving them into bas-reliefs of light and dark.

"This is the last scene, right?" she said. "Because I really need to get home before my dad does." She kept expecting to hear the familiar chime of the comm pad. It was nearly nine thirty. He tended to stay late at his meetings, which was the only reason she hadn't insisted they leave. But if she wasn't back by ten—

"Yeah, and it won't take long." Victor straightened up, grabbed his camera, and focused it on the village. "Could you adjust the lights? They're making some whining noise."

Evie frowned, glanced up at the lights. "I don't hear anything." She thumped the side of one of the spotlights and cocked her head to listen.

"You don't?" Victor looked up from behind his camera. "Sounds like a bee or someth—"

The sky lit up. Brilliant light washed over the cove, drowning out the spotlights. The clouds glowed purple and red and black.

"What the hell?" Victor scrambled around and held his camera up to the false dawn of the sky.

Evie heard it now. The whining. It was coming from far off, the direction of the water. It didn't sound like a bee at all. It sounded like a machine.

She stepped away from the spotlights, letting them drop out of formation, and drifted down next to Victor, who was filming. "What do you think's going on?" he asked. "Some kind of training?"

But Evie heard the tremble in his voice, the dissonant squeak of fear. Both his sisters were in the UNSC. He knew as well as she did.

Purple light streaked across the sky, from one cloud to another. Something boomed like thunder, and the cloud turned bloody and then rippled with black smoke.

"What the—" Victor said softly, dropping the camera.

Panic seized at Evie—was this why her father hadn't contacted her? Images intruded into her thoughts, of him lying slumped at his desk, a shadow with a plasma rifle lurking behind him. She scrambled for her comm pad. No messages. No alerts. She pulled up her dad's channel and tried to connect. *Searching*, the message on the screen said. *Searching . . . Searching . . .*

"The networks are down," she gasped. She felt as if she couldn't get enough air into her lungs, as if the Covenant were sucking the oxygen out of the atmosphere. But no, that wasn't how they attacked. Her mother had told her once, a few months ago, a serious conversation while she was home on leave, one that Evie tried her best not to think about—

Another boom in the sky. The brilliant light was fading, leaving spots in Evie's vision. But the clouds still flashed with streaks of purple light.

Victor was checking his own comm pad. "Yeah, the network's down for me too." He squinted up at the sky. "How far away do you think they are?"

Evie sucked in a deep breath. "I don't know." Far enough away that they couldn't see anything. But close enough that they could hear it. Which meant the Covenant had breached Meridian's atmosphere. "We need to get back to the village," she said. "The shelter—"

Victor nodded faintly, still gazing at the sky. Evie jostled his arm. "Victor!" she shouted. "We have to go!"

Victor blinked, shook his head, his hair falling into his eyes. "You're right," he muttered. "Help me get the stuff together."

Evie wanted to scream at him to leave it, but she choked the panic back and gathered up the dragon and set it in the box. Then she knelt beside Victor and fumbled with the village. Her hands were shaking. Every time something boomed up in the sky, she jumped and nearly dropped the delicate buildings.

"Slow down," Victor said gently, his mouth close to her ear. "You can't let yourself panic in a fight. That's what Camila told me."

"We're not in a fight." Evie's voice was shrill. But she slowed her movements. Her hands still trembled, but she didn't feel like she was on the verge of collapsing anymore.

"Focus on the task," Victor said. "Think about your training."

"Training?" Evie said with a strangled voice.

"Camila showed us how to shoot those guns," Victor said.

For some reason, this struck Evie as funny, and she started laughing. The sky was burning, the Covenant were attacking, she was crouched vulnerable by the ocean gathering up toys. The idea that an afternoon firing rifles on the beach was enough to protect her from death was absurd.

And so, she laughed.

"Evie? Stop." She felt the weight of a hand on her shoulder. She looked up at Victor frowning at her. Tears burned in her eyes.

"I don't know what to do," she said.

"We need to get back to town," he said. "That was a good idea. Get to town and get to the shelter. Go wait in the car. I'll get the rest of the props."

Evie took a deep breath. "I'm fine." She stood up. Did not let herself look at the sky. Did not let herself think about the stench of fire on the air, or the sting of smoke and tears in her eyes. "You told me to stay calm. I feel better now. I can do it." She switched off the spotlights and folded them up. Her hands weren't shaking anymore.

She walked toward the car with a blank numbness. Tossed the spotlights into the trunk. She thought idly about her dad, about how furious he was going to be when she got home. *You snuck out during a Covenant attack!*

She giggled, the hysteria bubbling up inside her again, although she shoved it back down. *Stay calm*, she told herself. *Stay calm.*

Victor tottered over with the box of props and shoved it into the trunk.

"Let's go," he said. "Straight to the shelter."

Tightness squeezed at Evie's chest. "What if no one went there, though? Should we go home first, see what people are doing?"

Victor frowned. "Let's see when we get into town. Okay?"

There was that tremble of fear in his voice again. Evie nodded.

They climbed into the car. Victor pulled away from the cove, and Evie watched the burning sky get eaten by the silhouettes of the forest as the car rumbled down the overgrown road. When the trees overlapped behind them, enclosing them in the forest, Evie focused her gaze on the road unspooling through the trees.

Neither Evie nor Victor spoke, and the silence was strangling. Everything looked eerie in the misty glow of the headlights. Vines and weeds seemed to crawl toward the car, as if they wanted to wrap around it and hold it in place.

A drop of water landed on the windshield. Another. Another.

"Great," Victor sighed, switching on the glass dryer.

The rain pattered against the car's roof. Evie sank back in her seat and checked her comm pad again. *Network could not be found. Try again?* She tapped yes.

Searching . . . Searching . . . Searching . . .

And then Evie was flung forward, the seat belt digging into her chest. Her comm pad clattered across the dash.

"Victor!" she shouted.

But Victor only sat trembling in the driver's seat, his face ashy, his hands gripping the steering wheel so tightly his knuckles had turned white.

Evie turned to where he looked and felt the bottom of her stomach fall out.

Something stood on the road, just on the edge of the headlights. It was tall and sinewy, and she might have mistaken it for a human except for its long, narrow snout, tall quills running along its head, and legs that seemed to bend the wrong way.

"Oh my god," she breathed.

It stepped into the light, the unnervingly pale skin on its bare arms gleaming wet from the rain. Although it was clad in some kind of armor, it stared at them with empty yellow eyes like it was a feral animal. Took another jerking, birdlike step forward. Its hands were empty, Evie realized. No weapon.

"Victor," Evie whispered.

"I don't know what to do." His voice vibrated in fear.

The creature crouched.

"It's going to jump on us!" Evie shrieked. "Go! Go!"

The engine revved, and the car shot forward, throwing rocks up around them into the rain. The alien shot up out of the way and landed a second later on the roof. Victor screamed and jerked the steering wheel, and the car careened into the thick underbrush of the forest. The creature pounded on the roof, denting the metal.

"Victor!" Evie screamed.

"I'm trying!" Branches slapped across the windshield. Cracks appeared in the glass. The thing—whatever it was—was still slamming into the roof. Evie heard the scrape of metal and a growly shriek. *Jackals*, she thought, remembering the conversations with her mother. *Mom called that one a Jackal.*

"Hold on!" Victor shouted just as the car rammed into the trunk of a golden rain tree. The Jackal hit the hood, bounced, slammed into the tree. It snarled at them, its narrow beak revealing a row of jagged, shining teeth. Then it slammed its forearm against the windshield. A spiderweb of cracks raced along the glass.

"Get in the back!" Evie screamed, and she scrambled over the seat. "We can get out through the trunk."

"It'll just chase us!"

"Don't let it see us!" She felt around in the cushions for the release latch. "Victor! Help me!"

He crawled on top of her, his body damp with sweat. "Dammit, Evie, get out of the way!"

"Get off me!"

Then came the melodic scatter of broken glass and a roar that pierced at Evie's ears. She rolled onto her back and kicked without thinking; her foot connected with the Jackal's beak, and its head jerked back. It slammed its three-fingered claws to its face and met her gaze, its eyes burning with rage.

"Got it!" Victor shouted. The seat popped out and hit Evie on the head. The Jackal lunged forward and Evie kicked out again, but this time it grabbed her by the ankle, its clawed fingers squeezing so tight she felt the bones of her foot grinding together.

Evie screamed and flailed, reaching out for Victor, who wrapped his arms around her torso and pulled. But the Jackal was stronger. It yanked her leg through the gap in the front seats. She stuck out her free leg, tried to catch herself. Pain burst up her leg, through her hip. Victor screamed in her ear. The Jackal leaned in and hissed. Pulled.

She slammed forward. The absence of Victor's grip burned more painfully than the hand at her ankle. She screamed and thrashed, but the Jackal grabbed her other ankle and yanked her through the windshield. Rain splattered across her face. The Jackal flung her into the bushes and then jumped, landing with a shuddering thud beside her. Evie screamed. Rainwater flooded into her mouth.

The Jackal crouched over her, muttering in hisses and squawks. Its teeth flashed, and Evie heard her mother's voice, staticky from the transmission feedback: *It was the damn Jackals. They'd eaten the survivors.* Eaten *them, Evie.*

Evie screamed and flung her body sideways, ferns and mud hitting her face. The Jackal roared and yanked her back by the arm, and Evie felt around in the underbrush with her free hand, fingers squelching in the mud. Everything was dirt and leaves, nothing she could use as a weapon.

Evie looked up at the Jackal. Her face was wet with rain and tears. She screamed in rage and shoved her fist into the side of its head. It roared, leaned back—

Something cracked in the forest.

Hot liquid spilled across Evie's face.

The Jackal froze, its eyes wide with surprise. Then it slumped and hit the ground and lay unmoving.

Dead, Evie thought.

With that, she realized what the liquid was, and she shrieked, trying to wipe it off with her hands. She scrambled up to her feet, dizzy with disgust and relief. The Jackal still didn't move.

"Are you okay?"

It wasn't Victor. It was a girl's voice. Evie looked up. Blinked.

Saskia Nazari stood a few meters away, cradling a sleek black rifle in her arms.

"Saskia?" Evie gasped.

Saskia turned her gaze to the Jackal lying in the underbrush. "Did I get it?"

"I—" Evie looked at the Jackal again. "I think so?"

"Evie?" Victor threw open the car door. "What happ—*Saskia?*"

Saskia glanced at him over her shoulder. She didn't look like herself, wearing nothing but a pair of ripped jeans and a baggy shirt, her dark eyeliner streaked, her hair straggly from the rain. Holding a gun. Then she looked back at Evie and held out one hand.

"Come on," she said. "We can go back to my place. It's not on the same energy system as the town."

Evie grabbed Saskia's hand, and Saskia pulled her forward, wrapping an arm around Evie's shoulder, propping her up. Evie's ankle felt weak beneath her weight.

"You too," Saskia shouted at Victor, who blinked at her in shock.

"But we need to get to town," Evie whispered.

"You can't." Saskia kept her gaze fixed ahead as they limped over the undergrowth. "The Covenant are there."

CHAPTER SIX

SASKIA

Saskia walked Evie through the woods toward her house, that boy Victor trailing behind them. The rain picked up, washing the blood and dirt from Evie's face. It also made it almost impossible to talk.

The woods now felt unfamiliar despite the hours Saskia had spent in them, sitting on a fallen tree and sketching, or listening to music as she strolled through the trees at night. The rain made everything shimmery and indistinct, and Saskia's thoughts were fuzzy. Already the memory of killing the Covenant creature was fading, replaced by flashes of sensations: the weight of the gun in her hands, the echo of Evie's screaming, the terror rising like bile in the back of Saskia's throat. Her ears were still ringing from the shot, which was louder than she expected. All the other times she had fired her parents' guns, she had been wearing sound dampeners. She wondered if her ears would ring for the rest of her life.

"How'd you know we were out here?" Evie mumbled. Her steps were heavy and confused. Saskia knew she'd need to look at her ankle when they got back.

"The security system," Saskia said. "You drove through the boundary and set off the alarms. When I saw what was happening on the holos—"

"You saved me," Evie finished.

"You would have done the same," Saskia said, having no idea if it were true.

The glow of her house appeared through the trees, the incandescent security lights bouncing off the massive iron walls. Saskia heard Evie gasp beside her.

"Is it always like that?" Victor asked, falling into step beside them. "No offense, but it looks like a prison."

"This is some kind of automated barricade system," Evie said, shifting her weight. "Isn't it? Don't your parents work for Chalybs Defense Solutions? I heard they were developing state-of-the-art security systems."

Saskia's face flushed. "Yeah," she said. "It's a prototype. New technology. That's how I knew about the—attack. The walls came up." She adjusted her weight, making sure she still had a strong grip on Evie. "Come on, let's get inside. In case there are—more."

Evie nodded. The two of them continued their stumbling walk up to the wall. Dirt and shredded plants lay scattered around the wall's base from where it had shot up out of the earth earlier. Saskia barely remembered where the security gate was—it had been designed to blend into the smooth, charcoal walls. But then she spotted the faint indentation, in the iron, and when she pressed her palm against it, a holography keypad materialized in the air. Saskia put in the entrance code. The entrance slid open.

"Wow," Victor said. "I couldn't even tell there was a door there."

Saskia shrugged and walked Evie up to the front door of her house. Victor's footsteps pounded on the pathway behind them.

With a sudden *whisk* and a violent *clang*, the entrance gate slammed shut behind them and locked tight.

"Whoa!" Victor whirled around, staring at the smooth wall. "That's crazy."

"It really is," Evie said. "I had no idea this kind of technology was even available yet."

Saskia's cheeks burned. She felt like Evie was accusing her of something. "I don't know much about it, just that they installed everything a few weeks ago. This is the first time I've actually seen it."

"Are your parents home?" Victor was still staring up at the wall, which must have been at least ten meters tall.

"No." Saskia didn't want to elaborate. "Come on, let's get inside. I have something for your ankle."

She and Evie hobbled up the steps, and Saskia put in the security code and pushed open the front door. The foyer echoed around them.

"Wow," Evie breathed, her gaze going up to the big glass chandelier hanging above the staircase.

Saskia didn't say anything, just kept walking, guiding Evie and Victor to the living room. She was aware of both of them gaping at the inside of her house, with its huge, airy rooms and her mother's immaculate artwork choices hanging on the walls. She was the only person in town who lived in a house like this. She supposed that made her lucky, but it also made her strange. And there was nothing worse in a town like Brume-sur-Mer than being strange.

She helped Evie onto the couch, then propped her foot up on the ottoman. Evie's ankle was swollen and red, mottled with angry, dark bruises.

"It grabbed me," Evie said weakly. "And dragged me out of the car." She laid her head against the couch's cushions. In the living room's bright lights Saskia could see the extent of her injuries, all the bruises and scrapes slashing across her bare skin. She was aware too of Victor hovering behind her, quiet and unmoving, his face pale. Apparently he'd been in the car the whole time—she hadn't even known he was there until he crawled out after she had killed the soldier.

She glanced back at him. His eyes were dark and solemn. He saw her looking and jerked his gaze away.

"You didn't have any weapons," she said to him, then immediately regretted it when he scowled at the floor.

"She's right," Evie said. "We're just lucky she saw us."

Victor shrugged, wandered over to the big picture window, even though it was too dark to see anything but his reflection.

"Were you able to get on a comm channel?" Evie asked. "Our networks were all down."

Saskia shook her head. "Mine cut out a while ago. I haven't tried since. Let me get the first aid kit and then we can try again."

She left the two of them in the living room. Her house felt big and empty and echoing as she bounded up the stairs to her bathroom, where they kept the health pack. Her parents had been gone for nearly a week—were, in fact, gone most of the time—but she still hadn't gotten used to being alone in such an enormous house.

It also did not escape her notice that her parents were conveniently gone when the Covenant attacked. Or that their fancy new security system had gone up right before they left. Her parents certainly had unique ideas about how to protect their only child.

The health pack was shoved into the back of the cupboard, and she had to pull out an entire pile of towels to get to it. She swiped her hand over the sensor and the lid popped open. A small holo-panel inside asked to contact emergency services. *Some good that'd do*, she thought. Luckily this health pack was military-grade: Her dad brought them in from work, and they were scattered around the house in various hiding places. Like the security system, another stand-in for actual parenting.

Saskia stood up just as something boomed outside, a thunderous rumble that went on too long to be actual thunder. She froze, listening to its roar and tumult, her fingers pressing against the health pack's metal box. Purple light flooded in through the single square window next to the toilet, casting everything into twilight shadows.

At least the alarms weren't going off.

Saskia bolted out of the bathroom and raced back downstairs. The purple light was starting to fade, but the roar was still there, a trembling in the air. She burst into the living room and found Evie and Victor huddled next to the window.

"What is it?" she gasped, jogging up beside them.

"I think it's a ship," Evie said numbly.

Saskia pressed herself in between the two of them and peered out the window. The trees slammed back and forth on the other side of the wall, their leaves swinging like hair. The clouds were low and churning and too bright.

Saskia's knees buckled; she pressed her elbow against the window to steady herself.

"You okay?" Victor asked, although he didn't move to help her.

"What are they doing here?" Evie was still staring out the window. "Why are they *here*?"

Saskia was seized with a violent, grasping fear. *The weapons*. Her parents' weapons, the prototypes for their company, tucked away in the storage facility down in the underground safe room. She staggered away from the window and slumped down on the couch.

The rumbling grew fainter.

"It's going away," Evie said.

"That low in the atmosphere, it's going to park somewhere close by," Victor said. "Are you sure that wall is going to hold?"

It took Saskia a moment to realize he was talking to her. "It's a prototype," she said, staring at the black viewing monitor set into the wall opposite the couch. "The house has a safe room, though. If we need it."

"A safe room!" Evie hobbled away from the window and sank back down on the couch. "Is it connected to the town shelter? We can check on—"

"It's not." Saskia looked down at the health kit. "Sorry."

Evie slumped back down, pressed her hands to her face. "My dad probably thinks I'm dead. I never should have snuck out without telling him."

"That ship looks like it's headed right for town," Victor said, his voice rough. "Maybe it's better we stayed out here."

Evie looked at him in horror. "I was attacked by the Covenant! That thing was going to eat me!"

"But it didn't." Saskia hated the sound of fighting. It set off discordant bells clanging inside her head. "Evie, let me look at your ankle, okay? And then we can decide what to do. We can try the comm channels again. My dad has a big setup down in the basement. We might have a better chance there than on the comm pads." She flipped open the health kit and pulled out a pack of MediGel. "Here, this should help."

"Yeah, the comm pads aren't doing crap." Victor paced behind the couch. "This is crazy! Why are they landing in Brume-sur-Mer?"

Brume-sur-Mer. Not Saskia's house, not her parents' stash of high-tech weapons. Would the Covenant even care about human weapons? In hindsight, it did seem unlikely.

"Are you sure they're landing there?" Evie said. "They could be headed for Port Moyne."

"They were landing," Victor said. "Listen."

Saskia lifted her head. It took her a moment—the ghost of that engine roar was still echoing inside her head.

"It's quiet," she said.

"It stopped," Victor said. "After it passed over us. It's in Brume-sur-Mer."

A chill came into the room. None of them spoke. Saskia pulled out a disinfectant pad and pressed it to Evie's ankle. Evie hissed in protest, jerked her leg away.

"I need to clean it," Saskia said. "If we don't take care of it, you aren't going to be able to walk."

"How are you so calm? Our entire town is going to die!" Evie shouted. "Doesn't that matter to you?"

Saskia flinched. "Of course it matters."

"Evie, calm down. The shelter is there for a reason." Victor stopped pacing and leaned against the back of the sofa. "Saskia's right. Let her fix your leg. Then we can try her comm setup. Okay?"

Saskia looked back and forth between Evie and Victor, the disinfectant stinging her fingertips. She was afraid if she said anything it would be the wrong thing.

"Fine," Evie said, pressing a hand over her eyes. "Fine."

Victor nodded, looking resolved. Saskia applied the disinfectant. This time, Evie didn't react at all.

Saskia tore open the gel next and pressed it into Evie's skin with two fingers. Evie let out a sharp gasp of pain. "I know," Saskia soothed. "I have to rub it in for a few seconds. But then you'll be fine."

"Where did you even get this stuff?" Victor asked, picking up the pack of MediGel. "Isn't this military-grade?"

"My parents." Saskia finished the gel application and looked up at Evie. "It usually takes a couple of minutes."

"It's already starting to feel better." Evie twisted her ankle around.

"My sisters told me about this stuff." Victor handed the pack back to Saskia, who set it into the medical kit. "Didn't think a civilian could get their hands on it."

Saskia shrugged. "CDS contracts out with the UNSC." She stood up, not wanting to explain any further, about how she was pretty sure the UNSC wasn't the *only* organization her parents worked with. "Let's get down to the safe room."

She held out a hand to Evie, who took it and then stood, tentatively pressing her weight against her ankle. "Wow," she said. "Yeah, it's totally fine."

"We can deal with those scratches and bruises later if you want," Saskia said. "But I figured you would want to try to get ahold of your parents first."

"My dad, yeah." Evie caught Saskia's eyes and smiled thinly. "Thank you."

Saskia gathered up the medical kit. "It's nothing."

"You saved her life!" Victor cried. "I'd hardly call that nothing."

Saskia blushed, turned away. She had saved Evie's life, but the enormity of that reality was too much. She understood it intellectually. Trying to grasp on to the implications just made her dizzy.

She led Victor and Evie into the kitchen, where she pressed her palm against the safe room sensor. Lines of light materialized around the door before it melted into the wall, revealing the safe room's entrance.

"Holy crap!" Victor said.

"Yeah, that's way more impressive than the town's shelter," Evie said.

Saskia smiled. "The town shelter is a lot bigger. I couldn't believe it when I went down there for the concert."

"You were at the Drowning Chromium show?" Victor asked as Saskia stepped into the dark stairwell. The lights blinked on with her movement.

"Yeah," Evie said. "I remember seeing you there."

"What'd you think of them?" Saskia asked, grateful to have something normal to talk about. "It's Dorian Nguyen's band, yeah? Who are the other guys in it?"

"They graduated a few years ago," Victor said, hopping down the steps so that he was right beside her. He talked quickly, his voice rising in excitement. "I actually filmed the concert for them. Dorian asked me to. I was going to put it on my channel, but . . ."

His voice faded into echoes. *But the Covenant attacked.* She couldn't blame him for not wanting to say it out loud. It made it seem more real.

"They were pretty good, I thought," Saskia said, wanting to go back to the normalcy of music and underground concerts.

"Too heavy for my tastes," Evie said from behind them.

"I thought they were great," Victor enthused.

They reached the end of the stairs. Saskia leaned forward so the scanner could pass over her eyes. A holo materialized in the darkness. The keypad. She pressed in her code, and the door hissed open.

"Vacuum-sealed?" Victor asked.

"My parents are pretty paranoid."

She led them into the safe room. As always, the door closed on its own, sealing off the air once Evie had come through. The safe room was small, really only one room, with an escape tunnel leading to the armory and then to the extraction point out in the middle of the forest. Saskia didn't mention any of this to Evie and Victor, though, and they didn't notice the door leading to the tunnel anyway, not with the comm station still lit up from when she'd checked the security cameras earlier.

"Look at this setup!" Victor cried, darting across the room and sinking into the chair in front of the station. The monitors flickered with the images from the security cameras: the forest, the beach, the road leading up to the house. All empty save the one monitor that showed Victor's abandoned car. The dead Covenant soldier was out of the frame, at least.

"Do you know how to use it?" Saskia asked.

"Sort of?" Victor frowned at the control panel.

"I do." Evie knelt beside Victor's chair and hit a key on the panel. A holo-panel shone up into the air. She glanced over at Saskia. "My dad has one like this at the university where he teaches. He lets me use it to talk to my mom sometimes."

"Where's your mom?" Saskia asked without thinking.

"Fighting. In the war." Evie turned away.

Saskia looked down at the floor. She should have known. Almost all the kids at school knew someone who had enlisted to fight the Covenant.

Evie's fingers flew across the holo-panel. A hiss of static burst out of the speakers.

"Hello," Evie said into the microphone, her voice tremulous. "Hello, is anyone there?"

Static. The whine and crackle of feedback.

"Hello?" Evie said. "We are looking for survivors in Brume-sur-Mer. Hello?"

The feedback intensified, transforming into a metallic screeching and then the babble of an unfamiliar language. Evie yelped and swiped her hand across the holo, switching to a different channel. Saskia's chest tightened with a pang of fear.

"What the hell was that?" Victor asked.

Evie didn't say anything. Saskia took a deep breath. "It was the Covenant, right? It sounded like them."

"The Covenant?" Victor jumped up and pushed his fingers into his hair. "Will they be able to track us here?"

"Probably not," Evie said. "They aren't using the same communications systems as us. It was just a weird fluke." She leaned into the microphone. "Hello? Anyone?"

The static that answered sounded like the ocean. Evie swiped the holo again, moved to a different channel. This time, a monotone voice blasted out of the speakers:

"This is an emergency broadcast," the voice droned in its mechanical timbre. "Seek shelter immediately. This is an emergency broadcast. Seek shelter immediately."

"Hello?" Evie shouted into the microphone. "Hello, can anyone hear us? Please, we're trying to get in contact with Brume-sur-Mer—with the AI Salome—"

"—emergency broadcast. Seek shelter immediately."

Evie cursed and tossed the microphone aside. She stood up and stalked across the room. Saskia reached over and turned down the volume on the broadcast.

"Let's leave this channel open," she said softly. "At least we know it's working."

"They could all be dead," Evie said, staring at the wall. "The whole town."

The air seemed to suck out of Saskia's lungs. "Maybe the comm station in the old shelter doesn't work," she said. "That seems more likely, don't you think?"

Victor looked over at her and nodded. His eyes were big and dark and frightened, and she wished she knew him well enough to give him a hug. To give both of them a hug. No one ever hugged Saskia, but she always thought it would be the best form of comfort.

"What are we going to do?" Evie turned around. Her cheeks glimmered with dampness, but she wiped at her eyes furiously.

"Look," Victor said. "We're safe here. Right, Saskia?"

She nodded.

"So we stay here." Victor strode across the room and threw his arm around Evie's shoulders and squeezed her. Saskia felt a twinge of jealousy that she cast aside. There was no space for it now.

"But what about our families?" Evie cried. "What about my dad? I need to know if he's all right! I need to tell him *I'm* all right!"

"We should do something," Saskia said. "Go into town. Something. But we should do it in the morning. All of us need to rest."

The emergency broadcast whispered in the silence. *Seek shelter immediately.*

"She's right," Victor said. "Especially you."

Evie shook her head. "I'm fine."

"You almost died," Victor said. "You need to sleep before we go marching into town."

Evie sighed. "Where are we going to sleep down here?"

Saskia walked over to the comm station, let her hand hover over the panel. What was the code again? Her father had pounded every code into her head since she was a little girl, but in that moment, the numbers swirled around her thoughts. She couldn't quite grasp onto them.

"Saskia?" Victor asked. "What are you doing?"

Three-seven-nine-four-one. It came to her with Victor's voice. She punched it in and immediately two hideaway beds snapped out of the ceiling.

"Two of us will have to share," Saskia said. "But we can sleep here. And there's food here too."

Evie stared warily at the beds. Saskia hoped she wouldn't protest, wouldn't demand to go back outside and march into town and find her father. She didn't know if she would be able to stop her.

But she didn't. She just tottered over to the larger of the two beds and flopped down across the mattress.

"Tomorrow," she said, her voice soft and slurred. "We'll figure out what to do tomorrow."

CHAPTER SEVEN

DORIAN

Dorian blinked, his eyes stinging. Something prickled against his cheek. He groped with one hand, his fingers sinking into damp sand.

Sand. The beach. He'd made it.

He rolled over onto his back and stared up at the gray sky. His mouth tasted like copper and salt, and his body seemed to move on its own, the ghost of the rhythm of the ocean rocking him here on the beach. And he ached. Every part of him ached, a dull throbbing tenderness that screamed every time he tried to move.

A few smudgy shadows of birds flew overhead. One of them cawed to the others. The air smelled like rain and salt and smoke.

How long had he swam last night? He had lost his sense of time when he plunged into the cold black water. He remembered the first shock of adrenaline propelling him forward; he remembered the glimmer of lights on the horizon. He remembered how eventually his arms and legs seemed to move on their own, how his mind had wandered far away from the roil of ocean water. At one point, he thought he was swimming through the universe itself, star systems clinging to his body like sea foam. He had even seen a starship, bathed in purple light, slicing the sky in half.

Dorian groaned, covered his face with his hands. Sand flaked off his palms and rubbed against his skin. He rolled, aching, to his side, and pushed himself up to sitting. He watched the ocean rolling in. There was no sign of Tomas's boat. No sign of Hugo or Xavier or Alex. But they wouldn't have washed up on some random stretch of beach. Not if they'd made it out on a lifeboat.

Thinking about them left a queasiness in Dorian's stomach. And Uncle Max and Remy—had that ship been heading toward Brume-sur-Mer? He couldn't imagine it. Probably it had gone toward Port Moyne, heading to Aagen. To Meridian's population centers.

That thought made him even queasier. At least Uncle Max and Remy were probably okay.

Dorian forced himself up to standing and swayed for a moment on unsure legs. His muscles felt as if they had been stretched out and tanned in the sun, tight and aching and wrong. He hobbled around, blinking at the lush thicket of forest behind him. He squinted down the beach. Spotted a communications tower. Close to town, then. And he had swum in the right direction after all.

Dorian hobbled toward the communications tower, a way station leading him into town. Once he was in town, he could borrow Uncle Max's comm pad and try to get in contact with the others. Report them as missing. The UNSC would have to go out there and search for survivors, right? They wouldn't let civilians just shrivel up and die on the ocean.

It took Dorian a long time to make his way down the beach. He couldn't walk very fast, not with the pain in his legs—although it did seem to get better, not worse. The sun limned the horizon with a pinkish-gold glow, but storm clouds crowded their way into the sky.

His feet thudded in the sand. Dorian passed another comm tower and one of the automated beach security stations before he came to the first of the seaside motels, its ornate walls faded from decades of salt and wind. Something hissed rhythmically, over and over, and it took Dorian a moment to realize that it was a door to one of the motel's rooms, sliding back and forth in its frame.

"Hello?" he shouted. "Anybody there?" He hobbled up to the building. Didn't see anyone. The door slid open, slid closed, revealing the room in flashes: an unmade bed, a single shoe.

He moved on, past the motel, and on to a cluster of old beach houses sitting precariously on their stilts. The rain started, a chilly gray drizzle. Dorian considered ducking beneath one of the houses and waiting it out, but he wanted to get home. Wanted to check on Remy and Uncle Max. Wanted to find out that the band was all okay, that they'd made it back. He kept picturing it in his head as he walked head down through the rain, his hair sticking to his cheeks. All three of them, Hugo and Xavier and Alex, lounging on his couch, music blasting out of their comm pads, annoying Uncle Max while they waited for Dorian to show up. Just like usual.

Dorian was almost to the main street heading into town when he heard it: an immense mechanical shuddering. In the sky above Brume-sur-Mer, a shape boiled through the clouds, tinged in a purple glow. The shape was too vast to discern its form clearly, but it loomed overhead like an impossibly large sea creature.

All the air went out of Dorian's body, and he swayed in place, sickness roiling around inside his stomach. The shape stopped, its engines thrumming deep in his chest, and for a moment, all the light was leached out of the world, and Dorian was back on Tomas's ship, crawling through the muck on the deck of the boat, plasma bolts streaking through the air above him.

He leaned over and threw up in the sand. Nothing but stomach bile—he hadn't eaten in hours. Then he stumbled a few meters backward and collapsed, his head spinning. The comforting daydream of everyone waiting for him at home was shattered by sudden flashes of broken bodies, bloody limbs, slack faces.

The Covenant hadn't gone to Aagen. They were hanging over Brume-sur-Mer.

Dorian peered up at the roiling clouds through the damp strands of his hair, following the vessel's silhouette. The ship was long and had a narrow neck with a large, wider body that fanned out, ending in a set of luminous engines. Immediately under the front of the ship were fin-like prongs that made the entire vessel look like a bottom feeder. A dizzying panic seized at his chest, and he remembered the video he had watched on one of the comm channels, a shaky, distant recording of a Covenant ship unloading a torrent of plasma onto some far-off world, blasting it with a heat so intense it turned to glass.

But this ship was just—sitting there, churning up the clouds. If they were going to glass the colony, wouldn't they want to get it over with?

Dorian stumbled forward, his thoughts numb. He wanted to charge into town and grab Remy and Uncle Max and get them out of there. He made it a couple of meters before he stopped, shaking. What did he think he was going to do? He was lucky he'd gotten off that damn boat, that he hadn't been shot by one of the aliens or drowned in the ocean. Now he wanted to run up to a Covenant ship? The town was probably crawling with ground troops by now—wasn't that how they worked? That was what they had done last night.

He didn't have a weapon. He didn't even have his full strength. He was sore and rain-soaked, and he felt a kind of madness creeping at the edge of his thoughts. He turned around and stared down the stretch of beach he'd just walked. His footsteps were already melting in the rain.

The houses along that way had all been empty and abandoned. He might as well keep going, see if he could get a better sense of what was happening in the town. It'd be useful when he tried to contact— someone. UNSC? He had no idea. Salome might know, if he could patch into her.

So he kept walking, more cautiously than he had before, skirting close to the overgrowth of the forest. There was a strip of trees between the beach and the town proper, but he figured it would be better to be closer to a potential scout than strolling along out in the open, where they could pick him off.

Like they did with the people on the boat.

He shook the thought off and focused on the shadows in the forest, looking for unfamiliar movements. Nothing. The rain slacked off, although the sky stayed that steely gray, the clouds shot through with purple. The light's quality shifted the beach and forest where Dorian had grown up, and everything was now as alien as that ship hovering over his hometown.

Something snapped off in the strip of woods between town and beach. Dorian froze, head tilted, listening. The constant rush of the ocean made it harder to hear, but he was able to pick out voices, the first he'd heard since last night. They were not speaking English. Or French, or pidgin.

He held his breath, not daring to move. The voices rose and fell with the wind, the language lilting in a strange rhythm. He had heard it before: in videos on the comm channels, in recordings at school. It was not a human language.

The voices moved closer, wreathed by the crackle of broken branches and snapped leaves. Dorian caught the gleam of something sleek and metallic amid the greenery of the forest, and his adrenaline finally overtook him.

He ran.

He ran down the beach, his feet kicking up arcs of sand, his muscles screaming in pain, his lungs tight and constricted. Each thud of his footfall echoed the thud of his heart. He bolted past the turnoff into town and kept going, past beachfront hotels and bars, their windows barred shut for the rainy season. He ran until his legs gave out under him and he collapsed face-first into the sand.

He lay still, gasping for breath, straining for the sound of footsteps or plasma rifles. But there was only the constant roar of the ocean. Eventually, he sat up, shook the sand from his skin. The beach was empty. He squinted out at the forest, trying to orient himself. He was nowhere near Uncle Max's house, that was for sure—it was around on the other side of the cove. He wasn't sure he'd ever been out this far on his odd jobs.

Might be a good sign. If he was far enough out, the UNSC might have set up somewhere. Especially since the Covenant had seen fit to invade Brume-sur-Mer, of all places.

Dorian stood up and took a deep breath, trying to slow his heart. He'd panicked back there and was lucky the Covenant hadn't seen him. Panicking wasn't going to do him any good from here on out.

He had to think.

If the UNSC were going to establish a camp, they'd want to be on a separate power grid from the town. They might just bring in their own equipment and set up in the woods, but it would be easier for them if they patched into one of those fancy houses on the edge of town, which ran separately from Brume-sur-Mer. So that was where Dorian needed to go. Over to the mansions.

He headed out, scanning the beach for landmarks. After half an hour, he spotted a boardwalk, jutting out of the woods. It was in good shape, the steel polished and glossy. It looked like it ought to belong to some expensive resort. Perfect.

He took the steps and began following the boardwalk. It led into the woods, tree branches drooping with rain weight. With each step, the branches trembled and showered him with old, green-scented rain. He moved cautiously, keeping his eye on the shadows. He saw nothing.

Then the woods ended abruptly, revealing an enormous iron wall, some kind of military-grade enclosure. Mounted guns perched on the top like wasps. He felt a surge of excitement—just like he thought. The UNSC had set up shop.

Except this didn't look like any normal UNSC base he'd seen from vids. The guns were unmanned, there was no interface or checkpoint as far as he could tell, and would the UNSC even be able to build a wall like that overnight, in the middle of battle?

His thoughts snapped into place then: the weapons manufacturer. Nazari. Dorian had seen his daughter around school. She never talked to anyone as far as Dorian could tell. And no one ever talked to her. A rich girl like that, in a town like Brume-sur-Mer? Dorian remembered when they'd moved in. Uncle Max had snorted at the news. "Tourists," he'd grudged. "Overstaying their welcome."

The memory sent a pain shooting through Dorian's core.

He jumped off the boardwalk and kicked around in the yard until he found a good-sized rock. Then he hurled it at the wall. It arced tall and wide and slammed into the steel without leaving a dent. He immediately realized the potential mistake of chucking a rock at a heavily armed fortification, but the guns didn't stir at all.

Dorian wondered if anyone was in there. A weapons manufacturer would have weapons lying around, wouldn't he? And Dorian could use some weapons, if he was going to go back into town.

He took a chance and cautiously moved across the perimeter, stopping a few meters away from the wall. "Hey!" he shouted. "Anybody home?"

The house stayed silent. Dorian threw another rock. He'd worked on smaller security systems, stuff like the SaRos array, but nothing this elaborate. He realized that he'd never be able to break in, but he also knew that with a security system this complex, someone must be monitoring it. Whoever they were, he hoped they were friendly.

Still, he found himself walking along the edge, looking for the gate. It would be worth a shot. Not that he found anything but the smooth, endless wall.

Then he heard a sudden, sharp slam. A gunshot? He froze and glanced slowly over his shoulder. He strained to hear the chatter of Covenant voices, but there was only the dripping of rainwater off the tree leaves.

Then, with a hiss of energy, a screen materialized on the security wall.

Dorian jumped in surprise. Saskia Nazari was on the screen. Saskia, looking exhausted and terrified. At least she didn't have a weapon.

"Hey!" he said. "Think you can let me in?"

She blinked at him, didn't otherwise answer.

Dorian sighed. "Can you hear me?" He took a deep breath and yelled, hoping his voice would carry over the wall. "I'm Dorian. We go to school—"

"I know." Saskia's voice crackled out of an unseen speaker. "I can hear you fine. They wanted me to make sure it was really you."

Dorian laughed bitterly. "Yeah, it's really me." Then: "Who else is with you? Your parents?"

Saskia shook her head, and the screen blinked out.

"Hey!" Dorian yelled. "Where'd you go?"

As if in response, an opening melted out of the wall, revealing a sprawling house on the other side, with a huge porch where Saskia stood, her arms crossed over her chest.

"Hurry," Saskia called out. "I don't want to leave the door open for long."

Dorian jogged over beside her, and she tapped at a keypad mounted on the column beside her and the wall's opening turned solid again.

"Pretty nice setup," Dorian said.

"It's a prototype. My parents put it in." She looked at him, and her eyes widened. "What happened to you?"

"Just noticed, huh?" Dorian grinned. "I escaped the Covenant attack, that's what happened to me."

"Oh my god, really? What do you know? Where are they? What's going on?"

Dorian held up both his hands. Her questions made his head spin. "Maybe we could get inside," he said. "And if you have some water, that would be great. And food."

"Oh, of course." She bounded over to the front door, hanging open to reveal a huge foyer. Dorian's footsteps echoed on the tile. Suddenly, all he wanted was to sleep.

Someone stepped out of the hallway, some girl Dorian didn't recognize. She was followed a moment later by Victor Gallardo.

"Whoa," Dorian said. It felt like a million years had passed since he'd asked Victor to record their show in the shelter. "Are you okay, man?"

"Are you?" Victor laughed nervously. "You look like you almost died or something."

Dorian shrugged. He had almost died—from a plasma bolt, from drowning, from exhaustion. And frankly, the girl next to Victor didn't look so great either. Her face and bare limbs were crisscrossed with tiny red scratches.

"He escaped the Covenant," Saskia said. "He's going to tell us what he knows, right, Dorian? Here, let's go into the living room. I'll bring you some water."

They shuffled down the hallway, into a cavernous room with big picture windows that revealed only that enormous wall. Saskia disappeared out a door on the other side of the living room and Dorian collapsed onto the brocade sofa in the middle of the room, not caring that he was smearing it with sand and mud and sea salt. He sank into the cushions and didn't think he'd ever be able to get up again.

"Do you know Evie?" Victor said, gesturing at the girl.

Dorian shook his head. Evie raised one hand in greeting. "Hey," she said.

"Hey."

"I liked watching your band the other night."

For a moment Dorian thought she meant last night, out on the water, when the Covenant attacked. *How'd you get back? Do you know what happened to the rest of the band?* But then he realized she meant the show at the shelter.

"Thanks," he said, and she smiled at him. The whole thing felt like awkward introductions at a party, not survivors meeting on the edge of a war zone.

Saskia breezed back in with a glass of water and a plate of cheese and crackers. Dorian grabbed the water and gulped it down. When he finished, he leaned back against the couch and looked up at the ceiling. "Thanks," he said.

"What's happened?" Victor asked.

Dorian closed his eyes, and then he told them, in short, sharp bursts. He stared at the ceiling the entire time, his stomach knotting from drinking the water too quickly.

"They're in the town," he said when he finished. "The Covenant. The ship is anchored overhead and they've got guards on the periphery."

One of the girls gasped. Dorian dropped his head. The three of them stared at him with wide, frightened eyes.

"They are dead," Evie whispered. "Just like I was afraid—"

"No." Victor spat the word out. "No way. We have the shelter. Salome would have made sure everyone got to them in time."

"The comm channels are dead!" shouted Evie. "How could Salome tell people to get to safety?"

Dorian's head buzzed. "The channels are down?"

Saskia nodded. "We only got an emergency broadcast last night. But it was after the ship passed overhead." She put an arm on Evie's shoulder. Evie's eyes glimmered, and she wiped at her face. Was she crying? Dorian couldn't tell. "If the Covenant are in the town, they would have cut the comm channels. But only *after* they arrived, right?"

"Or while they were heading that way!" Evie snapped. "It's not like you have to be on the ground to interfere with comm channels."

"Well, no," Saskia said hopelessly. "But if people saw what was happening, and they would have, I'm sure of it—I bet most people got to the shelter."

"The system is decades old." Evie shook her head, her hair flying into her face. "There's no way—"

"Look, why don't we just ask Salome?" Dorian snapped.

All three of them turned to him. He felt suddenly very tired.

"The comm system's down," Victor said.

Dorian rolled his eyes. "Yeah, but if we can get to one of the town computers, we won't need the comm system to talk to her. She'll be able to give us a better idea of what's going on."

Evie blinked at him. "That could work," she said. "Assuming the Covenant haven't destroyed all the computers."

Dorian shook his head. "Those things are well hidden, especially the older ones. I did maintenance on them with my uncle. There's one over on the east side, near the old tourist houses. No one ever uses it."

"The tourist houses?" Victor said. "You want us to go into town?"

"We have to," Dorian said, glaring at him. "We can't do anything until we know what's going on."

"The tourist houses are on the edge of town anyway," Evie said. "Talking to Salome is our best bet at finding out what's going on." She turned to Victor. "Don't you want to make sure your family is safe?"

Remy's grinning face flashed into Dorian's mind.

"We might find out they're dead," Victor muttered.

"Don't talk like that." Evie looked over at Dorian. "Are you sure you can access the old computers?"

"Yeah." Dorian laughed. "I'm sure."

"You said guards were patrolling," Saskia said, her voice small. Everyone turned to look at her. She had drifted away from the group, her arms crossed over her chest. "How are we going to get past them?"

"We'll fight them?" Dorian threw up his hands. "Don't you have weapons?"

The others looked at her expectantly, but Saskia only shook her head with a quick jerk. "There's the rifle I used last night. But other than that . . ." She shrugged.

"So we have a rifle," Dorian said. He leaned forward, forced himself to ignore the pain in his muscles. "That's something."

"Are we really going to do this?" Victor asked.

"I think we should," Evie said.

Saskia said nothing.

CHAPTER EIGHT

VICTOR

They decided to go on foot. Victor's idea—he figured scouts would be watching the roads more closely. Evie and Dorian agreed, although Dorian did so begrudgingly, digging his palms into his eyes and moaning, "Not more walking."

"Maybe we should wait," Saskia had said. Of the three of them, she was the one most reticent about going into town.

But Dorian shook his head. "No. I'll be fine."

They set out after a lunch of hot sandwiches from the food squirreled away in Saskia's refrigerator. She let Dorian take the rifle since he'd said he had used one like it before—it was some kind of hunting rifle, not like the military weaponry Victor's sister used. Saskia didn't say anything during their preparations—Victor couldn't shake the sense that she didn't want to go. Maybe she was scared, even though she had marched out into the woods and saved Evie. He wanted to tell her it would be fine, that they would stay together, that the afternoon storms would give them cover. But every time he tried, his tongue felt heavy in his mouth. Mostly because he wasn't sure he believed any of it himself.

The afternoon storms were actually the reason Victor had convinced them to go after lunch. It was a trick Maria had told him about during one of her visits home. "We always learn the local terrain," she'd said. "Study it. Use it to our advantage." It had been dry season and they'd been sitting out on the beach in the sun. She'd squinted out at the water and said, "If the Covenant invade here, you better hope they do it during the rainy season. That would give you an advantage. Rain hides things, and you're more used to it than they are."

At the time, Victor had just laughed and rolled his eyes, but he understood now she had meant it as genuine advice. So much of what she'd told him—Camila too—was training. He saw that now.

Not that he'd used any of it when it really mattered. All that time firing weapons on the beach and what had he done when an actual Covenant soldier had tried to rip his friend apart? Just froze in place, too terrified to move. Some fighter he was.

The four of them trudged through the forest, Dorian in the lead with the gun. He claimed he knew a path through the woods without going near the roads, saying that he and his uncle used it when they were doing repairs. And so far, he didn't seem to be lying. They snaked through the dripping trees, following a narrow strip of matted dirt.

"Did you know this was here?" Evie whispered to Saskia.

"Parts of it. I didn't know it went into town."

Victor stiffened at the sound of their voices. "We need to be quiet," he said softly.

"Sound isn't going to carry in this rain," Evie said. "That was your whole point."

Still, they both got quiet after that. Victor kept his head down so the rain didn't get in his eyes. His clothes clung to his skin, and he wondered if it was even going to be worth it to come out during the storms.

Dorian stopped suddenly, and Victor stumbled to a halt, nearly bumping up against him.

"I heard something," Dorian said in a rough voice, hoisting up the gun. "Did you?" Victor shook his head, and Dorian peered over Victor's shoulder. "How about you two? Did you hear anything?"

They hadn't. The four of them stood unmoving in the rain, and Victor strained his hearing against the constant rhythm of raindrops. They had *just* been saying you couldn't hear anything out here. It was probably just Dorian's imagination.

Leaves exploded up ahead, framed in blue-tinged light.

"Get down!" Victor cried, slamming into the mud and ferns growing around the path. The girls did the same. He could hear Evie breathing beside him. He had frozen up when the Jackal had grabbed her last night, and he didn't think he could bear it if it happened again.

Dorian stayed standing, peering through rifle's telescope. "Get down!" Victor hissed.

Dorian swung the rifle in response. He was shaking, his legs vibrating.

"Dorian," Saskia said. "He's right. We should just hi—"

Another explosion of leaves, another streak of plasma light. It was followed immediately by the *rat-tat-tat* of automatic fire. *Human* automatic fire.

UNSC? Or survivors from town, pushing back against the Covenant?

The gunfire grew louder, the streak of plasma bolts brighter. Dorian hit the ground in front of Victor, searching for cover.

"Get in the ferns," Victor said. "Hide."

An explosion of plasma fire. Scorched leaves and the sizzle of burning plasma streaking through the rain. A pair of squat armored figures rushed past, yelping like dogs. One of them turned around and fired into the woods, away from the place where Victor and the others were hidden. Immediately, there came another burst of automatic fire and one of the Covenant soldiers pitched forward, shrieking and gurgling and then falling silent. Victor pressed himself deeper into the ferns, his body aching with the need for stillness. The other soldier had veered deeper into the woods, vanishing into the trees. A shadow zipped past, too quick for Victor to make out who was following. More gunfire. A loud, strangled squawk.

Silence.

After a few moments, Victor tentatively lifted his head. Rain fell through the trees, but otherwise the forest was still. No sign of the Covenant. No sign of that shadowy figure either.

"Is it safe?" Evie whispered.

"I don't know." Victor pushed himself up, looked around, took a deep breath. Then he stood, his body tense, ready to fling himself back into the underbrush.

Nothing happened.

Saskia's head popped out of the ferns, her hair tangled with bright flecks of leaves. "We probably shouldn't stay here," she said. "There might be more Covenant on the way."

Victor nodded. Evie and Dorian both emerged from the underbrush, Dorian still holding the rifle. Their only weapon as they marched into occupied territory.

Their only weapon—

"Wait," Victor said as the others shook off grass and sticks and leaves. "Dorian, could I borrow the rifle?"

Dorian frowned. "Why?"

"I want to see something."

"What are you doing?" Evie asked. "We need to keep moving, like Saskia said."

"We need weapons too." Victor tilted his head toward the woods. "We saw one of these Covenant soldiers go down. We can grab his gun, or whatever they're using. Then we'll be more evenly matched before we go into town."

The others stared at him. Wordlessly, Dorian handed him the rifle. Victor grabbed it and marched toward the fallen creature with a determination he didn't actually feel, if he was being honest with himself.

The soldier lay like a pile of discarded machinery, nestled amid the wet ferns. Victor jabbed the rifle at its red armor. But the soldier didn't move. Victor leaned closer, his breath echoing in his ears. He had seen holos of this species of Covenant before, in classes at school, on the new channels, from recordings his sisters had shown him. They were smaller, apelike bipeds called Unggoy. Under their armor they had thick exoskeletons like crabs, and they needed methane masks to breathe.

This one's methane mask was twisted around its neck, revealing an open mouth with rows of jagged teeth. Its eyes stared unblinking at some point past Victor's shoulder. He shivered. It was definitely dead.

"What do you see?" Evie shouted. Victor jumped at the sound of her voice, then glared at her, pressing one finger to his mouth. He turned back to the Unggoy. Weapons—he needed to look for weapons. It wasn't holding anything. But there was something lying on the ground beside it, glowing pale pink. It didn't exactly look like a gun—more like an enormous arrowhead with what appeared to be a handle. Jagged crystal spikes jutted out from the top of it.

Victor laid the rifle on the ground and then picked up the Covenant weapon with both hands, staggering a little beneath its weight. It looked like it was intended to be a one-handed weapon, but Victor was forced to awkwardly hold it in two hands. He slowly squeezed his hand into a fist, and one of the shards vanished into the weapon's cowling. A series of smaller glowing shards simultaneously launched out of the weapon's mouth, and a few seconds later a tree exploded several meters away.

Victor shouted and dropped the weapon to the ground, then whirled around to face the others.

"I'm fine," he called out, low. "But I found something."

"No kidding," said Dorian, racing over to Victor's side and yanking Saskia's rifle off the ground. "We need to leave—something might have heard us."

"What is it?" Evie asked, frowning at the weapon. "Saskia? Do you have any idea?"

Saskia gazed at the weapon through hooded eyes, her face dewy with rain. Victor's chest constricted at the sight of her. In that moment, she looked so beautiful and strong.

"Looks like a needler," she said. "My dad told me about them. Guided munitions. The weapon fires those needles on its top, and they explode on contact. Dorian's right, though. We need to get out of here before the Covenant show up."

The name sparked something in Victor's head. Camila had described Covenant weapons to him once. *The Covenant needler can blow whatever it hits sky-high*, she'd said, kicking back in the over-stuffed sofa in their parents' hotel lobby. Ballistic munitions that detect heat signatures. *You point in the direction of a target, shoot—it tracks your enemy. BAM! Like that.*

"I know how to use this," Victor said.

"You almost shot us," Dorian said.

Victor scowled at him. "I lost my grip on it, okay? Look, it's heavy, but it's not that hard to use." He hoisted up the needler and pointed it at a tree ten meters away. Then he squeezed.

A series of glowing crystals streaked out of the weapon's mouth with a heavy lisping sound. They traced through the air, impaling the tree, which vanished into a plume of pink fire.

"You are making way too much noise," Dorian said.

"Dorian's right," Evie said. "But using their weapons—they won't be expecting it from us. Is there anything else?"

"Yeah, looks like it." Saskia was kneeling beside the Unggoy soldier. She stood up, cradling a vaguely circular object in both hands. "This is a gun."

"Doesn't look like a gun," Dorian said.

"Trust me," she said. "It's a gun."

She wrapped her fingers around the grip and pointed at a tree. There was a long pause, and then a bright green plasma bolt sliced through the air, steaming in the rain. Charred bark splintered and exploded across the ferns.

She glanced over at her shoulder at Victor, her eyes dark and unreadable. She was still pointing the gun at the tree. It was the hottest thing he'd ever seen.

"Plasma pistol," he confirmed. "Yeah, Camila told me about those too."

"Who the hell's Camila?" Dorian asked.

"His sister." Evie took the pistol from Saskia and held it awkwardly in two hands. "Show me how to shoot it. But quickly, like you said."

Saskia nodded. "Put your hand on the grip there." Evie did as Saskia said. "Now squeeze it to charge. It'll fire when you release."

Another plasma bolt echoed through the woods. Evie's arm jerked up, and she stumbled back a little.

"Yeah, you need to brace yourself," Saskia said.

"Like what Maria told us," Victor said. "When we were shooting assault rifles on the beach."

"Assault rifles on the beach?" Dorian said.

Victor rolled his eyes. "My sisters are in the UNSC. They've showed me how to shoot. We need to get going."

Evie looked down at the pistol. "Yeah," she murmured.

"Okay," Dorian said. "Who's getting what?"

Evie immediately shoved the pistol at Saskia. "You can use it better than me."

"I'll keep the rifle, thanks." Dorian lifted the rifle. "Sticking with human technology."

"I'll use the needler," Victor said. "Evie? You sure you don't want a weapon?"

"I'll be fine." She looked away. She still hadn't applied anything to the scratches on her face from last night, and they stood out red and angry against her pale skin.

They set off again, treading up Dorian's overgrown path. It was getting harder to make out against the mulch of the forest floor, the ferns reaching feathery fingers into the path that kept brushing against Victor's legs unnervingly. He tried not to think about the dead Unggoy reaching out one of its oversized hands and grabbing on to his ankle. The rain picked up again, pattering through the canopy of leaves overhead. Everything smelled like soil.

"We're here," Dorian said.

Everyone stopped. The forest was thick and overgrown around them, glimmering with rain. Victor didn't see any sign of a town computer—no ugly concrete slabs or metal boxes. But Dorian plunged off the path, wading into the ferns, and stopped next to a tangle of woody vines. He shoved them aside with the butt of the rifle, and something sparked in the thick murk of the forest.

"Wow," Evie said. "That is *really* hidden."

"Not hidden," Dorian said, propping the rifle up against the structure. He yanked on the vines with his hands and tossed them off into the woods. "Just old. I had to service it once, maybe three years ago? Only reason I know it's here."

Evie moved forward and began helping Dorian clear the vines away. Victor glanced at Saskia. "Shall we?" he said, then immediately regretted it. He sounded so *dumb*.

"Let's hope they can get it to work," she said.

Together, they stepped into the underbrush. The rain was ceaseless and Victor wondered if he'd ever feel dry again.

The town computer blinked with an arrhythmic pattern of yellow lights. Dorian hit one of the lights and a holo lock screen materialized in the rain. He tapped in a code, and the lights all switched to green.

Victor felt something twist in his stomach. Jealousy? Both Evie and Saskia were watching Dorian with something like admiration. Well, more Evie. Saskia was looking past the computer.

"Do you see something?" he asked.

She shook her head. "Just paranoid."

"Salome?" Dorian said. "You there?"

An excruciating pause. The wind kicked up, blowing the rain sideways. The trees rattled.

"Dorian Nguyen, you're alive!" The familiar figure of Salome materialized in the air beside the computer. "Oh, I was so worried."

"Were you?" Dorian's voice sounded tight. "Are there casualties? Is—"

"Oh, Dorian Nguyen, I didn't mean to worry *you*!" Salome swiped at him playfully. Her personality was so off. That was what happened when you got stuck with a non-volitional AI, though at least they lasted longer. "Seventy point two percent of the population made it to the shelter."

The breath strangled in Victor's lungs. Thirty percent of the town hadn't survived. His head buzzed. His parents, had they been part of the 70 percent? His friends from school?

He glanced over at Evie and her eyes were wide and glassy, her skin pale. She pressed one hand to her mouth.

"Seventy percent," she whispered hoarsely.

"Maximilian Nguyen is still safe!" Salome chirped.

Dorian's shoulders sagged. "And Remy?"

"Safe as houses."

Victor shifted his weight. He assumed these people were Dorian's family, but honestly, he was too scared to ask about his parents. Too scared to learn they were part of that 30 percent who didn't survive.

"So the survivors," Evie said slowly, "they're in the shelter? And they're safe from the Covenant?"

Salome's expression faltered. "Of course, Evelyn Rousseau. I designed the shelter myself, and it is impenetrable."

"My father?" Evie whispered. "Mikal Rousseau?"

"He's there."

Evie sagged and leaned up against the computer, her eyes closed. Victor squeezed his free hand into a fist and opened his mouth, but his tongue was too dry to speak.

But then Salome looked past Evie, the glowing lines of her form blurred by the rain. "Victor Gallardo, your parents are safe as well."

The world tilted. Victor let out a deep breath. *Your parents are safe.*

"Saskia Nazari, I am afraid to report—"

"My parents weren't in town," Saskia said, an edge to her voice. "They're fine."

"Why are the Covenant in Brume-sur-Mer?" Evie asked, bending in close to Salome.

"I don't know," Salome said. "But they aren't leaving."

Evie looked up, locked eyes with Victor. He'd never seen her look so afraid.

"Why not?" Dorian asked.

"I don't know. The motives of the Covenant are beyond my programming, I'm afraid."

"Why don't you get people out of the shelter?" Saskia said. "Get them to safety."

"They are safe in the shelter, Saskia Nazari. If I let them out, the Covenant would destroy them." Salome made an exaggerated frown. "I'm afraid I can't let any of you in the shelter either, because if I opened the doors, it would compromise the security. You should leave the area immediately."

"Noted," Dorian said. "Salome, I'm switching you off for a minute, okay?"

"Whatever you'd like, Dorian Nguyen!"

Dorian swiped through the holo, and Salome vanished. He looked up at the others.

"It sounds like most people made it to the shelter," Evie said. "That's something."

"Yeah. Most." Dorian looked away, his expression hard and unreadable.

"How equipped is the shelter?" Saskia asked.

Victor looked over at her. She was staring intently at Dorian, cradling the Covenant pistol against her chest.

"What?" Dorian asked.

"I was down there for the show the other night," she said.

"It's ancient. There's no way there's enough food or water for everyone—"

"They're fine for water," Victor said. "There's a whole river down there."

"But is there a working filter?" Evie frowned. "Rain runoff isn't drinkable."

"Yeah, there is," Dorian said. "Should still work. They have food stores too." He closed his eyes, tilted his head back. "But not enough for the whole town."

For seventy percent of the town, Victor thought.

Silence settled over the group. Victor's relief at his parent's survival was leaching out of him, replaced with the slow, creeping terror that they would starve to death in the shelter. "We've got to get them out of there," he said slowly, each word tasting like the rain.

"And how are we supposed to do that?" Dorian glared at him. "Go fight the Covenant ourselves?"

"We could talk to Salome." Evie put a hand on Dorian's shoulder, then snatched it away when he glared at her. "You and me. I might be able to get into her programming, convince her to open the doors."

"And just let the Covenant race in there and slaughter everybody?" Dorian snapped. "She's keeping the doors shut for a reason."

"We've got weapons." Victor's heart hammered against his chest. "My sisters—they showed me some things. And, Saskia, you can handle a gun well."

Saskia didn't say anything, and Victor's face flushed with heat.

"What are you saying?" Evie narrowed her eyes at him. "Victor, you can't—"

"Can't fight?" Victor laughed. "We'll have to, eventually. Look, there are shelter entrances all over the place. We'll go to one of the more hidden ones. You tell Salome to open *only* that door, and then we can get in and tell everyone what's going on. They probably have some weapons down there too. We might be able to actually fight back."

Everything spilled out of him in a rush. He breathed in, waiting for their response.

"That sounds like one of your holo-film plots," Evie said.

Victor grinned. "If it works."

"You kept saying *we*." Dorian gestured at Saskia. "You okay with this? Charging into town with just a plasma pistol?"

Victor turned to Saskia.

"No," she said.

Anger and disappointment jolted down Victor's spine. "What?" he said. "Why not?"

"We can't fight the Covenant!" she cried. "We should wait until the UNSC gets here. We'll tell them what we know, and *they* can—"

"It's been almost twenty-four hours," Evie said. "Don't you think they'd be here by now?"

Dorian gestured, and Salome materialized again.

"Are the UNSC in town?" he asked.

"The UNSC?" She shook her head. "No, there's no evidence of military involvement with the invasion."

"Thanks." His voice was strained. He swiped through Salome and looked up at Victor.

"Well?" he said. "What do we want to do? There's no UNSC. But Saskia's not wrong either."

Saskia looked down at her hands.

"She's not," Evie said slowly. "But we don't know how much time we have." She hesitated. "We have no idea why the Covenant haven't—why they haven't started glassing the colony yet. Maybe we have some time."

Victor shivered with fear. Saskia pressed one hand to her forehead.

"That's fair," she whispered. She looked right at Victor. "Your plan does make sense," she said after a time. "But I'll only go if you agree that we won't try to start a fight."

Underneath the blanket of exhilarated terror, Victor felt a swell of joy. He smiled at her. "Of course," he said. "We'll lie low. That's the whole idea."

"But if things look like they're getting too dangerous," Saskia said, "I'm coming back. Salome can track us so she'll know where we are. If we aren't at the shelter entrance, don't open the door."

"Which entrance should we use?" Evie looked over at Dorian. "Any ideas? You knew about this place." She gestured at the computer, the green lights brilliant in the gray mist.

Dorian looked at her for a long time without saying anything. Then he looked over at Saskia, then at Victor.

"You're really sure about this?" he asked.

Victor drew himself up. The needler felt suddenly too heavy.

"I'm sure."

CHAPTER NINE

EVIE

I'm going to be honest with you," Dorian said as Victor and Saskia disappeared behind a row of trees. "Saskia was right. This is a really stupid idea."

Evie glanced at him out of the corner of her eye. Like all of them, he was soaked with rain, his long hair plastered against the side of his face. Glowering there in his dark clothes, he looked more intimidating than either Saskia or Victor, and he didn't even have a weapon—he'd begrudgingly handed the rifle over to Saskia before she left.

"I kind of agree with you," she said. "But we don't have a choice." She paused. "I mean, we have to do something."

"Can't disagree there."

They crouched in silence for a few moments, rain pattering around them. Evie shifted uncomfortably, aware of Dorian's presence next to her. He was a stranger, really—she'd never spoken to him in school. But now they'd been lashed together by this invasion.

"I guess we should try Salome." He glanced at her. "You really think you'll be able to mess with her programming?"

Evie blushed. "I don't know. It's not exactly something I've tried before."

Dorian laughed. "Yeah. You never seemed like the type."

He turned and walked back over to the computer. Evie lingered a moment longer, watching the woods. Victor and Saskia were long gone. Evie dreaded hearing the whine of plasma fire.

"Hello again, Dorian Nguyen." Salome's voice chirped like a bird in the shimmering forest. "Oh! That rhymes a bit, don't you think?"

Evie tore herself way from her vigil of the forest. Salome's projection glowed in the rain.

"We just sent Victor Gallardo and Saskia Nazari into town," Dorian said, crouching so he was eye-level with her. "They're going to the shelter entrance at Rue Camélia and Rue Violette. Can you let them in?"

Evie moved over to Dorian's side. Salome made an exaggerated frown.

"You know I can't." She pouted. "I can't open the doors until the Covenant are completely removed from the vicinity. Why haven't you left like I asked, Dorian Nguyen and Evelyn Rousseau?"

Evie frowned. Her father was always complaining about Salome's programming—she was a dumb AI, meaning her intelligence had been built with code rather than by replicating the scan of a human brain. And while she'd been designed as a typical municipal infrastructure AI, over the years the city engineers had kept going in and messing with her programming. Cutting some focuses, adding others. Giving her this bizarre personality.

"Saskia and Victor have weapons," Dorian said. "They can clear out the Covenant in the area long enough to get inside the shelter safely."

"I can't open the doors for any reason." Salome jutted out a hip, tossed her hair over her shoulder. It was so unnerving, how flippant and obstinate she'd been programmed to be. "Not until the Covenant are gone. It's a safety protocol."

"You're not going to reason with her," Evie tried.

"There's nothing reasonable about letting the Covenant inside the shelter," said Salome.

"I'm going to turn you off now, okay?" Dorian flicked his wrist without waiting for an answer, and Salome vanished.

"I'm going to have to change that protocol," Evie said. Her thoughts whirred, going back to her AI classes at school, and to the chats she and her father would have over dinner, arguing about the best way to create a truly *artificial* intelligence, no brain scanning allowed. "It's probably part of her core programming, so it's going to be tricky."

"Can you do it?"

Evie took a deep breath. "Will the holo-menu work if I'm using it? It's not tied to your DNA or anything?"

Dorian laughed. "You're giving this town way too much credit." He tapped one of the blinking green lights, and the holo-menu materialized, shortcuts to access pathways floating around the air like butterflies. Evie could feel the electric prickle along her skin that meant Dorian was watching her, and she forced herself to concentrate. *It's just like Victor's dragon. You can do this.*

It was nothing like Victor's dragon. All of her experience with this level of AI programming was purely theoretical. Still, she reached out, tapped one of the icons. The computer's processing information bloomed in front of her. She scrolled through it, scanning, until she found the linkup to Salome. She tapped it.

Immediately, all the lights on the computer turned red, and the words *ACCESS DENIED* materialized.

"Should have known it wouldn't be that easy," Evie ground out. She swiped back, scrolled through the processing information, looking for an in.

Dorian, at least, didn't say anything. Evie leaned closer, squinting at the information—there. A back door. Municipal computers usually had at least one, since they were worked on by multiple engineers spanning decades. She tapped it, pulled up a holo-keyboard, and began to type.

This part was easy. Her father had shown her how to hack into a computer system like this when she was a little girl. It took her about five minutes to find the back door into Salome's code. When she opened it, the code unfurled in a loop around Dorian and Evie, drawing them together in a ring of binary light.

"Whoa," Dorian whispered.

But Evie just felt a stone sink into the bottom of her stomach. The code was a *mess*. The language looked like a baroque version of M-Tran, which was difficult enough. But there were layers of patches and programming protocols inserted at random, half in M-Tran and the other half in SASO for some inconceivable reason.

"No wonder she's so screwy," Evie mumbled.

"What is it?" Dorian turned, the holo-light shining golden across his features. "Can you change that protocol or not?"

"Maybe?" Evie threw up her hands. "It looks like thirty different programmers have been in here messing around. And the baseline code is—weird."

She spun through the code, trying to peel back its dense, compli-cated layers to get at the center. All dumb AIs began essentially the same way, with a core of programming that sparked them into intelli-gence. After that, everything that made them who they were was incorporated, starting with those infallible programming directives—like never opening the shelter doors once the town had been ferried away into safety.

Was that it? Evie squinted. She couldn't *read* this stuff. It was like the original programmer had used five commands when one would do. No, this wasn't tied to the shelter; it had to do with prepping the town for storms. But there was something about not letting the shelter flood? Evie followed the trail, winding through Salome's programming, as dense and overgrown as the surrounding jungle.

"You making any progress?"

Dorian's voice made Evie jump. The holo flickered as her hand sliced through it.

"Sorry," he said, not sounding at all like he meant it. "But they're probably at the shelter by now—I mean, if they didn't run into any trouble—"

"What?" Evie looked over at him. "It's been like five minutes. There's no way—"

"It's been half an hour," Dorian said.

Evie stared at him. Half an hour? But she always lost track of time when she was coding. It was the same with her father.

"Yeah," Dorian said. "You were looking pretty intense for a while there."

"I'm not—" Evie looked over at the glimmering code and surged with a sudden blast of hatred for it. "I'm not going to be able to hack into her fast enough. This stupid code makes no sense."

Dorian studied her, and she braced for him to insult her, to yell at her for overselling her abilities. But he didn't, and the silence was honestly worse.

"We need to get them back here." Evie stared at the code. The holo-light made her eyes water. She swiped one hand diagonally, and all the code was sucked back into its icon. "Salome," she said.

Salome flickered into existence. "Evelyn Rousseau," she said. "Did you find what you were looking for inside me?"

"Ugh, that is creepy," muttered Dorian.

"Salome, can you locate Saskia Nazari and Victor Gallardo?" The question tasted sour. "They should be near town. Or in town. At the shelter entrance on Rue Camélia, like Dorian said."

Salome tilted her head. Frowned. "I don't see them through any of my usual channels," she said. "But access to the town has been difficult since the Covenant landed."

Evie's knees felt suddenly as if they couldn't hold up her weight, and she stumbled backward, feet slipping over the mud. But Dorian grabbed her by the arm before she could fall.

"They're dead," she murmured. "We sent them off and they're dead."

"Not necessarily!" Salome perked up. "They're just not showing up on any of the town cameras. And many of those were destroyed by the Covenant."

Evie activated the computer's holo-keyboard again. "There's got to be a way to get to them—through the emergency broadcast, maybe," she said. "We've got to tell them to come back."

"I'll give them the message if I see them!" Salome said cheerily.

"Okay, I think that's enough," Dorian said. Evie glanced over, thinking he was talking to her, but she saw that Salome was gone.

"Didn't think she was helping the situation much," he said.

He didn't say *I told you so* and Evie was grateful for that. She dove into the town's warning system. Had either of them brought their comm pads? It seemed unlikely that Victor would have left his at Saskia's house—having his comm pad for the holo-camera was second nature to him.

Evie went in and changed the emergency message from *Seek shelter immediately* to *Return immediately.* It was the only thing she could think to do. When she finished, she leaned up against the vines growing over the computer and slid down to sitting. She couldn't believe that the one time she needed to hack into something for real, she couldn't do it. How did the city engineers update Salome?

Maybe they didn't. That would definitely explain some things.

A rustle of vines—Dorian was sitting down beside her. "That was impressive," he said. "Hacking in there like that."

Evie laughed. "Not that it mattered."

"You got into her code." Dorian looked at Evie sideways. His expression was still the same dark, serious one he'd worn since last night, but there was a light in his eyes. "And you did it like it was nothing. I don't know many people who could manage that."

Evie pulled her knees into her chest. The rain had stopped and the wind had picked up and she shivered in her wet clothes. She wondered what time it was. Probably late afternoon. If the Covenant hadn't attacked, she would just be getting out of school. Maybe meeting up with Victor to do homework and talk about his holo-film.

The normal world felt like a dream, fragmented and half-forgotten. She sighed.

"We shouldn't have sent them into town," she said. "We shouldn't have split up. That's the first rule, isn't it? Never split up."

Dorian frowned. "Yeah," he said, drawing the word out like he wanted it to lead into something else.

Evie looked at him. His hair had fallen into his face, hiding his expression from her as he glared into the forest. He had told them this morning about swimming to shore after the Covenant attacked the boat where he'd been the night before. But he hadn't told them why he was on a boat. And for the first time, Evie realized that his dark clothes were the same as the ones he'd worn the night she'd seen his band play in the shelter.

"You were performing," she blurted out. When his gaze swung over to her, she slapped her hand over her mouth. His eyes glittered.

"Yeah," he mumbled, looking away again.

"The rest of your band," she whispered. "Did they—"

"I don't know." Dorian lifted his gaze toward the gray sky. "We *split up*. We were in the middle of a set when the attack happened. I sent them backstage."

"Why didn't you go with them?" She cringed at the question—why would he want to talk about this? With her? But she wanted to know. Her ankle still ached from where the Jackal had grabbed her and dragged her out of the car, and the idea that maybe she wasn't alone in that kind of near death was a thin comfort.

"I was covering for them," he said. "So they could get to safety. But then more of those things boarded the boat and I had to get the hell out." He shook his head. "They might have escaped. Might have been able to get to a lifeboat or something. The Covenant probably weren't backstage. But I don't know if they would have gone to Port Moyne or here . . ." He gestured vaguely.

"You didn't ask about them," she said quietly.

He was silent for a long time. "I don't want to hear they aren't down in the shelter."

A pang stabbed at Evie's heart, and without thinking, she laid one hand on Dorian's arm. He looked at it, looked at her. Gave a slight nod.

They didn't say anything more.

CHAPTER TEN

SASKIA

The first Covenant soldier they spotted was right on the edge of the woods. Saskia saw him first, a squat, hulking creature of the same species they had found dead in the forest.

"Stop," Saskia hissed, throwing out one arm against Victor's chest.

"I see him," Victor said softly. He lifted the needler but didn't shoot. Saskia stood holding her breath, her father's rifle heavy in her hands. The Unggoy loped along, heavy arms swinging, oblivious to them, moving farther along the perimeter of the forest until it disappeared down a side street decorated with an ancient, flickering *Brume-sur-Mer: Town of a Million Sunsets!* sign.

Saskia let out a deep breath. "Thanks for not shooting him," she whispered.

"Yeah. I didn't want to draw attention," Victor whispered. "Do you think it's safe?"

No. There was nothing safe about Brume-sur-Mer. They should never have left her house.

"I don't see anyone else," she murmured.

They crept forward, stopping at the tree line. An open field stretched out to a street and then an outcrop of buildings, mostly abandoned warehouses. The perfect place to keep troops, Saskia thought, but then she caught sight of the Covenant ship through the trees. It was still hanging in place over the town, lights glowing faintly. Or the troops were up there. Waiting. For whatever the Covenant expected to happen here in the middle of nowhere.

"That's Rue Glycine," Victor said, tilted his head at the road separating the field from the warehouses. "It'll take us right to Rue Camélia, where the shelter entrance is. Are you ready?"

Saskia took a deep breath. "Are you?" She couldn't bring herself to lie and say no.

"Do we have a choice?"

So he didn't want to say no either. Saskia grinned, although it stretched uncomfortably at the skin of her mouth and she figured she must look like a madwoman. "I guess not."

They stepped out of the forest at the same time. Beyond the press of trees, the world seemed enormous, and Saskia's head spun with all that extra space. She was certain a million Covenant eyes were on her and Victor. Her whole body tensed with anxiety and she lifted the gun, pointed it at nothing.

The wind gusted, the trees rattled, no one attacked.

"This way." Victor skittered forward, and Saskia followed. He crossed Rue Glycine and made his way under the shadow of the warehouses, head flicking around. He moved like he'd done this before. His sisters had taught him some things about the Covenant, he'd said. They must have shown him how to creep along like a commando.

Something stepped out from between the buildings only a few meters away from them.

It was not an Unggoy, nor was it the avian species that had attacked Evie and Victor in the woods. This looked more like a walking blue tank, armored and seemingly faceless and massive, towering over them like a behemoth. Glowing bolts jutted out of its arms in studs, and large blue spikes shot up from its back like quills. In the gaps between its armor were flashes of orange flesh, what looked like writhing worms.

For a breathless moment, Saskia thought that it hadn't seen them, that it would just continue on its way without a glance in their direction. They were so small in comparison. But then it stopped, its bizarre head turning, a pair of inset bright green orbs locking on them.

Victor shouted and fired off a barrage of the needler's crystals. They coursed like a swarm of glowing insects through the air before impaling just to the left of the creature, exploding the wall of the warehouse.

"Run!" screamed Saskia. She shoved Victor into an alley between two buildings just as the monster lifted its tremendous arm and released a stream of green heat from what seemed to be a weapon. The blast bored a hole into the alley like a blowtorch on paper. The air rippled against her skin, left it hot and itchy, but she was still able to run.

Behind her, the alley began to collapse.

Burning scraps of metal showered down over Saskia's and Victor's heads; she ducked and threw her hands up in a worthless shield as the detritus rained over her. Her skin stung with blisters of heat, with cuts from the metal. She straightened up, scanned the wreckage. "Victor!"

"Over here!" He was struggling to his feet. Soot streaked his face. He lifted his gaze, and his eyes widened. "Behind you!"

Saskia whirled around to find the enormous blue-armored creature barreling toward her. It was at least twice her height, and looking up at it this close made her dizzy. She tried to fire off a few rounds from her rifle, just as the monster lifted its other arm—which had an unnervingly large shield on it—slamming it against the ground and easily deflecting her attack.

She screamed. Turned. Ran. Pink crystal shards darted down the alley behind her as she cleared the smoldering alley. It was Victor, trying to buy her time by firing the needler.

"It's not working!" he cried. "And we're almost out of ammo!"

"It's got a shield!"

"I can see that!"

She grabbed him and dragged him around the side of the warehouse. She knew that thing wasn't going to stop until they were dead. Green light obliterated the corner of the building with frightening ease, a thick beam of energy swiping across the industrial structure. Through the gaping hole, Saskia could see the remains of a robotic assembly line—the once sleek parts melted and mangled together. It was trying to find them with its weapon.

She shoved Victor down to the ground just as the closest wall exploded into a mass of smoke and flames and a scent like burning poison. Saskia's eyes watered and her throat ached and her skin stung. She rolled onto her back and fired off more worthless rounds from the rifle. Bullets shredded the smoking warehouse, what was left of it at least. The monster advanced toward them, plowing through the debris like it was tall grass.

"We have to run," she gasped, pulling at Victor, who moaned. He was bleeding from a cut above his left eye, and half his face was a mask of brilliant red. "We have—"

A supercharge on the air. A gathering of green light around the thing's arm cast dark shadows around her. This was it.

Saskia squeezed her eyes shut.

But instead of the searing blast that she expected, she heard what sounded like a violent head-on collision between two speeding vehicles. Her eyes flew open.

There was a humanlike soldier clad in dark blue armor, moving too fast to track. Saskia was not sure what it was—man or machine. Although it was significantly smaller, it had apparently barreled right into the Covenant monster at full speed, forcing the creature back before it could fire its weapon.

"Get clear!" the soldier shouted.

It was a man in that armor—a human being.

"Now!" he roared, as the Covenant monster launched itself at him with its shield. The armored soldier was thrown toward the adjacent warehouse like a rock, penetrating its steel wall with a shriek. Saskia wondered if there was any way a human could have survived a hit like that. Seemed doubtful. But at least the monster was preoccupied now—it charged through the wall after the soldier, and that meant she and Victor might escape after all. She wrapped her arm around Victor's shoulder and dragged him away from the fight. He sputtered and craned his neck, trying to look backward.

"Was that a Spartan?" he gasped.

Saskia stumbled out into the street. The warehouse smoldered and smoked from a quick series of green blasts that poured out into the air behind them. Debris and smoke flooded the sky, and that toxic chemical scent hung heavy on the air. Saskia's vision blurred. When she wiped at her eyes, they stung worse.

She was connecting the dots now. A Spartan—she'd heard of them before. Was it actually a Spartan, one of the UNSC's rumored super-soldiers? The thought of one in such a backwater town as Brume-sur-Mer felt disconnected from reality. Some kind of surreal nightmare.

Behind them came the rattle of gunfire. The Spartan was some-how still alive, but the sound only made Saskia realize that her own weapon was gone. So was Victor's needler. Stupid of them, coming out here, thinking they could fight. One explosion and they tossed their guns aside in the chaos. At least there didn't seem to be any other Covenant around. At least not for the moment.

She and Victor stumbled across the road, over to the cover of the woods. Another explosion blasted through the air, and Saskia froze, her heart in her throat—but it was followed by a volley of rifle fire. The Spartan was still fighting.

"That thing doesn't give up, does it?" Victor asked, his voice scratchy.

"The Spartan or that Covenant monster?" They had just crossed the tree line. Victor swayed against her, and she felt the hot wetness of his shirt, soaked through with his blood. She leaned him up against a coconut tree.

"Both," he said.

"I'm going to let you go, all right? Can you stand?"

Victor nodded. His eyes were too bright in contrast with the blood smeared across his face. Saskia dug around in her pocket for the pack of MediGel she'd brought with her.

"We've got to get out of here," she murmured, squeezing the gel onto her fingertip. "You think you can do that?"

"What about the Spartan?"

"The Spartan has his own problems." The gunfire had stopped. Saskia didn't know what that could mean. She pressed the gel to Victor's wound, and he gasped, jerking away in pain. "Stop," she said. "You've already lost a lot of blood."

Something flickered out of the corner of her eye. She froze, hand still outstretched. "Don't move," she whispered.

"It's fine," Victor said. "It's him."

Saskia forced herself to look. Through a gap in the trees, she saw the armored soldier strolling toward them, sun gleaming off his dark blue armor, turning it silver. His face was hidden behind the polarized visor of his helmet, which reflected dots of light into Saskia's eyes. She blinked, looked away. Dropped her hand.

"What are you kids doing out here?" The Spartan's voice crackled from the speakers in his helmet. "Why aren't you in the shelter with the other civilians?"

Saskia opened her mouth. She didn't know how to start. "It's a long story," she finally said. "And my friend is hurt. And we need to get out of here before more of those things show up."

"Agreed," he said. "Hunters always work in pairs. Be glad you arrived when you did. There were two of them just a few minutes ago."

Saskia shivered. She couldn't imagine facing two of those things, much less killing them.

"Do you have somewhere to go?" Was the Spartan looking at her? All she could see was the flat gray of his faceplate.

"Her house," Victor croaked. "It's safe there."

The Spartan nodded. "Let's go, then."

"There are two others," Saskia said. "Our—" She wasn't sure what to call them. Friends didn't quite feel right, but she went with it anyway. "Our friends. They were trying to talk to Salome, the town's AI—"

"We'll get them too." The Spartan pushed past her, cradling a huge black rifle in both hands. "We need to move quickly."

Saskia glanced back at the burning warehouses. The sky was black with smoke. All she wanted was to curl up in her bed and pretend the world outside didn't matter.

She wrapped her arm around Victor, led him back into the woods.

"Turn right," Saskia rasped out, her breath strangled. "We're almost there."

"You're fortunate the Covenant aren't interested in this part of the woods," the Spartan said. He'd walked in front of them the entire time, despite not knowing where they were going. Or maybe he did. Would the Spartans have a way of knowing about the town computers? "Otherwise all of you would be dead."

Saskia and Victor glanced at each other. The MediGel had sealed Victor's cut, although it looked dark and ugly beneath the blood. "Just lucky, I guess," he said, and twisted up his mouth into a pained smile.

The Spartan didn't say anything.

Saskia heard Dorian before she saw him: He shouted a string of profanity when the Spartan stepped out into the clearing.

"Those are our friends!" she shouted, darting over to the Spartan's side. He had lifted his rifle.

"Saskia?" Evie jogged forward. "What's going on?"

"You shouldn't be out here," the Spartan said. At least he wasn't pointing the gun at them anymore.

"We weren't able to get to the shelter entrance," Saskia said. "We got attacked on the edge of town and"—she didn't know what to call the Spartan—"he saved us."

"Where's Victor?" Evie asked, her eyes wide. "Is he okay?"

"I'm fine!" Victor stumbled out of the woods, one hand lifted in greeting. Evie gasped and slapped her hand over her mouth.

"I had some MediGel," Saskia said quickly. "He just needs to clean up."

"We don't have time for this," the Spartan said. "Where is your house?"

Dorian crept up to the rest of them, his gaze on the Spartan. "You sure we can trust him?" he asked, frowning.

"Of course," Saskia said. "He's with the UNSC. He saved our lives."

The Spartan's helmet turned. Saskia wondered what he saw when he looked at them.

"I don't know," Dorian grumbled. "They used to send those guys to root out rebel factions."

"There haven't been rebellions on Meridian since the twenties!" Evie said. She turned to the Spartan. "Sir—" She paused; he did not offer a name. "I'm sorry about Dorian. We really are grateful that you're here. Maybe you can help us. We're trying to free the town from the shelter—to evacuate them from the area. That's why we're out here."

Saskia's heart thudded. She wondered if a Spartan could even understand what it was to have a family. She wondered if he felt the way she did, knowing there was no one in the shelter waiting for him.

But needing to help anyway.

"It's not safe to do that right now," the Spartan said after a moment. "Your town is swarming with Covenant troops."

Evie's shoulders slumped.

"The safest place for your families is in the shelter. Now, we need to get to safety." He turned his head toward Saskia, and she tried to imagine what his face looked like behind that blank faceplate. "Are you sure your house is secure?"

"I—yes?" She glanced over at Victor, who shrugged. "Yes," she said, more firmly, squaring her shoulders. "I'm sure."

The Spartan nodded. "Then let's go."

There was such a decisiveness to his voice that none of the others protested. Evie and Dorian fell into step alongside Saskia and Victor. They didn't say anything as they trudged through the woods. The Spartan seemed to know where they were going. Saskia didn't know if he was just following the path, or if his helmet feed had located her house. Or maybe he could just read her mind. People told all kinds of stories about the Spartans.

A storm moved in, crashing cymbals of thunder and jagged sparks of lightning that threw the forest into harsh silhouettes. Saskia huddled up into herself, shivering. She had gotten dry during the fight in town. Now the rainwater seemed to soak straight through to her bones.

To distract herself, she concentrated on the Spartan, trampling his way through the forest, shredding fern leaves and flowering vines with every step of his heavy, armored feet. He didn't move as gracefully—as quietly—as she would have expected a super-soldier to move. He swung his body around heavily, a shower of broken branches following behind him.

"So much for stealthy," muttered Dorian.

Evie shushed him. The Spartan either didn't hear or didn't care. Probably the latter.

They walked. The rain fell harder, although most of it was caught in the forest canopy. Saskia kept watching the Spartan, and she realized that part of the reason he was making so much noise was because he walked heavier on his right foot, dragging his left behind him slightly. She almost didn't notice it because of his armor, which seemed to at least attempt to correct the imbalance. But after staring at him for thirty minutes, she was sure of what she saw.

He was limping.

He was *injured.*

She glanced at the others, wondered if they had noticed. Dorian had his head down, his hair falling into his face. Victor trudged along, staring out at the woods. Evie marched with grim determination, but she didn't seem to be looking at the Spartan at all.

Saskia turned back to him. He was definitely limping, which wasn't entirely shocking given the fight she saw. Not only that, but a patch of his armor was melted and twisted near his hip. She'd been so stunned by the sight of him she hadn't noticed the damage. Had he been injured fighting that Covenant monster? It would not have surprised her. A pang of guilt spread through Saskia's chest. Had he been injured because of them?

The woods began to clear, and Saskia's house materialized up ahead, the onyx-colored walls glimmering in the rain. The Spartan stopped, his head tilted back.

"You weren't kidding," he said. "Where'd you get the specs for this? Doesn't look civilian," he said, casting an eye toward the turrets.

"My parents." Saskia hesitated. The others were crowding around the gate, heads down against the rain. She looked up at the Spartan. "Are you hurt?"

He didn't say anything, and Saskia wasn't sure he would answer at all. Maybe she had overstepped some unspoken boundary here. Maybe Spartans weren't allowed to acknowledge their injuries. Who knew what sort of training the UNSC put them through.

But then the Spartan said, "I got taken down by the Covenant on the way in. The suit took up most of the damage, but—" He shifted in his armor, a movement sort of like a shrug.

"You're limping. And it looks like your armor is damaged."

His head turned toward her. His faceplate was dotted with raindrops. She wished he would take off his helmet. "It was a close call."

"Saskia?" Dorian called. "What are you waiting for?"

Saskia looked at the Spartan one last time, then jogged over to the gate and entered in the access code. The door materialized, and everyone stepped inside. The others ran up to the house, slamming in through the back door. But Saskia hung behind with the Spartan.

"I've got a medical kit," she said. "UNSC-issued. I can help you. You'll have to take that suit off, though."

"No, that can't happen. I wouldn't be able to get it back on again without a mounting machine."

Saskia took a deep breath. "Then maybe I can pry off the damaged part. Get in to treat you that way."

The Spartan stepped onto the porch and Saskia followed, grateful to be out of the rain. "Fine," he said. "But we're doing it out here. I don't want the others to see."

"Why not?"

"Bad for morale." He sat down on the porch, leaning up against the wall of the house. His left leg jutted out oddly, and Saskia wondered just how badly hurt he was.

"This whole day has been bad for morale," Saskia said.

The Spartan reached up and slid off his helmet. Saskia blinked in shock—he was *young*, his face unlined and boyish. He couldn't be more than a few years older than she was. But he did not have the eyes of a teenager, and his left cheek was marked with an angry red scar.

"Let me get the kit," she said.

He nodded, leaned his head against the house. Saskia ducked inside, went into the living room, and gathered up the medical kit from where she'd left it after treating Evie's wounds. She didn't see the others, although she heard water running through the pipes in the house. She trudged back outside. The Spartan had slid off the damaged panel of his armor, revealing the black bodysuit underneath. The armor panel was smeared with blood.

"I'm going to have cut this away," Saskia said.

"That's fine." The Spartan looked out at the yard, where the rain pummeled the grass in an endless sheet of gray.

Saskia pulled on the fabric of his bodysuit. It was thick and crusty with blood. She snipped at it with the kit's medical scissors and then peeled the suit away, revealing a startling patch of gray-black skin, mottled with purple and yellow. Saskia hissed through her teeth.

The Spartan laughed. "The armor took most of it. Lucky it didn't completely melt."

"No kidding." Saskia fumbled around in the medical kit for the canister of biofoam. "This is going to hurt," she said.

The Spartan glanced at the canister. "I've used it before."

"Just wanted to warn you."

She inserted the canister's needle into the edge of the wound; the Spartan's muscles tensed beneath her hands, but he didn't make a sound. She pressed the release, and the foam bubbled under the skin. She spread some extra across the top of the wound itself.

The Spartan leaned his head back and groaned, his eyes blazing, his jaw clenched. Saskia sat quietly, not sure how to react. Part of her wanted to reach over and smooth his short hair, a gesture that had calmed her the last time she'd had biofoam injected. But she wasn't sure it was appropriate. So she just sat, and waited, listening to the rain pound against the roof of the porch.

Then the Spartan let out a long, gasping sigh. His head dropped toward her.

"Thank you," he said, his voice strained. "It's working."

"You saved Victor and me," she said. "There's no point in letting you limp around."

"I'll need more than biofoam to get back to normal," he said. "But this helps."

Saskia smiled weakly. "Do you have a name? I'm Saskia, by the way."

"Saskia," he said, then closed his eyes and nodded. "I'm Owen."

It was such a startlingly ordinary name that Saskia broke into a grin. But then he said, "Owen-B096." Her grin vanished. A human name—but not quite.

"It's good to meet you, Owen," she said softly. He didn't protest.

CHAPTER ELEVEN

EVIE

The first thing Evie did when she came in from the woods was peel off her damp, clammy clothes and stand underneath the shower without moving. The hot, clean water soaked into her muscles and slowed down her racing heart. But whenever she closed her eyes she still saw the blood caked across Victor's face, his eyes bright and glittering and unfamiliar.

She didn't know what had happened to them. Only that they'd been attacked, that the Spartan had saved them somehow. Dorian had been right—they shouldn't have split up. Shouldn't have sent them into town.

When the shower started to cool, she switched it off, dried herself, and pulled out an old shirt and trousers from the stack of clothes that Saskia had brought her that morning. "My old stuff," she'd said. "If it doesn't fit, let me know."

The clothes did fit, even though Evie was smaller than Saskia. At some point they must have been the same size. Some phantom Saskia, from the time before she lived in Brume-sur-Mer.

Evie stepped out into the dim hallway. Rain pattered on the roof, although the rolls of thunder sounded far away. She knocked on

Victor's door, at the end of the hall—they had claimed rooms this morning, before they set out on their ill-fated mission.

"Yeah?" Victor called out.

"You okay?"

The door swung open. Victor looked like himself again, with no mask of blood. The long cut across his forehead was already turning pink.

"I've been better," he said, "but I'll live."

He pushed the door open wider and Evie stepped in. The room was big and airy and tastefully decorated—about as different as possible from the messy cave that was Victor's actual bedroom.

"What happened to you out there?" she asked.

"We ran into the Covenant." Victor leaned up against the wall, his arms crossed. He had on some of Saskia's dad's clothes, a button-down shirt and black dress pants that hung too big on his skinny frame. "We're lucky it was just one. I've never seen anything like it before. Probably close to four meters tall, like a walking tank, and it didn't stop coming for us."

"Good god," Evie murmured.

"It was pretty messed up," Victor said.

Evie nodded, and then they descended into an awkward silence, the rain beating out that constant rhythm against the windows. Her best friend had almost gotten blown up and all she'd done was hack into a town computer and then get stuck.

"You wanna go downstairs?" Victor said suddenly. "See what everyone else is up to?"

Evie grinned. "You think that Spartan has stuck around?"

"Where else would he go?"

Evie and Victor left the room together. A low hum of voices drifted up from downstairs. She glanced at Victor, who shrugged, then headed toward the narrow staircase curving its way into the front foyer. She followed him down into the living room, where she expected to find Saskia and Dorian and instead found Saskia and a man who looked like a robot, his body hidden beneath a layer of heavy armor.

"Are you—" she started.

"This is Owen," Saskia said. "Well, Owen and some numbers, but Owen is easier."

Owen smiled a little. Despite his height and hulking armor, he looked like he could be an athlete at the college in Port Moyne. It was startling, the idea that a Spartan could be so young. When she heard the rumors, she imagined grizzled old men behind those blank faceplates. Not a boy with dark, shrouded eyes.

Footsteps echoed against the walls, and then Dorian appeared, looking uncomfortable and strange in Saskia's father's castoffs. His hair hung in a wet ribbon down the center of his back.

"I see we've decided to commune," he said.

They all looked at one another for a moment, not saying anything. Owen radiated from the center like the sun.

"Owen thinks we should evacuate," Saskia said.

Evie's entire body went cold. "Evacuate?" she cried. "And leave our families behind?"

"Evacuation is the best course of action right now," Owen said.

"No!" Evie glanced over at Victor, and he seemed as horrified as she felt. "The whole reason we tried to go into town in the first place was because we know people can't stay in the shelter forever. And you want us to abandon them?" She felt her voice rising in pitch, her heart pounding against her rib cage. "We have family and friends down there! Our teachers and our neighbors—we can't just leave them to die. Not to mention Dorian still doesn't know what happened to his bandmates. We can't just leave."

She knew everyone was staring at her, but she kept her gaze on Owen, who looked back at her blandly.

"Evie's right." Victor lifted his head. "I'm not leaving Meridian without my parents. I'm not."

"You saw what that thing almost did to us!" Saskia said quietly. "If we stay, we're going to get ourselves killed."

"Better to die fighting than hole up like a bunch of rich cowards," Victor snapped.

Saskia froze, her eyes dark and glittering, her mouth tight with anger. It was the first time they'd acknowledged that unspoken truth— Saskia wasn't like the rest of them. A hundred years ago, their families had fought against the control that families like Saskia's had tried to exert over them. It was easy to forget when you had a common enemy. Easy, until it wasn't anymore.

"Stop it." Owen stood to his full height, and he suddenly seemed to take up the entire room. "You can't do anything for your families if you're killed. It's my job to get you to safety." He looked at them, his expression hard. "My job to get your families to safety too. Which is exactly what I'll do once you're at the UNSC shelter in Port Moyne."

He stalked toward the door. Saskia stood up and followed him. But Evie and Dorian and Victor all stayed put.

Owen stopped in the doorway. He didn't turn around to look at them. "You're just making this more difficult than it needs to be."

Evie glanced at Dorian. His expression was unreadable. She thought he almost looked angry.

"How do you feel about this?" she asked.

"I don't want to leave my nephew behind," he said softly.

Owen finally looked back at them. "You're not," he said. "I'll come back for him. I'll come back for all your families. Now let's go."

Evie thought about her father down in the shelter. The last thing she'd said to him had been a lie—as he'd left for his meeting, he'd asked about her plans for the evening and she'd told him something about staying in to study. Now he probably thought she was dead.

But she knew too that Owen was right. What could she and the others do? She thought of Victor stepping out of the woods, his face covered in blood. They weren't soldiers. They were lucky they'd survived this long.

She took a deep breath and moved toward the door. Owen stepped aside and let her pass through the threshold, into the hallway. She didn't say anything to Victor, or to Dorian, but she heard their footsteps behind her.

"It's going to be okay," Saskia whispered to her, but Evie just shook her head. She didn't want to talk about it with her.

They gathered in the foyer, everyone quiet, their gazes downcast. Owen's footsteps echoed down the hallway, and then he appeared, clutching his rifle in both hands. It was at least twice the size of Saskia's rifle, and much meaner-looking.

"Roads are likely being monitored," he said. "So we'll be going by foot."

Dorian groaned. "You expect us to walk all the way to Port Moyne?"

Owen glared at him. "We'll keep to the underbrush. Safest way. If we're lucky, we'll run into some UNSC or Meridian scouts and they can take us in."

"You can't call for backup?" Evie blurted. "Have someone come get us? Wouldn't that be safer than walking?"

"Yeah, good point," Victor added. "I mean, since you're so worried about keeping us safe and all."

Owen stared at them, unblinking. Eventually, he said, "The Covenant's jamming all comm channels, even the military's. There's no way to get calls out. The only way out is on foot."

Evie gasped, heard murmurs of surprise from the others too.

"Do you even know if there's a shelter in Port Moyne?" Dorian demanded.

"Yes," Owen said. "And to tell you how I know would be classified. We're moving out. No more questions."

He pushed past them, stepping out onto the front porch. Twilight had arrived while they'd been cleaning up, flashes of sunset peeking out from behind the heavy rain clouds. Insects chirruped off in the woods, shrill and keening.

"Here goes nothing," Victor sighed to Evie as they stepped out into the hazy light. Owen marched across the lawn, Saskia trailing behind him. She opened up the gate, and they went out into the open woods.

Owen stopped, turned toward them. "Stay quiet," he said. "Do as I tell you." He paused. "And I promise you'll make it out in one piece."

"More UNSC lies," Dorian murmured, and if Owen heard him, he didn't say anything.

For the second time that day, they clambered out into the humid woods. This time, Evie's dread was wound up tight with her guilt—at sneaking out, at leaving her father behind in the shelter. Maybe she'd be able to get a message to him once they arrived in Port Moyne. Owen had said the comm channels were scrambled. Maybe that wasn't entirely true. Maybe some were still working. At least the ones out of Port Moyne.

They walked single file through the lush, damp undergrowth for at least an hour, following the main highway out of town but staying clear of it. As the light dimmed, the shriek of insects grew louder, until it was the only thing Evie thought she'd ever hear again.

Up ahead, Owen froze, lifted one hand in a fist. The others all crumpled together into a stop.

"What is it?" Victor asked, and Evie slapped at him to be quiet.

"Stay here," Owen said in a dangerously low voice. Then he darted off into the foliage, vanishing into the green shadows.

But they did as he asked, and they stayed in place, not moving. Evie listened to the familiar screech of the insects. It seemed even louder out here, a kind of staticky hum reverberating underneath the chorus.

"Do you hear that?" Saskia asked softly, pressing close to Evie.

"It's just bugs," Evie said.

Saskia shook her head. "No. I hear something else—"

Something cracked and Evie jumped and one of the boys let out a shout. All four of them huddled together.

A soft rustling rang out from the undergrowth.

Owen reappeared. "Bad news," he said.

Evie exchanged worried glances with Victor and Saskia.

"What sort of bad news?" Dorian asked, breaking away from the others.

Owen's shoulders hitched. "Come and see. But stay quiet." He whirled around and vanished back into the growth, but this time Dorian followed. Evie glanced over at Victor. He shrugged, but his eyes were wide and bright and terrified.

Saskia edged forward, looked over her shoulder at the others. "He wouldn't do anything to put us in danger."

"I guess," Victor said, but he followed Saskia, and Evie followed him. They wound through the vines and dripping tree branches. The strange humming grew louder, and a sick weight filled up Evie's stomach. Eerie violet light filtered through the trees. The air felt strange. Like the way air felt right before a lightning storm.

And then Victor shoved some branches aside and bright purplish-green light flooded across them. Evie blinked. At first, all she could see was light. Then she made out the shapes of Dorian and Owen, darkened into silhouettes. Beyond them—light. Light shimmering fluidly. Plasma.

"Oh my god," she breathed.

It was an energy shield. Charred plant matter lay in heaps at its base, and when Evie lifted her gaze, she couldn't see the top. It was as if the shield had replaced the sky.

"We're trapped," Saskia said flatly.

"It looks that way." Owen kept staring at the energy shield. "They've put Brume-sur-Mer under a defensive canopy. It's a dome energy barrier. Nothing in, nothing out."

Terror vibrated up Evie's spine. For all that she hadn't wanted to leave her dad in the shelter, suddenly the thought that she was trapped here, with the Covenant, made her breath tight and panicky. She tottered to one side, her arm lashing out against Victor, who caught her, held her steady.

"Get down!" Owen shouted suddenly, whirling in a sudden flash of movement. The muzzle of his rifle lit up bright white, and the sound of gunfire bored into Evie's head. She yanked Victor down into the muddy ground as Owen jumped over both of them, firing into the woods.

Pale plasma bolts zipped overhead, melting into the shield.

"Retreat!" Owen shouted, but Evie didn't know where they could possibly retreat *to*. Shadows emerged from the trees up ahead. Incomprehensible chatter rose up from the brush. Evie sunk herself into the mud, her hands pressed over the top of her head. Energy from the Covenant's shield sparked over her skin. She knew she couldn't stay burrowed here in the mud.

She lifted her gaze in time to see Owen pound his fist into the mask of one of the Unggoy attackers. The glass cracked, and the Unggoy slammed into the ground, screeching. Owen fired off into the darkness and then glanced down at Evie. "Get out of here," he said. "Stay low."

"I *know*," she shouted as he slunk forward, still firing his rifle. Something darted out of the woods—another Unggoy? No, it looked too big.

Evie squirmed through the grass and fallen leaves and the puddles of dirty rainwater. The air was heavy with acrid smoke. Something behind her was burning, but she didn't look back, just pressed forward the way they'd come, into the safety of the trees.

She bumped into something warm and solid, and she let out a shriek of terror.

"Quiet!" the warm solid something hissed.

"Dorian?" she whispered.

"Yeah." Leaves rustled, and then his face was close to hers, his hair clotted with mud. "Where are the others?"

The rattle of Owen's rifle exploded through the woods.

"Some evacuation this turned out to be," Dorian muttered.

They crawled into a net of tangled tree branches. Evie propped herself up on her toes and peered out at the clearing: The energy shield glowed steadily, plasma rippling across it like ocean waves. A plasma bolt hit it, and the whole thing shimmered but stayed put; from somewhere she couldn't see came a strangled alien scream.

"I don't see anyone," she said, her voice tight with worry.

Something crashed in the underbrush, the steps too heavy to be human. Evie's body tensed, her hands curling into fists. Beside her, Dorian straightened his spine, his expression fierce.

The crashing came closer. Closer—

A flash of reflected light. A dark, urgent voice: "Move. Get back to the house."

"Owen!" Evie cried, then immediately slapped her hand over her mouth. Owen jerked his head, his eyes hidden by his faceplate.

"I've already sent the others ahead," he told her. "You can meet up with them there. I'll be right behind you. Now move!"

Evie looked over at Dorian. He nodded at her.

Together, they turned and ran back toward Brume-sur-Mer.

"So what do you know?" Dorian demanded.

They were in the safe room of Saskia's house, three layers of protection between the five of them and the Covenant crawling through the town: the fence, the expensive Erse auto-locks on the front door, the vacuum-sealed safe room. Evie pressed her knees to her chest. The mud had dried in a hard shell over her clothes.

Owen looked at them. He had removed his helmet, and his skin was still shiny with sweat.

"That could have gone better," he said.

"You didn't answer my question," Dorian said. "What's going on out there? Why do they have a *shield* around Brume-sur-Mer?"

"Seriously," Victor said. "Why aren't they going after Angoulême or Avignon?"

Owen held up one hand. "I don't know, and even if I did, I couldn't tell you."

Victor slumped back. He was sitting next to Evie, both of them sprawled out on the cold floor.

"I'll tell you what I can, though." Owen rubbed his forehead. "Since it appears we're stranded here for the time being."

Evie shivered. As much as she'd hated the idea of evacuating, the idea of being trapped actually felt worse.

"I'll start with this," Owen said. "The Covenant attack didn't actually begin last night."

"What?" Evie blinked. "What do you mean?"

"Meridian's Air Force have been fighting them off around Hestia V for the past week or so," Owen said. "Giving them hell too. But our people got overpowered. Last night was when the Covenant finally broke through. I've been fighting them for the last three days, trying to stop them from getting to the surface." Something in his demeanor changed: A shadow flickered across his eyes, his shoulders rounded slightly. "We let you down, and I'm sorry for that."

Evie looked down at her hands. Images from the last week flashed in her head: taking a test in history class, working on computer science homework at the café in the center of town, dressing up to go to the concert. All that time and the Meridian Air Force had been battling the Covenant up in the black. She thought of the flickers of electricity, the disruptions in the comm system. Suddenly, they were no longer random annoyances.

"Why weren't we told?" Dorian said. He was the only one who hadn't sat down, and he paced back and forth across the safe room. "Why keep it a secret like that?"

"To avoid panic," Victor said. "People would have rioted, or worse, tried to get off-world and jumped right into the middle of a battle—"

"People could have prepared," Dorian shot back. "You think I would have been out in the middle of the ocean if we thought the Covenant were on the verge of breaking atmosphere?"

"It's standard procedure," Owen said quietly.

"It's bullsh—."

"Stop," Evie said, even though she agreed with Dorian. "There's no point in fighting about it now. The Covenant *did* break through." She thought she could feel Dorian's eyes burrowing into the back of her head. "We can still find your bandmates," she whispered.

"They're dead."

Evie felt a flood of hopelessness. *You don't know that,* she thought, but it wasn't as if she knew they were alive—if they could even get to them, with that shield in place. Not like her father, who'd made it to the town shelter.

The room filled with a thick silence. It was Saskia who finally broke it, saying, "So are the Covenant all over the moon?"

Owen shifted in his seat and the couch groaned beneath his weight. "I would imagine so. They brought a fleet to Meridian, so they aren't focusing their efforts on one town."

"A full fleet," Evie whispered.

But Owen shook his head. "Not full, no. It actually had fewer ships than usual, which made it easier for us to hold back the Covenant."

"'Us,'" said Victor. "You mean UNSC?"

"UNSC and the Meridian military."

"So where are they now?" Dorian snapped. "There's a freaking energy shield around the entire town, and we didn't see a single military unit out there!" He narrowed his eyes. "Not to mention your backup. I'm sure the mighty *Spartans* could get through that perimeter." He spat out their title like a slur.

"We have a comm system." Saskia gestures at the station. "If you need to call someone."

Owen frowned. "It wouldn't matter. The Covenant is scrambling all the military comm channels. As for your question . . ." He nodded at

Dorian. "Both militaries are prioritizing the population centers. I imagine that's why they aren't trying to breach the perimeter."

"And your team?" Dorian demanded.

There was that flicker in Owen's eyes again. "Yes," he said. "We were separated when the dropship made impact. I have no idea if they're alive or dead, but protocol's pretty clear: I operate as if I'm the only one left."

The silence crept in again. Evie looked over at Dorian. He'd stopped pacing, and his eyes were dark and glassy. But then he nodded, once.

Owen nodded back.

"I did what I could," Owen continued, his voice straightforward, matter-of-fact. A soldier's voice, no hurt or emotion. "Particularly when I realized the Covenant were setting up in your town. They don't seem interested in the survivors—"

An exhale of breath filled the room, a rush of relief. Owen hardly seemed aware of it.

"—which means there's probably something about this place itself they want."

"Like what?" Victor asked.

Owen hesitated. "I'm not sure. But they haven't made any attempts to glass the colony, and their fleet is gridlocked outside the atmosphere. It's a good sign for the survivors."

He said it so casually—*glass the colony.* As if it were nothing for the Covenant to melt their home world into smooth, dark stone. As if it wouldn't mean that the molecules of millions of people would all meld together, frozen together in a tomb of destruction.

"So what do they want?" Dorian asked, peeling himself away from the wall. "What could be in Brume-sur-Mer?"

"Resources, maybe. I told you, I'm not sure."

"Well, we have to stop them," Evie said. "Whatever it is. If they get what they want, then they will—" She couldn't bring herself to say it. "You know. And everyone will be trapped underground. They'll die in the shelter."

"I'm not sure we can stop them," Owen said. "Sabotaging an entire Covenant operation without the rest of my team—"

"We can help," Evie blurted.

Everyone in the room stared. Her cheeks flushed with heat. Why had she said that? Victor and Saskia had almost been killed going into town, and all four of them had retreated from a firefight instead of helping.

And yet she didn't regret saying it.

"Are you crazy?" Victor asked. "Do you not remember what literally *just happened* to us?"

"No. I—what else are we going to do? Sit in Saskia's house and wait to die? You're the one who didn't want to evacuate in the first place."

Victor frowned.

"Well, now we're stuck here," Evie said. "So we might as well do some good."

Victor nodded. "Fair enough," he said, although he sounded scared.

"If you could help us learn how to fight," Evie said carefully, turning back to Owen, "we would be able to help you."

She took a deep breath. Her outburst made her realize how exhausted she was.

"This is crazy," Saskia said. "You can't expect him to train us into soldiers overnight."

"But we can't do nothing!" Evie cried. "We don't have to go into town again, but there's got to be something we can do." She looked at

Owen again. "I'm not asking you to turn us into Spartans. But we've got to fight back."

"I can't believe this," Saskia sighed.

"You're not going to get very far if you can't work as a team," Owen said. He nodded at Dorian, who'd slouched up against the wall. "And what about you? What are your thoughts on this?"

Everyone turned to Dorian, who pushed a hand through his damp hair. Evie pressed her nails into her thigh, waiting for his answer, certain he was going to side with Saskia.

"I'm not letting anything happen to my nephew," Dorian said in a flat voice. "Or my uncle. I'm not deserting the people I care about again." His gaze flicked over to Evie, then back to Owen. "I say we fight."

Saskia slid back against the wall, pressed her hands over her face. "This is so stupid," she murmured. "We're all going to die."

"So don't fight," Victor snapped. "Let us use your house as a base of operations. That can be your contribution."

Saskia glared at him. "If you didn't have my house, you would all be dead."

"Stop," Owen said.

They fell silent. Owen stood, although his legs trembled, and he kept a hand pressed to his side, to a spot free of armor. *He's injured,* Evie realized with a start. Had it happened during the failed evacuation? Or earlier?

But even injured, she bet he could help them. Spartans were the stuff of legend. Some stories claimed they could even heal faster than the average human. And even if it wasn't true, an injured Spartan was better than just about anything else.

"The three of you," he said, pointing at Evie and Victor and Dorian each in turn, "you have people in the shelter you're worried about?"

Evie nodded.

"And, Saskia, you don't have anyone."

Saskia frowned. "My family isn't down there," she said. "But people I knew from school—some of my teachers." She faltered, curling in on herself. Evie leaned forward, her heart fluttering. She hadn't expected this.

"I don't want to hide," Saskia murmured. "I don't. But you saw what happened to us in town. If you hadn't shown up—"

"Don't think like that," Owen said. "You two were up against a Hunter. A full squad of marines would have had their hands full."

The name chimed in Evie's memory—at school when they studied the Covenant species, the teachers never used the human shorthand names, but Victor's sisters would throw them around when they were home on leave.

"Which one's a Hunter?" she asked.

"A Mgalekgolo," Victor said quietly. "Right? That's what we were fighting."

Owen nodded.

"Oh." Evie leaned back, old lessons flooding into her head. The Mgalekgolo were colonies of some wormlike creature, formed into heavy armor in order to fight in combat. "That's bad, isn't it? They're one of the strongest species?" She frowned. "Aren't there usually two of them?"

Owen nodded. "I had already killed its partner before Victor and Saskia arrived." He glanced at them. "If the two of you had come up against a Grunt, you would have been fine. You knew how to use your weapons, and you did actually work together, even if you'd rather yell at each other right now. My mistake tonight was not arming you during the evacuation."

Victor looked down at his lap, his cheeks turning pink. Saskia just looked at the windows.

"The five of us are not going to be able to drive the Covenant out of town," Owen said. "But we can make things very hard for them. We can draw out their efforts until the UNSC can get through." He paused. "Like we saw tonight, we'll need weapons. Ammunition. And that means scavenging. So if this is going to work, then you will need to listen to me. You will need to do what I say. And you will need to work together."

Anxiety fluttered around in Evie's stomach, but so did hope. "You'll really help us?"

"I don't think we have much choice if we want to survive." His voice was strained; Evie didn't know if it was because he was in pain from his injuries, or because deep down he thought this plan was stupid, or both. "But we're going to need to act fast."

CHAPTER TWELVE

DORIAN

Their first lesson was that same night, after a dinner of reconstituted packets of stew from the stash in Saskia's pantry. They all filed outside and set up in the big expanse of Saskia's backyard, encompassed by the towering iron wall. She brightened the safety lights so they could see, although it was a harsh, unnatural light, making their skin look sallow and ill-looking.

"Tomorrow we do a reconnaissance mission," Owen announced, strolling past the four of them, all lined up as if they were in the military. Dorian scowled. The last thing he wanted was to end up like his parents.

Still, he had to do something. For Remy.

"Really?" Saskia asked. "A reconnaissance mission is exactly what we screwed up when you found us."

"No, you screwed up a rescue mission," Owen said. "But before we can rescue anybody, we need information. The more we can find out about why the Covenant are here, the easier our work becomes—not that it's ever going to be truly easy. Or safe."

Dorian shivered.

"The goal," Owen said, "will be to get you into town without being noticed. You'll go in teams of two. We'll practice tonight; send you off tomorrow morning."

Evie raised her hand as if she were in school. Owen stared at her blankly for a moment, then said, "You have a question?"

"Who are the teams going to be?" she asked.

"Same as before. Makes it easier."

"Before?" Evie blinked. "Oh. You mean your rescue mission."

Owen nodded.

"Guess it's you and me again," Dorian said, peering at her around Saskia. Evie smiled back at him, and for a moment, he almost felt better about this whole stupid situation.

"Okay, here's how this is going to work." Owen clapped his hands. "We're all going into the woods just outside the wall. Your job is to find me without me seeing you."

Victor snorted. "That's impossible—haven't you been genetically engineered? How are we supposed to see in the dark?"

Owen looked at him. "You went up against a Hunter this afternoon," he said. "And you didn't get yourself killed. Do you know why?"

"Because you showed up," Saskia said.

"Exactly. You got lucky. The Covenant are a coalition of species, all of them following an evolutionary track different from ours. The Elites have tremendous speed and strength. The Hunter, the one you fought? Their colony formation allows them to sense an enemy even if they aren't looking directly at them. You aren't going up against humans. So if it's impossible for you to reconnoiter me, then it's impossible to reconnoiter the Covenant, and if that's the case, what the hell are we even doing out here?"

The only thing to answer his question was the forest, the chorus of whining insects and chirping frogs, the rustle of tree leaves.

"If you don't have any more questions," Owen said, "let's get started."

They practiced through the humid, sultry night, creeping through the woods by the light of Hestia V, which barely seeped through the tree cover. The rain had let up, which made their training exercise all the more difficult. Dorian and Evie circled through the trees in narrower and narrower arcs, the way Owen had shown them, but every time Dorian thought he'd managed to finally slide in without notice, Owen would whirl around and flash a light in his eyes. "You're dead," he said flatly. "Try again."

"I never wanted to join the UNSC," Dorian said to Evie as they struggled through a tangle of fragrant moonflower vines, the big white blossoms drifting like ghosts in the shadows.

"Me neither," Evie said. They'd given up trying to be quiet at that point. Dorian had no idea how late it was—or how early in the morning. He felt like he hadn't slept for a million years.

"And yet here we are." Dorian yanked on a particularly tenacious vine and brought down a shower of wet leaves and broken sticks. Evie yelped.

A familiar sphere of light glimmered up ahead.

"Uh-oh," Dorian said. "He's up there. Run!"

Dorian leapt out of the vines, sliding in between a copse of narrow rubber trees. Evie was right behind him. She grabbed his hand, and they wove together through the trees, vines slapping Dorian in the face.

"I think we lost him," Evie gasped, slowing to a stop. She dropped Dorian's hand. Buddy system, she'd called it, like back in elementary school. Find a buddy and don't let go. Dorian didn't mind. He couldn't stand the thought of getting separated again. Not even during practice. Especially since they were now outside Saskia's enclosure and nothing stopped the Covenant from getting to them if they wanted to.

He peered through the darkness and didn't see any spots of light. "Yeah. Looks that way."

"This is pointless," Evie said. "It's just like what happened when we tried to evacuate. How are we supposed to see anything in town if we run at the first sign of the Covenant?"

Dorian sighed. "I have no idea." He slumped up against a tree. The night was cool and damp, and although he wasn't hot, his clothes were soaked with sweat. Everything smelled like soil and rotting leaves. He dropped his head back and looked up through the gaps in the canopy. A few stars twinkled, one slid out of sight. A ship, then. He wondered if it was Covenant or UNSC or even the Meridian Air Force.

He wished he could get to Mr. Garzon's scud-rider. Do an aerial sweep. Get a view of the town from up above.

"Oh," he said, straightening. "I know what we can do."

"What?" Evie was a pale smudge in the darkness.

"We go up." Dorian pointed. "Get close enough that we can see Owen's light; then we climb up into the trees. The forest is thick enough we might even be able to crawl from branch to branch, but honestly, we could probably just wait."

Evie moved closer to him, her eyes wide. "That could work. I mean, he'll still hear us—"

"If we go up high enough, the canopy should give us enough cover. It's at least worth trying." Dorian lifted his hair off the back of his neck, relishing the cool rush of air on his skin. "And maybe he'd finally let us go in and get some sleep."

"Seriously."

So they ventured out again, retracing their path, until Evie nudged Dorian in the side. "I see him," she whispered.

Up ahead, a yellow light blinked and flickered through the trees. Dorian nodded. "Let's go."

He hauled himself up a nearby cashew tree, scrabbling to the middle tier of branches. He crouched, listened to the rustle and scrape of Evie as she dragged herself up beside him. She panted a little, wiped at her forehead.

"You okay?"

"I'm fine. I haven't done that since I was a kid."

Dorian grinned. "You should come work for my uncle. He's got me climbing trees constantly."

Evie laughed, then clapped her hand over her mouth. "Sorry," she whispered.

Dorian leaned off the branch. The light still glimmered in the distance. "I don't think he heard us. Let's go."

It was slow work, creeping along the tangle of low branches. Leaves and flakes of bark rained down into Dorian's hair, and his arm muscles ached from having to pull himself along. Plus, Evie was overly cautious, debating each step before she took it, testing each branch with a few pokes of her foot before placing her entire weight on it. But the light grew steadily bigger as they approached. And it didn't move. A good sign.

They had scrambled through the trees for fifteen minutes when they came to a gap too large to jump. Dorian sighed with frustration.

"It was a good plan," Evie whispered, one hand braced against his shoulder. "We got closer to him than we have before."

That much was true, at least. Owen's suit cast a sphere of light up ahead, illuminating the sides of the trees. Owen stood in silhouette, clutching that rifle of his, but Dorian couldn't see much more than that. Some spy he was.

"I have an idea," Evie whispered. "Can we get up higher, do you think?"

Owen's silhouette shifted, didn't turn.

Dorian squinted up. They were currently crouched in a kapok tree, tucked in the hollow beneath the canopy. A particularly sturdy-looking branch jutted out like a stepping-stone into the leaves.

"Yeah," he said. "I think so."

"Okay. Get ready to climb." Evie snapped off an overhanging branch. The noise was like a gunshot, but Dorian realized instantly what she was planning to do. He swung himself up the stepping-stone branch.

Evie hurled the broken branch out into the woods. It clattered and cracked. Then she followed Dorian. They scrambled furiously into the middle layers of the tree, a few meters off the ground.

Down below, footsteps.

"I heard you," Owen called out. "I'm telling you, you need to be *quiet.*"

Dorian pressed a finger to his lips. Evie smiled at him. She looked wild and triumphant, her hair tangled up with leaves, her face smeared with dirt.

Moving slowly, carefully, Dorian eased aside the curtain of leaves. Owen was right underneath them, his armor reflecting the light. He swiveled his head: left, right—not up. *He's underestimating us,* Dorian thought. He didn't think they would know to climb into the trees.

Owen walked forward, vanishing from Dorian's line of sight. Dorian glanced over at Evie, gave her a manic grin, and jumped.

"We caaaught you!" Dorian screamed. The tree slapped him on the way down, and although the ground was soft and mulchy, electricity jolted up through his feet. "Oh, ow."

Light shone in his eyes. He peered up to find Owen smiling and shaking his head. "You went up," Owen said. "Good job."

"Wasn't expecting that, were you?"

"I expected to catch you before you climbed up there."

Leaves and old rainwater showered down around them; Evie was descending, as careful as always. "Why'd you do that?" she shouted at Dorian. "I thought you'd fallen! You're lucky you're not hurt!"

"Element of surprise," Dorian said.

Owen shook his head again. "If you can manage to avoid any surprises tomorrow night, you might actually find something out for us."

"Assuming we're in the woods," Evie said. "I don't know how this is going to work in town."

"There are trees in town," Dorian said. "And buildings. Roofs. Trust me, I know my way around." He sounded too confident, even to himself, but he was riding on that thrill of getting the drop on Owen—a Spartan! A Spartan who didn't think Dorian was smart enough to climb up in the trees, but still.

"Go back to the house," Owen said. "Get some rest. We'll be heading out at nightfall tomorrow."

Dorian woke up at sunset, orange light spilling through the open curtains in his bedroom. They'd started out on the cots in the safe room, but Owen thought it was okay for them to sleep in the bedrooms since there didn't appear to be an immediate threat. He was less sore than he expected, and he rolled out of bed, refreshed and bright-eyed. For a moment, everything seemed to glimmer with possibility. It came crashing down soon enough: His best friends were possibly dead, Uncle Max and Remy were trapped in the shelter, an energy shield was covering Brume-sur-Mer like a shell, and he was going to have to sneak into town and spy on the Covenant without getting caught.

He dressed in the black clothes they'd scrounged up last night and brushed his teeth and went downstairs, where he found Victor sitting at the dining room table poking at a mess of scrambled eggs and fried sausages. Dorian's stomach grumbled at the scent, even though the packets of emergency supplies mostly just tasted like water and aluminum after they were reconstituted.

"How'd it go for you two last night?" Dorian slid into the chair across from Victor.

"Okay. We managed to sneak up on him once, although we weren't able to watch him for long. He said it would probably be fine."

Dorian nodded. He knew he needed to eat something. Keep his strength up for the reconnaissance tonight. He looked over at the big grandfather clock towering in the corner. Almost seven thirty. They'd be in full dark soon enough.

He pushed away from the table and went into the kitchen without saying anything more to Victor. He figured Victor felt as much like talking as he did. He pulled open the pantry, where they kept the food rations, slim packets stacked haphazardly on top of each other. Behind them were the sorts of things you'd see in any pantry—rice, flour, a few jars of dried spices. Saskia had told him they'd brought the rations up from the house's safe room the morning after the invasion. Easy access.

He picked one packet at random and dropped it in the reconstituter, the power cell still glowing from when Victor had used it. Dorian ate standing up, scooping the food straight out of the reconstituter's pan with a big wooden spoon. He watched the yard grow darker. Moths fluttered up around the iron wall, dark flickering shadows in the security lights. No rain.

It wasn't long after Dorian finished eating that Evie showed up, dressed in dark clothes, a black hat pulled tight over her hair. "It's time," she said. "Owen wants us all out front in five minutes."

"I'm ready now." None of them were *ready* ready, and Dorian knew that. He suspected Owen did too. But as much as he dreaded going back toward town again, he knew he couldn't sit in the house and pretend everything was normal. And if they waited too long, the Covenant would find what they were looking for and then it'd be over.

Saskia and Victor were already outside by the time Dorian and Evie arrived. Owen paced in front of them, helmet off, his armor gleaming in the floodlights.

"What's your mission?" he said, his voice stern. Dorian glanced over at Evie, but she had her gaze fixed firmly on Owen.

"Well?" he barked. "We talked about this last night."

"Reconnaissance?" Victor offered.

Owen nodded. "What are you looking for?"

"Anything we can find," Evie said.

"Without getting caught," Dorian added.

Owen looked at him. Was he smiling a little? It was hard to tell in the dark. "Yes," he said. "That's the key. *Without getting caught.* What do you do if you're at risk of being seen by the enemy?"

Silence. The others shifted, their shoes rustling the grass.

"Well?" Owen stopped pacing and stared at them.

"Run," Dorian said.

Victor gave a sharp, shrill laugh.

"That's correct," Owen said. "You four aren't soldiers, and I'm not sending you in there to get killed. What we want is information. But do not put your lives at risk, do you understand?" He paused, then added softly, "That's my job."

Before they ditched him for the UNSC, Dorian's parents had told him stories of the Spartans like they were boogeymen, monsters come to snatch up misbehaving colony children. He realized then that part of him had still been thinking of Owen that way. But a boogeyman didn't put his life at risk for the sake of his victims.

So Dorian's parents were wrong about something. Big surprise there.

"What exactly are you going to be doing?" Saskia said. "You know your wound hasn't totally healed—"

Owen held up one hand. "I'll be looking for weapons. We'll need as many as we can get."

Something tightened in Dorian's stomach. He didn't know if he could bring himself to really face the Covenant again. Not after what he'd seen on board Tomas's boat—

But he knew too, if we wanted Remy and Uncle Max back, he didn't have much of a choice. At least he didn't have to worry about fighting yet—assuming he and Evie could do their job right.

"Are you sending us in unarmed today?" Saskia asked.

Owen sighed, a slight movement beneath the bulk of his suit. "No," he said. "But that doesn't mean I want you to go in there shooting. We are looking for *information*. I can't stress that enough." He jerked his head toward the porch. "What weapons we have are over there. I'd suggest the rifle and the pistol. The needler would compromise us."

Dorian looked over at Evie and gestured to the weapons. "Which one do you want?"

"I'm not sure I really know how to use either of them."

Dorian smiled. "I thought you went shooting with Victor."

"I sucked at it."

He laughed in spite of the heavy tension soaking through the air. "I call the pistol," he said to Saskia. "You can take the rifle. Fair?"

"Sounds good to me," Victor said.

None of them moved, just looked warily at each other.

"Let's go," Owen said. "Find out what you can. And stay alive."

Thirty minutes later, Dorian and Evie were nestled up in the thick branches of a banyan tree, peering through the leaves at the stretch of Brume-sur-Mer's main street. Owen and the others were somewhere on the edges of downtown—not far, really, but enough to feel risky.

Down below, the twisted remains of cars lay in broken heaps along the sidewalk, and the storefronts were streaked with black scorch marks. The glass in the windows had melted into gleaming, transparent lumps that glistened in the light cast by the tall, strange pylons that the Covenant had set up along the road like streetlights. They looked like some kind of comm system, though it was impossible to tell.

"Why did they do this?" Evie whispered. "What's the point?"

Dorian shrugged. What was the point of the Covenant slaughtering everyone on Tomas's boat? They were civilians. They weren't a threat. And yet they were all dead anyway.

"It's just what they do," he said. "They hate us."

"But why?" Evie's voice rasped. "It's so—so illogical."

"The UNSC used to kill colonists," Dorian said. "And they were the same species."

"They killed insurrectionists," Evie said. "It was war."

"This is war too."

Evie sighed and fell quiet. For a moment, they just sat in that thick silence. Then Dorian heard the whirring sound of heavy pneumatic joints slowly approaching from the east.

"Crap," he said.

"I hear it too." Evie pulled back from the leaves and tilted her head, listening. "It's coming from that direction." She pointed off to her left.

Dorian nodded, then pressed a finger to his lips. Evie nodded gravely. He moved into a crouch, and then, balancing himself against the tree's trunk, crept closer to the origin of the sound. He peeked through a gap in the trees.

Bit back a shout of fear.

It was some kind of purple-armored ground vehicle, not a ship, that crawled on four legs, tottering like a crab. Atop its main chassis was an armored cowling, narrow and swept back—which might have been the operator's cabin. It was also too wide for the road, and Dorian suddenly understood why the shops and the cars were all so damaged.

The vehicle lurched down the street, scrabbling over the wreckage of the town. Smoke billowed up into the air. Dorian watched the vehicle's movements and then he jumped back into place beside Evie, who was staring with her mouth hanging open.

"We should follow it," Dorian breathed into her ear.

Evie jumped. "What?"

"That thing's huge," he whispered. Noise from the vehicle's movements swelled, drowning out their conversation. "It's got to be going somewhere important."

Evie looked back out at the street. Her eyes narrowed into that look of determination Dorian had seen when she hacked into Salome's system.

"The roofs," she said.

"That was the plan." They had chosen that particular tree for their stakeout because its branches brushed up against the roof of the nearby bank. They wouldn't have cover on the roofs, not like they did in the trees, but if they stayed behind the vehicle, they should be okay. He hoped.

The tree branches trembled as the Covenant vehicle rumbled

past them, and though it moved somewhat like a spider, each footfall made its size and weight very clear. Dorian peered out at it again. No soldiers anywhere, although he could see what looked like a large plasma device at the front end of the vehicle's cowling. The toxic scent of plasma filled the air, making Dorian's eyes water.

And then the vehicle was on the other side of the tree, moving away from them. The lack of visible Covenant soldiers actually unnerved Dorian for the first time. He guessed that it meant they were there somewhere, just unseen—which was worse. He and Evie likely wouldn't have a better chance if they missed this opportunity.

"Now," Dorian whispered. He didn't wait for a reply, just darted over to the branches that connected to the bank's roof. They were thinner than he'd thought. Flimsier. He took a deep breath and a couple of cautious steps. The branches bent beneath his weight. He thought he heard Evie gasp behind him, but it might have just been a gust of wind.

He grabbed the overhead branches and swung himself forward. For a moment, it was like flying.

Then he landed hard on his knees, pain ricocheting up into his hips. But he was on the roof. From here he had a wider vantage point, and he swiveled in place, looking for more vehicles or more soldiers. He didn't see anything.

Evie was already inching toward him, her face screwed up in concentration. He scurried over to the side of the roof, keeping himself low. The lack of plasma fire was enough to convince him his little free fall hadn't been spotted, but he was still playing it safe.

Evie lifted her face, her eyes wide and bright in the darkness.

He nodded at her.

She jumped, arms and legs pinwheeling, and Dorian's heart seized up—she wasn't going to make it. The arc of her leap wasn't the right shape. He jumped to his feet and snapped out his arms and grabbed her. She slammed against the side of the building, the impact shuddering in his biceps.

"I've got you," he said through his teeth, then yanked her up, pulling her over the ledge. She was gasping, wheezing, her eyes wild.

"You're fine," he said, patting her on the shoulder. "We won't have to jump like that again."

"I almost died," she said.

"But you didn't."

She closed her eyes. "But I didn't," she breathed.

The whine of the Covenant vehicle grew quieter, with only the crunching sound of its footfalls remaining.

Evie's eyes flew open. She took a deep breath. "Let's go."

Dorian smiled at her. She almost smiled back.

Dorian held out one hand and helped her to her feet. The vehicle was clambering its way toward the three-way stop that would either send it deeper into town or down toward the water. He and Evie jogged along the roofs, jumping easily over the narrow gaps between buildings. Up ahead, the Covenant machine slowed.

"It's going right," Evie said. "Why would they want to go into town?"

She was right; the vehicle was headed toward the narrow street leading into the residential part of Brume-sur-Mer.

"Are you serious?" Evie looked at him, her damp hair whipping out of her hat and sticking to the side of her face. "They're trying to get into the shelter."

"Then why not go for the main entrance? Down at the old tourist houses?" Dorian shook his head. "They're after something else."

The vehicle turned again, left this time, heaving itself into the old neighborhood next to downtown. It had clearly been this way before; even in the darkness, Dorian could see the path that had been cleared for it, the downed trees and demolished houses. The Covenant had done this before. Maybe that's why there were no soldiers. Whatever they were up to, it had become routine.

Evie and Dorian slowed; they had reached the last main-street building. Dorian walked over to the far edge, his lungs filling with breath. He wished he had some fancy top secret UNSC equipment, or his uncle's old analog binoculars, anything that would let him see what was going on.

A series of blue lights on the vehicle cast a soft, cool glow around it as it crept through the darkness. Dorian and Evie stood on the roof, unspeaking, as the vehicle moved deeper into the neighborhood.

And then it stopped.

"Are you sure there's not a shelter entrance there?" Evie asked, her voice edged in panic.

"I'm sure," Dorian said. "There aren't any entrances in the older parts of town."

"Then what are they doing?"

The vehicle sat unmoving for a moment. The neighborhood was blanketed in shadows and pale wisps of smoke.

"You think we can get closer?" Evie asked.

Dorian glanced at her. Grinned. "Someone's feeling more adventurous."

She glared at him. "I want to know what's going—"

A flare of pinkish light erupted from the neighborhood where the vehicle had stopped, brilliant and blinding. Dorian ducked, pulling Evie down with him. A loud whining started to build up, the pink light blooming with its intensity. Evie pulled away from Dorian and peered over the edge of the roof.

"Look," she said.

He did, moving shakily to his feet.

The vehicle's large carapace was pointed down, sending a narrow column of pink energy straight into the ground from its nose. The beam disappeared into the hole below the vehicle, but its glow lit up everything around it, casting wild shadows across the neighborhood.

"That's not what glassing looks like, is it?" Evie whispered frantically. "Why would they glass the moon while they're still on it?"

"They're not." Dorian pressed his hands against the railing of the roof, squinting out into the darkness. "They're—*drilling*."

Evie looked at him. Looked back out at the neighborhood.

The Covenant's light burrowed deeper into the soil.

CHAPTER THIRTEEN

VICTOR

his is pointless," Saskia said. "We're not going to find anything out here."

Victor sighed with annoyance. "We've only been out here an hour. And we're not supposed to talk."

"Then why are you talking?"

"To tell you not to."

Saskia peered over at him through a curtain of her dark hair. She'd had it pulled back when they left, but during their trip, it had come loose, and she'd shaken it out of its ponytail entirely. Victor felt a flare of heat and looked away. There were more important things to worry about. And Saskia didn't seem to really care about any of them.

They crunched through the forest, branches snapping beneath their feet. Victor cringed at every crack and rustle, but it was impossible to be truly silent in the forest. He and Saskia had learned that last night. Every time they spotted Owen's light in the distance, they would try to move forward without making a sound. And every time, Owen would shine the light in their faces and tell them they'd lost. Again.

At least there didn't seem to be any sign of the Covenant out here tonight. Owen had said that they tended to patrol closer to town, which was where he was surveilling now. Victor figured there wasn't going to be anything of interest out here in the forest. But this was where Owen sent them, and Victor wasn't in much of a mind to try to sneak into town again anyway. Not after what happened last time.

They continued on in silence. Victor swept his gaze around, alert for the soft glow of alien light. Nothing. A whispering brushed through the tree leaves, and Victor felt drops of water on his skin.

"Great," he mumbled.

And then, as if the clouds had been waiting for him to speak, water poured out of the sky in a thick curtain, shredding the tree leaves and soaking Victor and Saskia instantly.

"We should just go back," Saskia said.

"Easy for you to say," Victor snapped. "You don't have anyone in the shelter."

She recoiled and looked away, and Victor felt a sting of guilt. But *just* a sting. Saskia was the only one of them who seemed to not care that all the survivors were trapped in the shelter while the Covenant crawled over their hometown.

It's not her hometown, Victor thought. He plunged forward into the forest.

"We're not going to find anything," Saskia called out to him, after a pause. Her voice was small and plaintive against the rain. "If I thought there was a chance, I wouldn't—"

Victor stepped through a gate of trees, into the brunt of the storm. A clearing, big enough that the wind was blowing the rain at him sideways. Why was there a clearing like this in the forest? The forest was protected by the Meridian government. It was supposed to be untouched.

Of course, there had been a city computer nestled in it. People in Brume-sur-Mer weren't great at following the rules.

He pulled the rifle off its sling and carried it loosely in front of him. The clearing was *huge*—he'd almost think it was the edge of the forest if it weren't for the dark wall of trees off in the distance.

"Saskia!" he hissed.

"What?" She materialized beside him, then let out a little gasp.

"I know, right?" Victor fumbled for his comm pad and switched on the light. But the clearing was so big it swallowed up the light, and all Victor illuminated was a bunch of wet grass drooping in front of him. When it was dry, it probably came up to his knees. "I think it's been like this for a while."

"Yeah, it doesn't look recently cleared." Saskia had brought out her comm pad as well, and her light blinked and shimmered in the rain. Victor imagined Owen jumping out of the woods, shouting, "You're dead! Put that light out!" But there didn't seem to be any sign of the Covenant out here.

Saskia waded forward through the grass. Victor stayed closer to the trees, moving around the perimeter of the clearing. He wanted a sense of how big it was. Maybe that would give him an idea of what exactly a massive clearing was doing in the middle of a protected forest.

His light bounced off something and reflected back at him. He froze, his body prickling with fear. The rifle tucked in the crook of his elbow felt clumsy and useless.

They should have listened to Owen. They should never have brought out their light. He was a Spartan and they were just—what? Kids?

Except no one was attacking. There were no incomprehensible alien screeches. Victor tilted his comm pad and set off another shower of light.

Metal. There was something metal over there.

He moved closer. The sphere of light revealed things in pieces—a slab of cement, a scatter of rusted mechanical parts lying half-hidden in the grass. A metal wall.

It all looked very human. And also very old.

"Saskia!" he hissed. "Over here."

He moved closer, whipping his light around, trying to piece together the fragments. Everything was blurred by the rain, but he was fairly sure he was looking at some kind of enormous metal building. It was nestled into the tree line and was largely overgrown by the vines and vegetation, but the glint of metal was inescapable.

Saskia jogged up to his side.

"You're seeing this, right?" he said.

"It looks like a hangar." She strode forward, up on the slab. Victor followed. The slab was broken and cracked, plants pushing their way through the decay. He kicked at one of the cement chunks.

"This place is ancient," Saskia said. "Look at this lock."

Victor stepped beside her. They were underneath an awning, and it was a relief to be out of the torrent of rain. Saskia had her light fixed on a rusted metal keypad.

"It's not a holo?" Victor leaned forward, frowning. "This is old."

"Did you know about this place?" Saskia looked over at him, her eyes big and luminous beneath her stringy, wet hair.

Victor shook his head. "Did you?"

"Is it some of my parents' work, you mean?" Saskia laughed a little. "No. This is way too old." She peered up at the wall in front of them. "It's freaking huge!"

Saskia was right about that. The building stretched far out of the net of Victor's light, disappearing into the woods and the rain.

"Do you think we can get in?" Victor said.

Saskia shrugged. "We can try." She reached over and pressed the number seven on the keypad. It lit up yellow, the light pale beneath the coating of dust.

"Please enter your access code," said a polite female voice. Not Salome.

"Too bad Evie's not here," Victor said. "She could hack into this like it was nothing."

Saskia wiped her hand over the keypad's base, smearing the dust into mud. She shone her light up close to it, squinting. Then she broke into a grin.

"Sweet," she said. "Watch this."

She hit the 0 key several times in a row—Victor lost count, but it was long enough that he thought she might have been messing with him. But then there was a long, low beep, and that mechanized female voice said, "Override accepted. Enter access code."

"What'd you do?" Victor asked.

Saskia grinned at him. "This is a CDS name keypad."

"Your dad's company?"

"The company he works for, yeah. They've been around forever, although under different names. I took a risk on the override codes not changing, though. Anything from the last fifty years or so would have triggered an ATLAS protocol and shutdown." She turned back to the keypad, fingers hovering above it. "Now I just need to remember the base code to open it up."

Victor's early irritation with Saskia vanished, replaced by that warm feeling that had followed him around the halls of their high school, before the Covenant had invaded.

She entered a code but was immediately blasted by a buzzer and the voice saying, "I'm sorry, I don't recognize that code." Victor flinched; the buzzer seemed to reverberate through the woods, even with the pounding rain.

"Crap!" Saskia muttered. Then: "Oh wait, I think I put it in wrong."

Victor straightened up. "Let's hope so. That buzzer was—loud."

"I know." She looked at him sideways, the way she did. "I'm sorry."

She entered another keystroke, and this time the keypad's light turned green and instead of a buzzer there was a scraping, groaning noise that was just as loud.

"This is *worse*," Victor said, clutching at the rifle.

"Yeah, but the hangar door is opening."

And it was. The wall in front of them was being drawn slowly into the building. Dust billowed out and clung in streaks to Victor's wet clothes. It was accompanied by a chemical scent, sharp and pungent and blessedly not at all like the toxic scent of plasma. This scent was unpleasant enough but still recognizably human. It was a scent Victor associated with his sisters, because every time they came to visit, he and his family would meet them at the landing pad where the UNSC dropships came in.

It was the scent of starship fuel.

Victor ducked into the hangar as soon as the door was high enough. The rhythm of rain on the roof was thunderous, and the door was still screeching its way open, but there was a stillness in the place itself. Like a tomb. Like a place no living thing had been in decades.

Victor lifted his light, but the space was too big for him to see anything. Something lurked in the darkness. Something big. His heart fluttered.

There was a buzz, a loud electrical whine, and the hangar flooded with sickly yellow light. Victor yelped, and his eyes watered as they adjusted to the sudden brightness.

"Turn that off!" he said. "It'll be a beacon—"

"I closed the door," Saskia called back. "We should be fine." Her footsteps echoed across the space. Victor took a deep breath. Looked up.

A starship. It was clearly human, but it didn't look like any of the UNSC ships Victor had seen in holos. It was an enormous vessel, several dozen meters in length and almost completely filling up the length of the hangar. The nose was rounded and it tapered toward the rear, where there were four engines at its tail. The craft hunched over like an old man, wings jutting out at its sides with an exaggerated set on its tail. It wasn't a capital ship like the ones Meridian was fighting the Covenant with, but it was clear it once carried hundreds of passengers.

It was also as ancient as the hangar, covered with a film of dust. Victor's heart fluttered again.

"Wow," Saskia breathed beside him. "You think it still works?"

"I don't know." Victor moved closer to it. He'd never seen a starship like this up close, having never gone off-world. It was bigger than he expected. Bigger than the dropships that brought his sisters home. But was it armed like they were? He couldn't tell.

"Why is this here?" Saskia said. "I mean, how could this be here all this time and no one knows about it?" She swiped her fingers against the ship's side. "Look at this dust! And the cobwebs." She pointed up at a net of fine white silk draping between the engine turbines on its wings. "Who just forgets about a hangar in the middle of the woods?"

Victor stopped. Beneath the dust was the familiar outline of a symbol he'd only seen in school holos: a lopsided circle bisected by two lines.

"The Sundered Legion," he said.

"What?" Saskia laughed. "They haven't existed for fifty years! How could they possibly—"

"I don't know," Victor interrupted. "But that's totally the Sundered Legion's insignia. Look."

Saskia walked over to him and tilted back her head to peer up at the symbol. "I can't believe it," she said. "You think this place has been here for half a century? Or more? Without anyone finding it?"

Victor shrugged. "It's pretty far into the woods. And people may not want the UNSC knowing how loyal Brume-sur-Mer was to the insurrectionists back then. It's a lucky find for us, though."

"Assuming someone can fly it." Saskia strolled down the length of the ship, running her fingers along the side. A cloud of dust trailed in her wake.

"I'm sure Owen can," Victor said. "Those Spartans can do everything."

Saskia stopped and looked over her shoulder at him. In the harsh, buzzing light, her skin turned ashy and pale, and she looked like a ghost. "I hope you're right."

She turned away, continued her slow walk around the perimeter of the ship. She moved like a dancer, soft and graceful, and Victor felt the heat of his old crush like he was still staring at her from the far corner of calculus.

She disappeared into the shadows, and Victor turned back to the starship. He wished his sisters were here. They'd probably know how to fly this thing. Victor didn't even know where to start without a holo-panel and voice commands.

"Victor!" Saskia's voice echoed from the back of the hangar. Victor went cold—had something happened to her? He jogged down the length of the ship, his heart pounding, his palms slippery against the stock of the rifle.

But when he found her, she was crouched in front of an antique comm station.

"Check this out." She peered over at him, grinning. "It still works."

Victor knelt down beside her. The comm was coated in the same thick layer of dust as everything else, but there were definitely a row of lights glowing beneath the grime.

"But the channels are all jammed," Victor said. "We couldn't even get your comm station to work."

"Yeah, but the one at my house isn't military-grade. This is." She thumped the side of the comm and dust billowed up in a cloud. "If we could get word to Port Moyne, maybe they could send backup to help get people out of the shelter."

"That would be awesome, except Owen said the Covenant were scrambling everything."

"It's still worth *trying*." She ran her fingers along the side of the station. Suddenly, the lights flared and a crackle of static shot through the hangar. Victor winced.

"I'll turn it down," she whispered, pressing the control keys along the side. The static roared on, though, filling the room like an alarm bell.

"Do something!" Victor hissed. "Turn it off!"

"I'm try—"

"—any word on the situation in Brume-sur-Mer?"

The voice was tinny and far away and shimmered with static and for a moment Victor thought he'd imagined it. But Saskia had frozen in place, her eyes wide.

"Working on it." The second voice came through more clearly, and both Victor and Saskia pressed closer to the comm. Victor no longer cared about the noise—it sounded like someone was coming to help them after all.

"Report."

A crackle of static. Victor held his breath.

"Shield still up. Can't see what they're doing in there, but we've got our suspicions."

Victor and Saskia looked at each other, eyes wide.

"Go on," crackled the first voice.

"We're thinking there's an artifact under the town. Can't confirm, of course—"

"An artifact?" Victor whispered.

"So we're in the safe window, then? While they're looking for it, we've got a low risk of glassing for the time being, correct?"

More static. Victor's heart vibrated against his rib cage. *Answer,* he thought. *Answer.*

"With forces still on the ground, absolutely. But if they get what they came for—"

Suddenly, the static flared up, swallowing both voices. Victor stared at the comm in horror. "What about the survivors? What did they mean 'artifact'—"

A brush against his arm: Saskia. "At least they're not just leaving us alone," she said softly. "At least they're acknowledging us. That means there's still hope."

Victor nodded. Saskia pressed a few buttons again, but all it brought up was static. Whatever wires had crossed to give that fragment of a conversation had unraveled themselves. There was only white noise.

They regrouped a little after midnight, meeting in the dining room of Saskia's house, all of them still dressed in their dark clothes, their hair stringy and wet from the rain. Dorian and Evie reported what they'd found: a Covenant vehicle drilling into the old neighborhood in the center of the city.

Victor went cold, his body prickling with sweat.

"Drilling?" Owen leaned forward on the table, his armor clanking against the stone tabletop. "Are you sure?"

"I don't know what else it could be," Dorian said. "They were shooting a beam of energy into the ground, like they were boring a hole."

Owen narrowed his eyes. "What did the vehicle look like?"

"Weird," Dorian said. "You could tell it was Covenant. Maybe five, six meters front to back."

"It walked on four legs," Evie added. "It moved more like a robot."

"It's a Locust," Owen said. "I'm familiar with it. If we can get enough firepower, we might be able to take it out. What else did you see?"

"They'd clearly been there before," Evie added, and then described the state of the main street, everything scorched and crushed. Victor couldn't stop thinking about the drill, though. He kept hearing the staticky voice on the comm, talking about an artifact.

"Could the drill hit the shelter?" Owen asked.

Dorian looked over at him. "The shelter doesn't go under the old part of town," he said. "That's not what they're doing."

"Are you sure?"

"Of course I'm sure. I've spent the last five years working with my uncle. I know the entire layout of this place."

Owen accepted this with a curt nod. "Fine. So they aren't interested in the civilians. That's good."

"There's something else they want, though," Saskia said in a small voice.

Everyone turned to look at her.

"She's right." Victor's voice was rough, scratchy. "We found this old military comm station and we—we overhead something."

"A military comm station?" Owen frowned. "Where?"

"It was in a hangar in the woods. Covered over with vines and stuff. We think it's from the old insurrectionist days." Saskia took a deep breath. "We found a starship too."

"What?" said Dorian. "And you didn't lead with that?"

"We're pretty sure we overheard a UNSC military channel," Victor snapped. "And they were talking about some kind of artifact in Brume-sur-Mer."

The room went still, the air electrified with a jolt of terror. The only sound was the rain pattering against the glass, and Victor wondered if he'd ever be able to hear that sound without thinking of the Covenant and the invasion.

Owen was the first to move, the floor creaking as he shifted his weight. "What else did you hear?" he asked.

Saskia and Victor glanced at each other. "Not much," Saskia said, turning back to Owen. "Just that they were searching for some kind of artifact, and that as long as they were searching for it, the colony was safe from glassing—" She shook her head, her eyes wild. "What does it mean? What artifact could possibly be in Brume-sur-Mer?"

Owen didn't seem to be paying attention, though. He had turned toward the window, and two Owens, the real Owen and the ghost of his reflection, gazed out at the rain.

"Well?" Dorian said, breaking the silence.

"How much do you know about the Covenant?" Owen asked.

Victor blinked, glanced over at Evie, then at Saskia. Both of them looked as baffled as he felt. Dorian, of course, was just leaning back in his chair, scowling.

"We know the species," Evie said. "They teach us that in history at school."

"Mrs. Elwin told us about their religion," Saskia said. "Weren't you in her class, Victor?"

He blushed again. Mrs. Elwin's current events class was the first time he'd ever laid eyes on Saskia Nazari. "Yeah. It's all tied up with their government. Most species they try to convert, but not us—"

"Yeah," Owen said. "Not us." He stood up, paced across the dining room, his armor strange in the soft glow of the chandelier. "Did your teacher tell you who the Covenant worship?"

Victor glanced over at Saskia, who shrugged and shook her head. He tried to remember. "Some old aliens, right? They're dead now?"

"Yes." Owen stopped. "We call them the Forerunners."

The name chimed in Victor's memory. It was such a bland word for a race of gods.

"What does this have to do with anything?" Dorian demanded. "Does it matter what aliens the Covenant worship?"

Owen whirled around. "This entire war is about who the Covenant worship. It's the entire reason they want to exterminate us."

"They have a reason?" Evie said. "In school—"

"Of course they have a reason," Owen said. "But ONI keeps as much key information out of civilian ears as possible. It's for your own benefit."

Dorian snorted, but the others all leaned forward, eyes wide with interest and fear. Victor felt the way he did whenever he wrote the scripts for his movies, like he was on the verge of uncovering some unimaginable secret.

"So are you going to tell us or not?" Dorian said. "What exactly is the artifact they heard about?"

Owen sighed. "The Forerunners left artifacts behind. One of the central tenants of the Covenant's religious belief involves seeking out these artifacts."

Victor felt dizzy. "You're saying there's a Forerunner artifact in Brume-sur-Mer?"

"I don't know," Owen said. "But the drilling would suggest as much, yes. As would the energy shield." He paused. "I suspect what you saw in town was an archaeological dig. The Covenant think there's something here, and they're looking for it."

Silence, and the rain. The Sundered Legion ship seemed suddenly absurd now, compared to the possibility of some ancient alien *something* buried beneath the rows of shabby wooden houses that

Victor had known his entire life. Strange enough to think of a hangar hiding in the woods, but here was something older and even more bizarre, something Victor couldn't even imagine.

And the Covenant had come and destroyed his home for it.

"What sort of artifact is it?"

Evie. She spoke in a raspy whisper, barely audible over the rain.

Owen shook his head. "I couldn't even begin to tell you. And the voices you heard on the comm are right. The artifact's presence here must be keeping the Covenant from glassing the planet."

He fell quiet, the cold reality sucking all the air out of the room. Victor glanced at Saskia. "Even if we got that Sundered Legion ship to work," he said. "Even if we had a pilot—"

"You've got a pilot," Dorian said roughly. "I know how to fly."

"Really?" Victor blurted out.

Dorian glared at him.

"Well, it doesn't matter. We're blocked in by an energy shield. And we can't just leave everyone in town here to die."

Saskia shifted in her seat, her gaze tilted downward. Owen watched them for a moment, unspeaking, then said, "I agree." He lifted his chin, planted his armored legs hard on the floor. The damaged section of armor stood out stark and angry, a melted mass on his hip. But the rest of him looked like a weapon.

"This artifact—it's our leverage. We can't let them to get to it."

"How exactly are we going to do that?" Dorian said. "Fight them? We barely even have weapons."

Owen gave one of those disconcerting smiles. "Not fight. Not exactly."

Then he leaned forward, pressing his palms on the table, and began to talk.

CHAPTER FOURTEEN

SASKIA

Saskia crouched in what had once been Brume-sur-Mer's only coffee shop. She thought she could still catch the earthy fragrance of coffee beans beneath the stink of plasma and smoke. And the rain. Sometime while they had slept, it had started to rain, and when they woke up, the driveway outside Saskia's house was rushing like a river. "This is good," Owen had told her, the two of them eating a reconstituted breakfast in the kitchen. "Gives us cover." Saskia had only nodded in agreement and stirred her soupy eggs. She still hadn't told him about her father's armory. She hadn't told any of them. Before, she hadn't been sure she trusted them; now she had waited too long, and she was afraid they would kick her out if she revealed she'd lied. Victor seemed convinced she wanted to abandon the town to the Covenant—they all did.

And part of her had wanted to. *Part* of her.

Rain blew in through the shattered coffee shop window, pooling on the dusty tile. Saskia hunched a meter away, the rifle propped up on a pile of broken chairs. Her comm pad rested on the floor beside her, the screen black.

Saskia shifted her weight, moving her legs out from under her. They tingled as the blood rushed back in. How long had she been sitting here? It seemed stupid to think the Covenant would come out to the drilling site in this rain. But Owen had positioned her in the coffee shop anyway. "Just in case," he'd told her, pressing one armor-heavy hand on her shoulder. It hadn't felt like a human touch.

Somewhere out there in that rain, the rest of them were making their way through the old neighborhood with Covenant weapons. Owen had been able to procure a fully automatic plasma rifle. Saskia wasn't sure how he got it, but she could guess. Right now, Owen and the others were taking position at key spots, and she was the backup. If the Covenant showed up: Shoot them.

The rain pounded harder and blew into the coffee shop in misty clouds. Saskia peered through the scope of the rifle, zeroed in on an empty place out in the street. Raindrops glowed green from the night vision. She wasn't sure exactly what her father had in his armory, only that most of them were prototypes, things that hadn't been officially approved for production yet.

She should have told them about the armory the first night. The situation was life-or-death, not just for her and the others, but for the whole colony. She shouldn't have let her parents' warnings about the classified nature of the weapons and corporate espionage and intellectual property theft get in her head. They'd raised her to never get too close to anyone, that she was never part of the town, not really. At first, she convinced herself that the invasion hadn't changed that.

After all, she was the only one without family in the shelter. The only one with nothing to fight for. That was how the others saw her, wasn't it? And she could see the truth to it.

Saskia heard the faint whirring of a large machine in the distance.

She stiffened, crouched lower behind her wall of broken chairs. Her heart hammered and a sickness rose in her stomach. *They're going to need me after all.*

She felt around on the floor for her comm pad. The noise grew louder; a pale light spilled across the street. Evie had set up a local channel for them to use when they were split up like this. They'd tested it back in Saskia's safe room, after the military channel Owen had given them access to didn't work—still scrambled, he'd said. Evie's local channel wouldn't be strong enough to reach outside of Brume-sur-Mer, but at least it could keep them in contact with one another.

She tapped in the code, hit send, threw the comm pad aside, and peered through the scope again. The night vision was washed out. She switched to normal view. It was murky and violet, but she thought she could see well enough.

She *hoped* she could see well enough. She would only have one shot.

The Covenant vehicle crept into view, the light from Covenant pylons that lined the road casting everything into harsh shadows. It looked like a large metallic insect, crawling over everything in its path. Saskia pressed her finger against the rifle's trigger. Owen had told her what to do. "The Locust has weak defenses. Concentrated fire should take it down, as long as you act fast. Aim for the generator lights. They're small, but you're a good shot." She'd wondered how he knew that—had someone told him about her shooting the Jackal back when she saved Evie? The compliment made her blush regardless, and she thought about it now, shrouded in darkness, surrounded by the thrum of rain and the Covenant Locust.

The vehicle filled up her line of sight. It was very large and threatening this close.

For a moment, she panicked: All she saw was the mass of the Locust, its enormous armored body that sat atop its chassis and four legs. No lights.

You're a good shot.

But as the Locust crawled closer, she saw flashes of blue glow from cylinders behind its chassis. They were small and mostly protected by the vehicle's armor. Even in the scope, they looked impossible to hit. From her current position, this was as good a chance as she'd have.

Saskia sucked in a deep breath of air. Exhaled.

Squeezed the trigger.

The rifle kicked back and slammed into her forehead, and she forced it back down again, her finger pressed against the trigger, releasing a stream of gunfire.

Alien voices erupted out of the rain, chattering and indecipherable. A plasma bolt sliced through the light fixture overhead, sending shards of glass raining down on her. She choked back her fear and held her place.

But then the Locust's turret started to turn.

No, she thought, just as she saw a dazzling burst of light. But the dazzle didn't fade, and then she smelled smoke, and she realized the vehicle was burning.

She'd gotten through the defenses.

Saskia grabbed her comm pad and her rifle and darted behind the counter. More plasma fire. Had they seen her? Or were they just firing into the space? It didn't matter. She had to get out of here before they fired on her with the vehicle's cannon.

She charged into the shop's back storage room. Unlike the front, it was pristine, untouched, plastic tubs of synthetic coffee beans lining the shelves, waiting to be brewed. The sound of Covenant voices followed her as she pushed out of the storage room and into a tiny back office. More plasma fire, although it sounded distant.

I'm going to get out, she told herself. *I'm going to get out.*

She slammed out of the back door and into a wall of rain. She faltered for a moment, blinking at the darkness. But then she heard the hissing pulses of a plasma rifle and she took off again, feet pounding against the cement. Dorian had given her the escape route—out the back, through the delivery parking lot, into the wooded area that cut between the shops and the houses.

"It'll be easy to lose them back there," he'd said. "Especially in the rain."

Saskia hoped he was right. She leapt over the edge of the parking lot and landed in a mess of soft, sucking mud.

Behind her, everything illuminated.

She didn't turn around, didn't look back at her attackers. She only ran, slipping and stumbling over the mud and grass. The trees seemed a million kilometers away until she darted past the first of them. A plasma bolt winged past, close enough that she felt the heat of it on her cheek. She veered left, into the tangle of underbrush, and flung herself onto the ground. Her lungs burned; her side stung with a sharp cramp.

Footsteps pounded past. Someone barked out something in the Covenant's language, and Saskia pressed her hand over her mouth to keep from crying out. Then someone answered, farther away. Footsteps retreated.

For a long moment, Saskia lay motionless in the undergrowth, rainwater sluicing over her. The Covenant soldiers' voices faded away until there was only the sound of rain. Saskia straightened up, shaking. Then she plunged off into the underbrush, fighting against vines and tree branches until she emerged on the other side. A fence rose up in front of her—on the other side were houses, the edge of the neighborhood where the Covenant were digging. Saskia ran along the perimeter of the fence until she found an unlocked gate—Dorian had sworn there would be at least one—and slipped into the house's backyard. It was small and neat, a flare of amaryllis growing in the corner. Untouched by the fighting.

She pulled out her comm pad and her heart sank. No confirmation message from Victor. She opened up her message—had it sent? It said it had, but they hadn't confirmed receipt. Maybe they just forgot? Or maybe Evie's local channel wasn't as foolproof as they thought.

Saskia's head buzzed. She shoved the comm pad back in her pocket and jogged around to the front of the house. The street number glowed faintly on the bricks: 23. What street was this? She pulled out her comm pad again (still no confirmation) and checked the map. Rue Cascade. She was on the right street. She just needed to get to number 57. Their rendezvous point. Dorian's suggestion—he said no one had lived there for years. It went unsaid that it was a good choice because they wouldn't risk finding bodies when they went inside.

Saskia ran down the empty street, past the rows of dark houses. The streetlamps burned like always, but the houses seemed to be sleeping. Or dead.

Number 57 was as dark as the others. But that didn't mean anything. They would want to blend in. Saskia went up to the front door and pushed it open. Unlocked, just like Dorian said it would be. She stepped inside and dripped on the tiles in the foyer. Kicked the door shut.

"Hello?" she called out low, her voice tremulous. "I'm here."
Nothing.

Saskia slumped up against the closed door. Her head spun with terror.

They hadn't made it.

They hadn't gotten her message.

She didn't let herself think of the other possibility. That was the possibility she would have to prevent.

She opened up the map on her comm pad. Evie and Dorian had estimated the location of the dig to be on Boulevard du Lac, near Rue Montagne, a few blocks over. If the Covenant were scouring the coffee shop or the wooded area looking for her, then they wouldn't have found them yet.

Saskia raced out of the house, back into the pounding rain.

CHAPTER FIFTEEN

EVIE

E vie nestled the bomb at the base of a towering tangle of alien-alloyed beams. It was a narrow metal canister, palm-sized and ordinary. It sat there like an egg, inert until it wasn't anymore.

The rain was falling in sheets, and even the Covenant's sleek, organically shaped drilling infrastructure didn't provide any real shelter. She hated this part. She'd done it five times already, with five different bombs, and every time she felt like her body was collapsing in on itself.

She leaned down, pressed her thumb against the activation button.

The bomb lit up red.

She darted away, stumbling over charred bricks and wood, their ashes turned muddy from the rain. Half the houses on this block had been destroyed, left in tall blackened piles. And then there was the drill site, where the rubble had been cleared away and the strange alien infrastructure constructed—a network of scaffolding and observation platforms that had somehow assisted the Locust in the Covenant's extraction efforts. Evie couldn't tell how it worked. She could barely even look up at it because of the rain.

"Is the package secure?" Owen asked, his voice mechanized behind his helmet.

Evie nodded numbly. "Activated and ready."

"I see it." Dorian was standing beside Owen, hunched above an oversized, militaristic data pad. The glow stained his face blue and illuminated the fat drops of rain thrumming around them. He tapped at the screen. "Still waiting on Victor."

The bombs had come from Dorian's house. He called them *explosives* and said his uncle always kept a set around in case they were needed for construction projects. But they were designed to blow up old buildings, he'd argued, not Covenant technology.

"It's better than nothing," Owen had said. "And we'll use as many as we can spare. A big enough explosion, in the right place, could even take out a Covenant shield."

"What about the rain?" Evie had asked. "Won't that dampen the effects?"

Dorian and Owen had looked at each other. Dorian shrugged.

"Let's hope not," Owen had said.

They were about to find out. Evie wrapped her arms around herself, trying to fend off the torrent of rain. Dorian tapped his screen. "Looks like Victor's activated his. As soon as he gets back—"

Owen jerked around, whipping his gun off the holster fixed to his back. "Get down."

Evie dropped into the mud and broken bricks, pulling Dorian down with her. She fumbled around with the comm pad—she had to send a message to Victor, tell him to stay put.

Owen stalked forward through the rain. Evie took deep, panicked breaths. Then she felt a warmth on her shoulder—Dorian. It was easier to breathe then.

Owen stopped. Crouched down a little.

A figure burst out of the shadows and barreled toward them.

"Covenant!" it shrieked. "The Covenant are coming!"

"Saskia!" Evie gasped, clambering to her feet. Owen had already thrown his weapon down. Saskia slammed into him. He put his hands on her shoulders to steady her.

"You didn't get my message," she said, each word punctuated by a harsh breath. "The Covenant—they're on their way."

It was like a switch in Evie's head. She suddenly registered what Saskia was saying.

"Then we need to get out of here," Owen said. "Now."

"What about Victor?" Evie asked.

"He's here," Dorian said. "Let's go. I can set these things off once we're clear."

Dorian gestured—Victor's silhouette bobbed its way over the rubble of houses, moving agonizingly slow.

Rising up out of the roar of the rain came a low, droning whine. Evie's entire body turned to ice. She recognized the sound of a Covenant engine instantly.

"It's them!" Saskia shouted.

"Go," Owen said. "I'll get Victor." He took off, legs arcing in huge, inhuman strides.

"This way," Saskia said. "They're coming from the south." She ran off down the bombed-out street. Dorian and Evie followed. The whine grew louder. Evie didn't dare look back to see if Owen had gotten to Victor or not. She just ran, head down against the beating rain, her lungs screaming.

A Covenant light swept across the street. Evie strangled a cry.

"This way!" Saskia veered sharply to the left, darting in between two still-standing houses. The gate to one of them hung open, revealing a tidy backyard thick with canna lilies and banana trees.

"Wait!" Dorian shouted. "We need to detonate the explosives."

"What about Victor and Owen?" Evie screamed, just as Victor came barreling through the gate, Owen sliding in behind him, gun out.

"The Covenant!" Victor choked. "Why did you stop?"

"Because of this," Dorian said, tapping the screen of his comm pad.

There was a still and silent moment, the rain hanging like jewels in the air.

Then: a blast of orange light, a shudder through the earth that knocked Evie sideways. All sound was sucked out of the world; for a moment, she couldn't even hear the rain, only a constant, crystalline ringing deep inside her eardrums.

Flames licked up at the black sky, shining warm, yellow, *human* light over the entire neighborhood.

"Holy crap!" Victor shouted, his voice muffled and far away. Dorian watched the flames without saying anything. So did Saskia. So did Owen, his faceplate dancing with light.

"Good job," he said. "Now let's get the hell out of here."

All five of them sat dripping around the table in Saskia's kitchen. Evie wasn't sure how long they had been sitting there in silence, breathing in the warm, dry air of the house. All of their exhilaration had burned away while they fled through the woods, the intermingling scent of rain and fire following behind them.

"No backup," Owen said suddenly, lifting his gaze. One hand was pressed against the damaged portion of his armor—had he reopened his wound? Evie didn't want to ask. Not now, not when they'd had something like a victory.

"Well, yeah," Victor said. "Everyone's down in the shelter."

Owen shook his head. "No, I meant the Covenant didn't have any backup. It's been, what? Thirty minutes since we set off those explosives. I haven't heard any ships coming in. Have you?"

They all looked at one another. Evie remembered the Covenant ship sliding into Brume-sur-Mer the first night, the horrible roar of its engines.

"You hear better than any of us," Saskia said.

Owen dipped his head in acknowledgment. "Fair enough. There wasn't anything."

"Is that unusual?" Evie frowned.

"An explosion at an artifact dig site like that?" Owen grinned, his eyes glinting. "Yeah, it's unusual. They would have sent a team if they could spare one." He leaned forward. "You know what that means, don't you?"

No one answered.

"The Covenant's not getting past the human defenses. They must be trapped here too. It makes our job a hell of a lot easier." He laughed, slapped one hand against the table. The whole thing shuddered.

"You really think the Meridian Air Force stopped the Covenant up there?"

Owen nodded. "I think they're doing their best, anyway."

They all fell silent, and Evie imagined the Meridian Air Force winging through the atmosphere above the storm clouds dumping water on Brume-sur-Mer, beating back the Covenant ships trying to make their way to the surface. Surely UNSC was still out there too, and she thought about her mother. Would UNSC have sent her back to Meridian, to protect her home world? It gave Evie a warmth inside her chest, the thought of her mother blowing away the Covenant's backup after the drill station exploded from bombs Evie had laid with her own hands.

Owen stood up, chair scraping. "We do need to figure out what went wrong, though," he said.

"Went wrong?" Victor cried. "It worked! We blew up the drill!"

"Yeah," said Saskia, "only because I ran there to warn you the Covenant were coming. The message I sent didn't go through at all."

Evie's cheeks flushed. "I'm sorry about that," she said. "I thought it would work—I mean, we tested it—"

"And it worked fine here," Owen said. "There could be any number of explanations. That's what I want to look into. I doubt the Covenant would have scrambled an ad hoc channel like that, but if the fighting in the atmosphere is bad enough . . ." He sighed. "We need to know for certain before going into another situation." He looked at Evie, then at Victor. "You two contact Salome. Find out what you can."

"We'll have to go out to the town computer again," Dorian said. "And no offense, but I need the rest. We all do."

"You can use my comm station," Saskia said. "It worked the other night, when we were testing Evie's channel. We might have had better luck because we were farther from town."

"It's worth a shot," Evie said, when Dorian scowled at Saskia's answer. She stood up, tilted her head toward the safe room entrance. "C'mon. Let's try it. After our daring escape tonight, what else can we lose?"

"I'm not going back out there," Dorian grumbled. "Not tonight."

"If it doesn't work, you can go in the morning," Owen said, and Evie knew he really meant the next day's sunset. They'd been sleeping during the day since he arrived.

Dorian pushed away from the table with an exasperated sigh, but he did follow Evie down the narrow safe room stairs. The two of them had been down here last night, tapping into the local comm channel Evie had set up. She still couldn't believe it hadn't worked in town.

But Saskia had beat the Covenant to the dig site. The second time in three days she had saved Evie's life.

The comm station glowed forlornly in the corner. Evie sank down in the chair in front of it. Dorian slouched against the wall. She didn't need his help with this, but Owen always insisted they travel in pairs. Even in the safety of Saskia's house.

Evie's comm channel was working fine, crackling with distant, distorted voices. "Salome," Evie said. "Can you hear me?"

A burst of static.

"Evelyn Rousseau," came Salome's cheery voice. "I see you still haven't left town."

Evie sighed, slouching back in her chair. "I see you still haven't done much to stop the Covenant. They've got us blocked in with an energy shield now."

"Oh, come on," Dorian said. "Leave her alone."

"What can I do to stop the Covenant?" Salome said, her voice rippling with the distortions on the channel. "I'm afraid that falls outside of my purview of experience. But you know what doesn't?"

"Keeping the comm channels open?" Evie asked. "We tried using this one in town, and it didn't work. Saskia's message didn't go through."

"The Covenant are blocking all comm channels in the vicinity of Old Brume; their scrambling system is proximity based."

Evie groaned and looked over at Dorian, who shrugged. "Guess that explains it."

"But that wasn't what I was going to say." Salome's voice reverberated out of the speaker. "I have been trying to contact you," she went on.

Evie's heart fluttered. "What? Why?"

"It's been difficult, with the fighting. But there is an impending emergency situation."

Dorian laughed. "The last three days have been an impending emergency situation."

"Well, yes, Dorian Nguyen." Salome's voice rippled like an ocean wave. Evie's hand shot out to adjust the channel.

"What's the emergency situation?" she asked, fumbling with the controls. Static swelled. Salome's voice emerged like a cloud.

"—the storms," she was saying. "The shelter wasn't designed to function under this kind of weather emergency."

"What?" Dorian darted forward, kneeling beside Evie's chair. "Weather emergency?"

"The shelter is in danger of flooding."

Salome said it so matter-of-factly that Evie's first thought was that there wasn't time to deal with the situation right now. But then Dorian shouted, "How soon? Has it started flooding already?"

"No," Salome said. "But water levels are rising dangerously high. If the rain continues—and it likely will, given the atmospheric disturbances from the fighting—"

The Covenant's not getting past human defenses.

Evie gasped. Her entire body went cold.

"We've got to get them out of there," she whispered.

"Well, yes," Salome said. "But the Covenant are still present. They are a greater threat than the flooding."

"Are you insane?" Tears stung at the corners of Evie's eyes, and she wiped at them furiously, not wanting Dorian to see her cry. "If you let them out, they'll at least have a chance—"

"The chance of flooding is currently at ninety-eight percent," Salome said.

Evie shrieked wordlessly. In her anger she had forgotten how to speak.

"While the Covenant threat is currently at one hundred percent. That's a two percent difference! Enormous!"

The tears escaped, streaking down Evie's face in long hot rivers. Her father had survived the Covenant attack only to drown in an ancient, faulty shelter.

"Salome." Dorian's calmness was shocking. "How is the Covenant risk at a hundred percent? They don't even seem to care about the shelter. It's not like people would be walking into an ambush."

Silence crackled. Evie swiped at her eyes. She doubted it would be that easy. You didn't reason with an AI through rhetoric.

"The Covenant risk is currently set at one hundred percent," Salome said. "I cannot open the doors."

Dorian slammed his fist onto the table. Evie jumped, wondering what happened to his earlier calm.

"Damn it, Salome," he shouted.

"Sorry!" she chirped.

Dorian shut off the channel, plunging them into the true silence of the safe room. He stalked away, footsteps echoing off the walls. Evie just stared at the comm station. You couldn't reason with an AI, unless you spoke the AI's language.

It hadn't worked before, trying to change her programming. But maybe they didn't need to change Salome's programming. Evie just had to make her believe the Covenant weren't a real threat. Then she'd open the doors.

"What the hell are we going to do?" Dorian shouted. "I'm not letting Remy die down there."

It took Evie a moment to recognize the name: his nephew. He'd told her about him. Only eight years old, trapped underground in a shelter a hundred years out of date. She twisted her damp clothes around her fingers, still staring at the comm station.

"We might—I have an idea," she whispered.

Dorian's footsteps fell silent.

"You want to try to reprogram her again?"

She shook her head. "I don't think I would be able to. But we don't need to reprogram her."

Dorian was suddenly at her side, kneeling beside her chair, one hand on her arm. "If you've got a plan," he said, low and dangerous, "spit it out."

"A virus." Evie's heart pumped, but her voice didn't waver. "A virus to make her think the Covenant have gone."

CHAPTER SIXTEEN

DORIAN

I can't believe it," Dorian said.

Owen glanced at him, his face as unreadable as always. A starship had been stashed in the middle of the forest *his entire life*, and he'd had no idea. Hearing about it from Victor and Saskia had been one thing, but seeing it in person—he could hardly believe it.

All those times flying Mr. Garzon's rickety old scud-rider and he could have been learning on this?

"We don't even know if it works," Saskia said.

"Dorian says he can find out for us," Owen said.

Dorian ignored both of them. He jogged up to the side of the ship and thumped his fist against the cool metal. The *clang* it made echoed through the hangar, and Dorian thought of all the times Mr. Garzon had given him his flying lessons. Every time he climbed aboard his rider, he thumped the side. Some old Brume-sur-Mer superstition.

"It looks to be in good shape," Dorian said. "Not rusted or damaged or anything." He climbed up a ladder to the pilot's door and pulled on it. He half expected it to be locked, but it swung open with ease, revealing an old-fashioned interior, the control panel smooth and sleek save for a scatter of artfully placed warning lights and a holographic ignition.

He climbed in, sinking into the seat. The ship smelled like must and rocket fuel, a softness and a harshness that wound its way around Dorian's throat. He pressed the ignition.

At first, nothing happened. The dash stayed smooth and dark and empty. Dorian cursed under his breath.

But then the warning lights twinkled one after another like stars, rippling in the discordant pattern of all start-up systems. Holo-light flickered.

"So far so good!" Dorian bellowed out the door.

Owen jogged over to him, his steps heavy against the hangar floor. "The engine's not on."

"No duh." The holo-light had settled into the familiar pattern of a keypad. "You think the Sundered Legion's just going to leave their starship where anyone can hop aboard?" Dorian leaned out of the cockpit. "It wants a password."

Owen frowned. "Of course."

"Hey, you're the one who was designed to fight these guys."

"The Insurrection?"

Dorian stared at him.

"That wasn't me," Owen said. "I'm third-generation. I've been fighting the Covenant since day one—they're the only threat that really matters now." He paused, eyes glinting. "It was the second-generation Spartans who fought the insurrectionists."

Dorian scowled and pulled back into the cockpit. Looked at the keypad. It was numeric 0–9 glowing lazily in the dusty light. Too bad Evie wasn't here. He figured she could hack into a century-old Sundered Legion lock without a problem. But she was back at the house with

Victor, the two of them working on a virus to trick Salome into opening the shelter doors. Owen had brought Dorian and Saskia out into the field, first to check on the vessel, then to scope out the shelter, to decide the best course of action to get the villagers out of the shelter and into the woods.

Dorian reached out and pressed the 7. Lucky number. Not that he'd been particularly lucky this last week.

He expected a warning blast, maybe a polite but insistent voice informing him that the password was incorrect. Instead the keypad dissolved away.

"What the—" he said.

"What happened?" Owen pulled himself up the ladder. "Where'd the holo—"

"DNA match confirmed," said a man's voice. "Welcome, Quinn Butain."

"Whoa!" Dorian shouted.

Holo-light rippled across the cockpit, materializing into dials and controls far more elaborate than anything Dorian had worked with on Mr. Garzon's scud-rider. Owen poked his head into the cockpit and gave Dorian a stiff smile. "Good job, soldier."

"I didn't do anything!" It was Dorian's first instinct. Deny everything. "I didn't—"

Owen leaned farther in.

Immediately, a monstrous howl poured out of the ship, louder than any show Dorian had ever played in his life. The holo vanished.

"Enemy detected," the man's voice said. "Self-destruct sequence begins in ten . . . nine . . ."

"Stop!" shrieked Dorian, swiping his hand through the air above the cockpit. "What the hell happened?"

"Run!" Owen bellowed over his shoulder.

"Six . . . five . . ."

He grabbed Dorian by the arm and jerked him sideways. Dorian's hand slammed against the cockpit.

The warning siren stopped. Silence rang against Dorian's ears. Then:

"DNA match confirmed. End sequence, Mr. Butain?"

"Yes!" Dorian screamed.

A pause. Then the keypad appeared again. Dorian glanced over at Owen.

"Hey, Spartan," he said. "Maybe stay out of the rebel starship next time."

Owen didn't say anything, only dropped down off the ladder. Saskia crept closer, her eyes wide beneath her dark, wet hair.

"I guess it works?" she said.

Dorian reached over and tapped the 7 again. Again, the ship accepted his DNA, called him Quinn Butain.

"Who is that?" Saskia asked. "Quinn Butain?"

"Hell if I know." Dorian watched the controls reappear in blue lights. He slumped back in his seat, suddenly exhausted. *Quinn Butain.* It sounded familiar.

"You probably had a relative who fought in the Sundered Legion," Owen said. "Your DNA was enough of a match to fool the system."

"Dumb thing," Dorian whispered, although he couldn't complain. Not if it got them their ship.

Quinn Butain. Hadn't his grandmother been a Butain? She would have been too young to have fought with the Insurrection, but maybe her father had.

Not that it mattered now. The insurrectionists couldn't have conceived of a threat like the Covenant. Humans had all been too worried about fighting each other back in those days.

Dorian leaned forward, studying the controls. The ignition wasn't where he was used to, but he found it lurking in the far left-hand corner. "Here goes nothing," he said, pressing down on it with his thumb.

The controls flickered. And from somewhere deep in the craft came a low, throaty rumbling.

"Oh my god!" cried Saskia. "Is it really working?"

"The engine's working." The strength of it rumbled up through the ship's structure, pounding along the bottom of Dorian's feet. He checked the fuel gauge; it was at about half, but they could grab some fuel from Mr. Garzon's place if there wasn't any lying around here. The air pressure looked good too. At least considering he was sitting in a hangar, not moving. There were also about a hundred other readings, and Dorian couldn't even begin to guess what they might mean. A ship this size wasn't going to exactly fly like the scud-rider. If Dorian was being honest with himself, the thought of even attempting to lift this thing into the air was pretty nerve-racking.

He slid out of the seat and leaned out of the cockpit. "What do you want to do now?" he shouted down at Owen and Saskia.

Owen gestured at him to come down. Dorian sighed, killed the engine, jumped down to the floor.

"A prowler like that," Owen said. "It should have a stealth mode."

Dorian wasn't sure he liked the sound of that. "I guess. I didn't exactly learn to fly on one of these things."

Owen's flat expression didn't change. "It'll be easier to get a view of the town from the air," he said.

"Not if I'm flying."

"You would need someone else with you." Owen tilted his head toward Saskia. "I doubt the system will register her as a threat. It was more than likely registering the energy signature from my armor. It doesn't like Spartans."

Dorian and Saskia looked at each other. She was as hard to read as Owen.

"We're running low on ammunition," Owen said. "Reconnoitering the shelter by land is—it's going to be dangerous."

"And flying over the town won't be?" Dorian said. "The Covenant will shoot us down in a heartbeat. Even if there is a stealth mode, it's fifty years out of date."

"You think a ship like this doesn't come equipped with weaponry?" Owen's eyes were steely. Hard. "If you can fly as well as you said you could, it'll be safer for you to do this from the air. My guess is that the Covenant don't have significant anti-air implements, otherwise we'd have seen them. Stay away from the shield and the Covenant ship and you'll be fine."

Dorian narrowed his eyes.

"Make a low pass over the shelter entrance locations," Owen said. "Get a bird's-eye view. See where the Covenant are. See where the paths are." He nodded at the ship. "This looks like it was a Naval Intelligence bird before the rebels got a hold of it. I guarantee there's infrared capabilities in there."

"He's thought of everything," Dorian muttered.

"That's my job," Owen said flatly.

"And if the Covenant see us while we're doing this?" Dorian said. "What then?"

"I told you, a ship like this will have weaponry. But activate the stealth mode. The Covenant will be too focused on the drilling to notice you." Owen jerked his head toward the ship. "The insurrectionists were guerrilla fighters." His voice softened. "Just like you. Like us."

Dorian shifted his weight, unsure of what to say.

"It'll have stealth mode," Owen said, more confidently now. "Use it and you'll be fine."

Dorian looked over at the ship, ten times as big as Mr. Garzon's scud-rider and almost as old. Then he looked at Saskia. She was staring up at the ship with a dazed bafflement. She glanced up at him. Must have felt his gaze on her. She smiled.

"I guess I'm an insurrectionist now," she said.

Dorian didn't know why, but it made him laugh. No way her family would have fought with the rebels back during the war. But here they were.

"Here goes nothing," he said.

The starship lifted off from the overgrown runway with an uneasy bobble from its vertical thrusters. Dorian guided it up through the rain, the holo-map glowing in the top of the viewport. He tilted the ship around until they were heading not toward town but back toward Saskia's house. He needed to figure out how to manage a safe distance between the dome energy shield that compassed the entire town and the lone Covenant ship that still hung somewhere in the thick clouds. Owen said it was a corvette, one of their smaller capital ships. If that was small, Dorian didn't want to see what their larger ships looked like.

"You're a good pilot," Saskia said from the copilot's seat. "Where'd you learn to fly?"

"From a friend of my uncle." Dorian kept his eyes on the controls, gaze flicking around between readings. He kept reaching for things in the wrong place.

"I've flown a few times," Saskia said. "Not anything like this. It was one of our classes at my old school."

"Flying?"

She nodded.

"Damn," Dorian muttered. "What kind of school did you go to?" He was vaguely jealous—there were schools where they taught you to fly as a course?

But then Saskia said, "It was a UNSC prep school."

Dorian snorted. "Figures." They were cruising over the forest now. Dorian lowered the speed and put the ship on autopilot.

"My dad wanted me to be an officer in the UNSC," Saskia said, staring straight ahead, at the windshield seeming to melt with rain. "I think he expected me to be some kind of contractor for his company." She sighed. "But then we moved out here. So who knows."

"Parents suck," Dorian said.

Saskia laughed.

"You think you can activate the stealth mode Owen was babbling about?"

"Oh yeah, easy." Saskia leaned forward, the holo-lights illuminating her face. "There." She pointed at a blazing red icon. "That looks like the old artillery icons from school. I'm not touching it, though." She half smiled, glanced at Dorian out of the corner of her eye. "Don't think it would like my DNA."

Dorian laughed at that, tapped the red icon. Sure enough, it blossomed with a new range of different controls, including one labeled, helpfully, *Stealth*.

Dorian tapped it.

The ship tilted; the engines whirred in the distance. Saskia gave a yelp of protest and clung to her seat. But then the control turned green. *Stealth mode activated*. The ship steadied out again.

"Let's hope it's working," Dorian murmured, pulling up on the throttle. The ship lifted. Turned. Dorian's heart beat faster. He couldn't believe he was just going to fly straight into town.

"It looks like the missiles are armed," Saskia said. "I guess I should go take up my position."

Dorian nodded. Saskia tottered into the rear of the cockpit. Dorian heard her slide open the view window on the cockpit floor.

"Any sign of trouble," Dorian said, "and you get back up here. I'm not going to be able to fire and fly at the same time." He hoped the ship would let her work the controls. And as far as he could tell, the DNA lock was really only on the activation screen. Not in the controls themselves.

"Sure thing." Her voice sounded far away, muffled by the rumble of the engines. Dorian brought the ship down a little lower. Brume-sur-Mer glimmered on the holo-map, although he had zero visibility of the town itself. Everything was shrouded in black storm clouds, which ran smooth and uninterrupted up until they hit the Covenant ship anchored in town. Dorian's heart pumped. *Let's hope this stealth mode works.*

The energy shield shimmered overhead, bathing everything in purple light.

"Gonna have to go lower," he said. "Because of the clouds."

"Got it."

He tilted the ship down, plunging deeper into the clouds. Raindrops streaked across the windshield in angry rivers. The cockpit trembled. Dorian gritted his teeth, kept pushing on the throttle—

They burst out of the clouds, into the brunt of the storm. A smear of light gleamed up ahead. The Covenant ship. Dorian told himself not to worry about it. Reconnaissance was Saskia's job.

"We should be right over the old tourist houses," Dorian said. Where he and Drowning Chromium had played in the shelter. Had it really only been a few days ago? He gripped the throttle, squeezing until his knuckles turned white. Nearly a week and still no sign that any of them had made it off Tomas's boat.

"I see them," Saskia called out. "Can you get lower? I can't tell if the area's clear or not."

Dorian glanced at the altitude. Two thousand meters. He had no idea how effective the stealth mode on this thing was. Even if it weren't fifty years old, anything lower than two thousand would be pushing it. Still, he dropped down a hundred meters, then pulled back around in an arc.

"How about now?"

"Yeah, I can definitely see better now—it looks like—" A pause. Dorian held his breath. "Maybe five Covenant vehicles? Locusts. Like the one they were using to drill."

"Five?" Dorian asked. "Why would they have so many?"

"Who knows? But we won't be using this entrance, that's for sure."

Dorian took that as a sign to increase altitude. No one was firing on them, at least. Maybe the stealth worked better than he thought.

He cruised around the edge of town, dropping lower anytime they came closer to another shelter entrance.

"I can see them moving around down there," Saskia said. "The Covenant. The view window lets me zoom in—I feel like there are more patrols than there were before? We were always able to get into town pretty easy."

"Well, we did blow up one of their drills," Dorian said. "I can't imagine they were pleased about that." Probably out scouring the woods for them and not even thinking to look up. Just like he and Evie had figured out during their training.

"We should fly over the drill site," Saskia said. "See how they're dealing with it."

Dorian knew they shouldn't. It wasn't worth the risk. But the part of him that had gone cloud-diving before the invasion couldn't resist.

"Just once," he said. "We need to figure out how to get people out of the shelter."

"We will," Saskia said. "I just want to see."

Dorian tilted the ship to the right, went soaring straight across the town. Straight across Covenant territory. They were low enough that he could see the glow of their machines seeping through the dark below, streaking his home with veins of blue light. A brighter patch glowed up ahead. He checked the map.

The drill site.

They zoomed past. Dorian braced himself for a flood of plasma fire. But the stealth was still working.

"Hope you saw what you wanted," he said. "'Cause it's probably not a good idea to do it again."

"They're repairing it." Saskia's voice was small.

"At least they're distracted," Dorian said. "If they bring their patrols in to help with the repairs, it'll be easier for us to get to the shelter."

They flew in silence for a few moments as Dorian wove his way toward the edge of town again.

"Your brother's down here, isn't he?" Saskia asked the question too lightly.

"I don't have a brother." Dorian tilted the vessel toward one of the older shelter entrances, one that was built out in the woods. When the shelter was for the Sundered Legion, and not rich tourists.

"Oh, I thought—"

"I have a nephew. Remy. He's—he's like my brother. Do you see anyone down there?"

"No." She almost sounded surprised. "Are you sure there's a shelter entrance here?"

Dorian glanced at the holo-map again. "Yeah, I'm sure. Any sign of a patrol?" He didn't let himself get excited.

"Not like earlier, no. Could we do another loop?"

Dorian soared out over the forest. The rain misted across the viewport. Still pounding down, overflowing the basins that helped keep the waters regulated in the shelter. A system as old as this ship, though not nearly as effective.

"We'll be able to save him," Saskia said suddenly. "Remy."

Hearing his name in her voice was a shock. Dorian flinched and was grateful she was peering out the window and not looking at him. "I don't know how we're going to do this," he finally said. "Without any real weapons. Even if we do find a clear path back to your house."

She fell quiet. Must not have anything to say to that. Dorian didn't like thinking about it himself. If there were any way of landing this ship near the shelter, he'd do it in a heartbeat. But they'd have to go by foot. And he didn't think carpet-bombing a bunch of evacuees to get at the Covenant was much of a defensive strategy.

"I'm still not seeing any signs of Covenant patrols out here," Saskia said after a time. "The woods look pretty undisturbed, although it's hard to tell from this far up."

Dorian looked at the map again. "We're only about a kilometer from your house," he said.

"That's not bad."

"It could be better." He thought again about the rifle, the plasma weaponry. Worthless without ammo. "I'm going to loop us around again," he said, knowing it was a risk. "Just to be sure."

"Sounds good."

Dorian pulled up on the throttle. The engines groaned. The rain pounded against the cockpit. The world below was pitch-black. No sign of Covenant activity.

"It's clear," Saskia said, for the third time.

CHAPTER SEVENTEEN

SASKIA

Saskia listened to the hum of voices carrying over from the next room. The others were mapping out a strategy for the shelter rescue. She'd told them she was going to the bathroom, but she'd gone halfway down the hall before she stopped and leaned against the wall, her eyes closed.

She and Dorian might have managed to find a way to get the survivors to her house. But all she could think about was Dorian mentioning the weapons. How they were fast becoming worthless without ammo.

She should have told them about her father's prototype room at the beginning. She should have trusted them.

The voices swelled; it sounded like Dorian was yelling about something. Saskia took a deep breath. Then she slipped down the hall, looping around into the kitchen. It was easier to hear them in here—the yelling was definitely Dorian. Now he was calling someone crazy. Victor? It could be any of them, really.

Saskia stepped into the safe room, slipped down into the main room, then off into the narrow little hallway that led to the prototype room. They never bothered to come down here except when they needed to use the comm station, and even that was rare. None of them had ever mentioned the door to nowhere.

She stopped in front of the door leading into the prototype room. Pressed her fingers to the lock. It thrummed beneath her touch but didn't snap open. They'd have to hack in.

"What are you doing down here?"

Saskia jumped and whipped around, her heart pounding. Owen stood a few paces away, almost too big for the confined space of the safe room.

Saskia didn't say anything.

"What's that door lead to?" Owen nodded at it. "I noticed it my first night here. Noticed the lock."

Saskia's mouth went dry. Her tongue flopped around uselessly. Owen's dark gaze bored into her.

"Why didn't you mention it before?" she finally said.

Owen raised an eyebrow. "I assumed it was unimportant. After all, you would have told us otherwise, right?"

Saskia trembled. She pressed her back against the cool wall. Owen just stared at her.

"I'm not like the others," she finally said.

Owen tilted his head. She was struck then by how much of the wrong thing it was for her to say—*he* wasn't like the others. He was an urban legend that turned out to be true. She'd just been a rich girl living in a poor town, so unusual that everyone hated her for it. And she didn't really blame them, honestly.

"What's behind the door, Saskia?" Owen said.

Saskia tilted her head toward the room. Her heart pounded. She could feel the heat of Owen's gaze on her, and she knew she'd been so stupid, and so selfish.

"Weapons," she whispered.

Owen said nothing.

Saskia gestured limply. "Prototypes of my parents' designs." Confessing was like throwing up. She felt worse and worse until it was out, and then she felt better. "They keep them locked down here for safekeeping. I don't—I don't have the code—"

"Is that why you kept it from me?" Owen stepped forward. "From the rest of your team?"

Saskia laughed. Shook her head. "They're not my team."

Owen took another step forward. "Why do you say that?"

Saskia shrugged. "Isn't it obvious?"

"Not really." Owen sounded genuinely confused, something Saskia hadn't thought he could be. "You've been working alongside them. You warned us about the Covenant during the mission the other day—I mean, you *ran* through the woods to get to us in time."

"Well, I didn't want anyone to *die*." The hallway felt too narrow, the air too stale. Owen took up too much space. "But I'm not—I don't have anyone in the shelter. I'm pretty sure my parents knew about the invasion before anyone else and took off when they could—"

Owen's eyes flashed. "Why would they do that?"

"They're contractors with Chalybs Defense Solutions for weapon design," Saskia said. "They make weapons for UNSC, but—" She hesitated. "I'm pretty sure they don't make weapons *just* for UNSC, if you know what I mean."

Owen went silent for a moment. Saskia looked down at the lock, the light turning her fingers red. She was still waiting for him to grab her by the arm and throw her out of the house, into the storm.

"I see," he finally said. Then: "They still left you here."

Saskia looked at him. Her skin felt clammy and shivery, and she wrapped her arms around her chest.

"They tend to forget about me," she said. "Especially when things start to get—more questionably legal. Before we moved to Brume-sur-Mer, they actually left me alone for like three months. Never sent anyone to check on me."

A shadow slid across Owen's face. "You think your team upstairs will just *forget* about you too?"

Saskia looked at the far wall.

"You saved Evie's life before you even were a team," Owen said. "You belong here more than you belong with your parents."

He strode across the hallway and put a hand on her shoulder. Saskia looked up at him, on the verge of tears.

"I would have died if you hadn't treated those injuries," he said softly. "You saved my life." He paused. "And there aren't many people who can say that."

Saskia blushed. She looked down at the floor.

Owen crouched down until they were eye-to-eye. He stared at her, his gaze piercing. She couldn't find it in herself to look away.

"I was a war orphan," he said. "ONI found me on Jericho VII, eating bugs in the countryside. Half the planet had been glassed. My parents had been in town when it happened."

Saskia pulled back. "I'm—I'm sorry," she whispered.

"I lost my family," he said, "but I was given a new one. Your parents—they might have left you here. But you have a new family now. They're upstairs." He jerked his head up. "And you've been lying to them for the past week."

Saskia sighed, dropped her head back against the wall. Owen straightened up.

"What are you going to do?" he said.

"They're going to kill me."

"No, they're not."

Saskia looked down at her hands. Her thoughts thrummed. Were Victor and Evie and Dorian really her family? Maybe. She certainly couldn't imagine racing through the woods to warn her parents about an impending Covenant attack. Something in her chest tightened. She took a deep breath.

"They still have their families," she murmured. "Down in the shelter."

"You have more ties to those people in the shelter than you think you do," Owen said. "You aren't your parents. You didn't abandon this town to save your own skin the minute the Covenant showed up."

She lifted her gaze to him. She realized he was right.

Her parents had ditched her so they wouldn't go to jail. But she wasn't like them.

"Let's go upstairs." Owen held out one hand, thick from his armor's gloves. Saskia took it and let him lead her back up the stairs, into the bright kitchen. The voices of the others spilled in from the dining room. Still arguing, but there was a lightness to it. A familiarity.

Owen nodded at her. Saskia stepped into the dining room, flush with rosy light from the chandelier. The others didn't pay her any attention, just continued with their argument. They were talking about some holo-film, she realized, not fighting about the invasion or the rescue or anything related to the Covenant. For a moment, they may as well have been in the high school cafeteria.

But then Owen clanked into the dining room, and everyone fell silent.

"Saskia has something to tell you," he said.

The others looked back at her, eyes wide with expectation. She took a deep breath. Easiest to just spit it out.

"I have weapons," she said.

Silence. Evie frowned, Dorian narrowed his eyes. Victor was the first to speak.

"What do you mean?"

Saskia glanced at Owen, hoping he could give her some strength. But he just stared at her with his flat expression, his dark eyes.

"My parents," Saskia started. She looked at the window. Still raining. She couldn't remember the last time it had rained for so long. "There's a compartment in the safe room. It's locked. We'll have to hack in—"

Dorian leaned over the table. "Are you saying you've had weapons all this time? And you didn't tell us about them?" He laughed hoarsely. "Why not?"

Saskia shrugged hopelessly. "They're prototypes," she said. "And they might not be, um, totally legal. I guess I didn't—" *I didn't trust you.* But the words dissolved on her tongue. "I was being stupid," she finally said. "And paranoid. And then it had gone too long without telling you, and—" She flung her arms out.

"We have had a stash of *prototype weapons* this entire time?" squawked Victor.

"It's not like we really needed them," Evie said. Saskia gave her a thankful look.

"Of course we needed them!"

"You got your hands on Covenant weapons," Owen said. "Dorian had the explosives at his house. You were fine."

"But we need weapons now," Saskia said, her face hot. "If we're going to get people out of the shelter and take out that shield. I couldn't—I had to tell you. If you hate me, it's fine. But we have the weapons." She slumped against the wall, suddenly exhausted. "I mean, once we break the lock."

"You sure you're not keeping the password from us too?" Victor asked.

Saskia glared at him, and he turned away, sheepish.

"Evie, I bet you could break into the lock," Saskia said. "It's not that complicated."

"I'll give it a shot." Evie stood up. The boys were both scowling. Evie rolled her eyes.

"You want to save your families or not?" she said. "We're running out of time. Saskia didn't want to tell us about the weapons. Big deal. It's not like any of us had been friends with her before this all started. Not even you, Victor."

Victor's cheeks reddened. "C'mon, Evie."

"He had a crush on you," Evie told Saskia. "Back before the invasion."

"What the hell?" shouted Victor.

Dorian started laughing.

Saskia looked at Victor, who was burying his face in his hands. She had to laugh too, although she immediately slapped her hand over her mouth. "I'm sorry," she mumbled.

"That's why he's been so crummy to you," Evie said in a conspiratorial whisper. "Couldn't handle his feelings."

"Evie, I will *kill* you!"

Dorian leaned sideways on his chair, still laughing.

"It's not that funny," Saskia said.

"I know." Dorian wiped at his eyes. "It's just so—*high school bullcrap*, you know?" His laugh trickled away, and he slapped a hand on Victor's back. "Cheer up, man. I can show you how to talk to girls sometime if you want."

"Shut up!" Victor slid down in his chair. For a moment, his eyes flicked over to Saskia, and she smiled at him. He'd been the one she'd thought trusted her the least. She supposed he'd just been overcompensating.

Saskia wasn't sure she would ever understand boys.

"Enough," Owen said. "Evie, Saskia, you two go figure out the lock. Gentlemen." He looked at Dorian and Victor, who both straightened their spines, although Dorian had to smother another laugh. "We're going to work out a strategy now that we know the lay of the land." He clapped his hands together once, and Evie ducked out of the dining room. Saskia glanced over her shoulder at Victor one last time. He wasn't looking at her. But Owen was.

He nodded. Saskia knew what that nod meant.

Good job.

"Don't let Victor get to you," Evie said. She was sitting in front of the door leading to the prototype room, a snaky wire connecting her comm pad to the lock. They hadn't had much luck with it yet.

"What do you mean?" Saskia sat cross-legged next to her, watching the readouts on the holo-projection.

"He's never had a girlfriend before." Evie's finger tapped against her comm pad screen. "I'm not sure he even knows how to talk to a girl that isn't me." She laughed. "Seeing you all the time, it was too much for him to handle."

Saskia smiled. "He seemed nice until he started accusing me of not wanting to save people in the shelter."

Evie rolled her eyes. "Sounds like Victor. He'll figure it out someday." She sighed. "God! This would be so much easier with my computer."

"You can borrow mine."

Evie shook her head. "Doesn't have the right software on it. I mean—" She glanced at Saskia sideways. "I'm guessing you don't have JLM installed."

Saskia laughed. "You would be correct."

"It's fine." Evie tap-tap-tapped on her screen. "Ah! Now we're getting somewhere."

Something in the lock clicked. The red light switched off.

"Whoa," Saskia said. "Did you get it?"

"Not yet." Evie tapped and code flew past on the holo-screen. "Try now."

Saskia pressed her hand against the lock. Nothing happened. She tried to push on the door, but it wouldn't budge.

"Nope," she said. "Not opening."

"Hmm." Evie's forehead scrunched up in concentration. Holo-light flashed off the walls. "Try now."

Saskia reached out and touched the lock. This time, it lit up bright green, and there was the *hiss-whirr* of the door pulling open.

"You got it!" Saskia cried, jumping to her feet. "That was fast. You're freaking amazing."

"It was actually that Sundered Legion craft that gave me the idea." Evie unfolded her legs, and Saskia held out her hand to help her. "I mean, it's a DNA lock, so why shouldn't it recognize your DNA? I just had to expand the parameters until it recognized you."

"Brilliant," Saskia said. She felt more at ease with Evie than she had before, Evie being the only one who hadn't gotten mad about the whole keeping-unnecessary-secrets thing.

"So what kind of weapons are in here, exactly?" Evie asked.

Saskia frowned. "I'm not sure," she said. "I know this is where they kept all their prototypes because they were always taking clients down here, but I don't really know the specifics or anything."

"I guess we'll find out," Evie said, pushing the door open.

The light in the room was pale and sharp and cold. It reflected off the weapons resting on the glass shelves. Everything was unfinished and looked like raw steel, dramatic in the light.

"Wow," breathed Evie.

Saskia drifted forward. The last time she'd been in the room was four months ago, when her dad had been out of town and her mom asked her to meet with some clients that night, a pair of tall, angular men who never smiled. They had come down to the room after dinner, pulled a grenade launcher off the shelf, and gone out into the backyard to demonstrate it.

That grenade launcher was gone now. It had been replaced by a pair of complicated-looking pistols and a large rifle that vaguely looked like a pair of long, steel blocks connected to a grip.

"I'm going to tell the others we got in," Evie said, interrupting Saskia's thoughts. "You grab anything that looks good and meet me upstairs. We've got to figure out how all this stuff works."

Saskia nodded. Evie vanished into the safe room, and Saskia turned back to the shelves. She knew, from eavesdropping on conversations, that CDS had reversed-engineered some Covenant technology. She wondered how many of these weapons were energy based, rather than ballistic. The grenade launcher had been, in her mother's words, "old-fashioned." The clients were only interested in human tech, she'd said later.

Saskia picked up the twin-block rifle. It weighed more than she expected. She turned it over in her hands, looking at the two long blocks that seemed to represent the weapon's barrel—in between were studs that looked like teeth.

Footsteps thudded overhead. The others, coming down to see what they'd found.

She curled her fingers around the grip, and instantly felt the weapon surge with power, as a series of targeting displays projected around the rifle's stock. Saskia yelped and dropped it. The displays vanished. The weapon looked cold and dead again.

She knelt down to pick it up, this time gingerly.

"Railgun," Owen said.

Saskia glanced at him over her shoulder. "Stop sneaking up on me."

He actually smiled at that. "We need to work on your situational awareness." He nodded at the rifle. "It's a recoilless carbine. Or, at least, a CDS version of it. I thought only Acheron Security made these. Looks like I was wrong." He took the weapon from her and activated its displays, examining the weapon closely.

"Have you used one before?" Saskia asked.

"Once. Against a battle lance of Sangheili. You know about Elites?"

"The warrior class, right?" Saskia smiled a little. "Some use energy swords that can cut through solid steel? That's what they taught us in school. Even though all of the Covenant seem to be warriors."

"That's what happens in war," Owen said.

"Did it work?" Saskia asked. "Your railgun?"

"It got the job done," Owen said. He put the rifle down.

"Come on," he said. "Let's see what else we've got here."

CHAPTER EIGHTEEN

VICTOR

Owen dropped a military crate full of weapons at Victor's feet.

"You know how to shoot," he said. "And you worked out how to use the needler without killing yourself. So you're going to help us figure these things out." He paused. "Be cautious, however. They're prototypes, and they might not function as you'd expect."

They were on the front porch, rain shimmering around them. It had slowed to a drizzle, and Victor hoped it would stay like that for at least a couple of days. Give a chance for the flooding to recede, buy them some time to open up the shelter.

He knew he couldn't operate on hope alone, though.

The front door slammed. Saskia slipped out with another crate. Victor went still, his face burning. He couldn't believe that Evie had said that about him liking Saskia. *In front of her.*

Saskia didn't look at him, only set the box down next to Owen. More weapons. Mostly guns.

"You're going to work together to get these figured out," Owen said. "We don't have time for whatever"—he waved his hand around—"relationship issues you're having."

"We weren't in a relationship," Saskia said.

"Not a romantic one." Owen pushed the crate of weapons toward them with his boot. "But you were partners. And you're part of a team. Work it out."

He stomped across the porch and went back inside.

"I guess we should get started." For the first time, Saskia met Victor's eye. "I don't want anyone in the shelter to drown."

"I never thought . . ." Victor's face flushed.

Saskia just shrugged. She reached into the box and extracted a long rifle that appeared to have a strange amalgamation of Covenant technology mechanically grafted along the stock and barrel. "I've heard this one before," she said.

"Heard it?"

She laughed. A little bitterly, Victor thought. "Yeah, while I was trying to sleep. My parents were showing it to a client. They'd pulled it out before I went to bed."

She stepped off the porch, into the glow of the safety lights. Held the rifle up to her shoulder and pointed it toward a clump of trees growing on the far side of the interior.

"It almost looks like the marksman rifles my sisters were issued." It was easier to talk about weapons.

"Yeah, guessing it's easy to modify existing stuff rather than create it whole cloth. At least, in the beginning."

Victor jumped off the porch and held out his hands to her. She gave him the rifle, and he put its butt on his shoulder, the way he had Camila's marksman rifle, during one of his shooting lessons on the beach. It felt natural, although this weapon was heavier than Camila's had been. He removed the safety, toggling to a semi-automatic, before giving the weapon a once-over to make sure he was firing it correctly, although given its bizarre, cobbled-together design, it was impossible to know for sure. Once he felt confident enough, he pressed his finger on the trigger. Squeezed.

A single round jacketed in what appeared to be plasma streaked out of the rifle with a sudden, echoing crack, nailing one of the trees, which violently exploded into microscopic splinters on impact. The gun jerked up, the kickback stronger than he expected.

"That's the sound I remember," Saskia said.

"It's powerful," Victor said, examining the Covenant tech woven into the weapon. "Do you know what it's called?"

"No clue." Saskia shrugged. "Probably just a string of letters and numbers right now."

Victor smiled. Glanced at her. Her hair was damp from the misting rain, her skin dewy in the shield light. Evie was right. He had felt betrayed, thinking Saskia didn't care about the townspeople. And not just in a normal way, but in, like, a boyfriend way.

The minute Evie got him alone, she was going to tell him what a creep he was. He could just feel it.

"Hey," he said, and Saskia looked at him, her face bland and as expressionless as Owen's.

"I'm sorry," he said.

She stared at him for a long time. Then she nodded. She didn't have to say anything else. It was enough.

Victor set the rifle down at his side. Saskia bounded back up the steps and pulled a pistol-like weapon out of the box.

"Let's try this one next," she said. "They call it a sticky detonator."

Victor woke up to the filtered gray light of rainy season daytime. Raindrops pounded against the glass of his window. He sighed. It had been too much to hope for a reprieve from the rain.

He lay in bed, staring up at the ceiling. Even the dim light felt too bright for him. In the last few days, he thought he'd gotten used to this whole sleep-during-the-day, attack-at-night routine. But for the first time, the light was just—*distracting* him. It seemed to illuminate all the thoughts in his head, dragging them to the forefront: testing the weapons, Saskia and him silently working out how each prototype functioned. Showing the others. Practicing on trees. He'd fallen asleep earlier with rifle blasts behind his eyelids. But the weapons test made him think of Saskia, and Evie blurting out, *He had a crush on you*. Dorian almost falling off his seat from laughing.

The rain. His parents in the shelter. The Covenant boring a hole in the middle of the town.

He grabbed his comm pad and checked the time. 2:15. He sighed, listened to the constant pattering of the rain. He knew he wasn't going to fall back asleep. Maybe he could have ignored the rest of it long enough to drift off, but not with the rain. Salome had told them about the potential for flooding a day ago. A lot could happen in a day.

He kicked off the blanket and swung out of bed. He could get a hold of Salome on Saskia's comm system. Ask if the shelter was still safe. The not knowing was gnawing away at the edge of his thoughts.

He threw on some clothes and went out into the hall. The house was silent save for the rain. He took the stairs carefully, afraid they would creak beneath his footsteps. Let the others sleep if they were able.

When he went into the kitchen, he was surprised to find the safe room door was hanging open, a narrow band of yellow light spilling out across the tile floor. Had they forgotten to close it up last night? Or maybe it was just Owen. Saskia had told him she didn't think he ever slept, back when they were working together as partners.

Partners. He really had been unfair to her. It was just that his thoughts got all twisted up around her, and the last thing he wanted was for her to abandon them, and him to have to hate her. So he'd started mistrusting her. Some kind of stupid defense mechanism.

He pushed open the door. "Owen?" he called out.

"Victor?" Evie's head popped into the doorway at the base of the stairs. "What are you doing up?"

Victor grinned. "Um, what are *you* doing up?"

She vanished out of the doorway. Victor jumped down the stairs and found her sitting in front of the comm station, Saskia's computer glowing beside it. The same computer she'd been using to work on the virus for Salome.

She hunched over the keyboard, fingers flying. The holo-projection glowed with rapid-fire code. Victor could almost follow it, but she was too fast, and his eyes glazed over a few minutes in. "Looks like it's coming along," he said, not wanting to embarrass himself.

She kept typing.

"I kind of wanted to use the comm station." Victor shifted his weight. "I was worried about the flooding, and that's the only way to contact—"

"I think I have it."

Evie spoke so softly Victor almost couldn't hear her over the typing. "What's up?"

"I have it. The virus." She stopped, her hands poised over the keys, the holo shining across her face. "I think." Back to typing.

"What?" Victor crouched down beside her, squinting up at the code. Still too fast. "Are you serious? What are you doing now?"

"Adding some finishing touches." She leaned forward and

scanned her work. "I woke up about an hour ago, and I just—knew what I'd been missing." She laughed, hit a key, leaned back in her chair. "I couldn't wait till morning."

Now that the code was still, Victor could read it more clearly, more slowly. It was pretty elegant work, the way Evie's code always was. Deceptively simple. A worm that could enter into Salome's system and change a single piece of information: the Covenant threat risk.

"Have you tested it yet?" Victor said.

Evie shook her head. "I tried. But the comm station wasn't connecting to her. The system's too patchy. We'll need to upload it at the town computer." She looked over at him. "I'm glad you're here, though. I wanted someone to check my work. Normally my dad does it, but—"

"Sure," he said. "And maybe I can get the comm system to work too. Maybe we won't have to upload at that old computer."

Evie shook her head like she was doubtful, but she ceded her chair over to him. Victor read through her code as quickly as he could. It looked fine to him. Better than anything he could do, at any rate. But it would be so much safer to upload over the comm system.

"Let me try to bring up Salome," he said. "I bet I can do it." He thumped the side of the comm station.

"I really don't think it's a hardware issue," Evie said. "Seriously, the comm system is just—down." For a moment, she seemed to tremble. Seemed to draw into herself. "I hope the Covenant hasn't noticed that local comm channel out here."

"Yeah," Victor said. But he was already focused on the comm station, switching it on, fiddling with the switches on the side. Nothing was connecting.

"I told you," Evie said.

Victor reached back behind the station. "Maybe if I can just turn it off—"

He pressed a switch, and the entire room lit up, every overhead light flooding on with searing intensity. A siren wailed up out of the speakers in the station and from someplace set into the wall.

"Warning," said a dull, mechanized voice. Not Salome's. "Warning. Warning."

Evie was shouting something, not that Victor could make it out over the racket of the siren. He hit the switch again, and the noise cut out, the silence afterward buzzing in his ears. The lights faded back to normal.

Evie knocked him in the shoulder. "Way to go!" she laughed. "Waking up the whole house."

Victor grinned back at her. "I just wanted to bring them down here to tell them you got the virus ready."

She laughed again, shook her head. Her smile lingered, but there was a sadness to it. "Let's hope it works."

Footsteps pounded overhead. A door slammed. Someone released a litany of curses.

"Dorian's up," Evie said. She unplugged the computer and snapped it shut. "Let's go find them before Dorian starts shooting up the place with Saskia's guns."

"Dorian's not that stupid," Victor said.

Evie made a face at him. "Dorian's not stupid at all. You're the one who activated a warning siren for no reason."

Victor bumped against her, knocking her into the stairwell.

"Hey, Saskia!" Evie called out as she began to ascend the stairs. "We're fine!"

"Oh my god." Saskia's voice echoed as it rebounded down the stairwell. "I haven't heard that old warning system in years."

"It was Victor." Evie's voice was far away, at the top of the stairs. Victor slunk into the stairwell, his face hot with embarrassment. Evie grinned down at him.

"There's the genius now," she laughed.

"You hit the switch in the back, didn't you?" Saskia was silhouetted against the kitchen lights. Victor couldn't see her face. "I should have warned you about it."

"What the *hell* is going on?" Dorian, marching shirtless into the kitchen. Victor sighed and clomped up the stairs.

"Actually," he said, breaking through the pack the others had formed around the safe room entrance. "I did it on purpose."

"I hate you," Dorian said.

"He didn't really," Evie said. "He was trying to bring up Salome."

Dorian and Saskia glanced at each other.

"You should tell them," Victor said.

Evie smiled a little.

"Tell us what?" Dorian asked.

"I think I've finished the virus." Evie let out a long rush of air. "I'm going to have to upload it at the town computer, but—"

"Are you serious?" Dorian asked.

Evie nodded.

Dorian let out a whoop of excitement and threw his arms around Evie's shoulders. She blinked in surprise.

"We can get them out of there," Dorian said. *"Finally."*

Evie smiled against his shoulder. He let her go and Saskia said, "Good job."

"And we've got your weapons," Dorian said. "We know an entrance to use. We should go out now."

The others laughed nervously, but Victor didn't think Dorian was joking. "We need to go at night," Victor said. "Like we've been doing. And we need to tell Owen, anyway."

"Where *is* Owen?" Saskia asked.

"Seriously," Evie said. "That alarm should have woken him up."

Saskia shook her head. "He doesn't sleep much. But I mean, if he thought something was wrong—" She moved over to the kitchen window and peered out at the gray yard. Victor felt a twinge of jealousy.

"Oh," Saskia said, the relief audible in her voice. "There he is."

Victor and Evie and Dorian crowded up next to her around the window. Owen was cutting across the yard. He had his helmet on, which always made him seem inhuman. You had no idea what was behind that mirrored visor. You couldn't help but feel a little bit afraid, even when he was on your side.

"Tell him the good news," Dorian said to Evie, sliding away from the others. Owen disappeared around the corner of the house. A few minutes later, the front door slammed shut. Victor and Evie and Saskia made their way toward the foyer, where they found Owen dripping on the tile. He pulled his helmet off.

"Why are all four of you awake?" he said.

"Evie finished the virus," Dorian said. "Right, Evie?"

She nodded. "I couldn't test it," she said. "We couldn't get ahold of Salome on the comm station. But the code itself checks out. It should work." She glanced around, and Victor saw that mask of anxiety she always wore before big tests at school. An overachiever afraid of failure.

"It will absolutely work," Victor said. "Evie's the best comp sci student in the whole school. Even if she's the one usually fixing the viruses, not making them."

Evie grinned at him, ducked her gaze away.

But Owen didn't look as pleased as Victor would have expected him to. Not that Owen ever *truly* looked pleased, but there was an extra grimness in his features, a glint of worry in his eyes.

"I'm happy to hear that," he said, "because I have some bad news."

Immediately, everyone seemed to slump. The sparkle of excitement went out of the room. Owen set his helmet on the expensive foyer table. The incongruity of the scene struck Victor. It was the sort of shot he always wanted to put into his films.

"I was checking the perimeter," Owen said. "Like I always do while you're asleep. Making sure we don't have any scouts encroaching on our position. And I found—" He paused, looked at each of them in turn. "There's some pretty massive flooding out on the edge of the woods, heading into town."

Silence. The rain pounded on the roof. Victor hated it in that moment.

"Where?" Evie's voice was shrill. "Parts of town always flood, it doesn't mean—"

"Near Rue la Marde." Owen was calm. "And Rue la Florêt. In the woods. The entire road was underwater."

Evie gave a little gasp and covered her mouth. Victor just tasted a sourness in the back of his throat. He couldn't remember Rue la Marde ever flooding before.

"What are you saying?" Saskia asked. "That we're too late? That they've already drowned?"

"No." Dorian stepped forward, shaking his head. "No, the shelter doesn't go out to Rue la Marde. But if it's flooding there, that's not a good sign."

"We need to act," Owen said. "Get ready. We're going out now."

"It's still daylight," Victor protested.

Owen shook his head. "We don't have a choice. The rain should cover us, and the flooding will likely impede Covenant movement as well. Suit up!"

He barked out the last order, and it reverberated around the room. For a moment, no one moved.

But then they erupted, a flurry of activity, all four of them bounding toward the stairs.

They were going to take back their town.

CHAPTER NINETEEN

EVIE

wen held up a fist. They were trained well enough by now: All of them stopped. Evie didn't even bump into Dorian, who was marching in front of her with the needler carefully strapped to his back, holding one of the rifles Saskia's parents had kept down in the safe room—it was a strange-looking human rifle modified with Covenant bits. It didn't look like a natural fit, but according to Victor it would do the job.

"What's wrong?" Saskia whispered in Evie's ear.

Evie shook her head, her stomach too twisted up in knots for her to say anything. It was the first time she had been out in the woods during the day since the invasion, and she felt exposed and vulnerable in the pearly gray light.

Owen turned around, his own rifle in hand and Saskia's railgun magnetically anchored onto the back of his armor. He depolarized the visor on his helmet, revealing his eyes. "We're almost to the split point," he said. "And I thought—"

He squinted at some point in the distance, and Evie's hand dropped down to the plasma pistol hanging from the holster on her belt. She'd take one of the Covenant pistols, but also had a large pistol-like weapon latched to her back with a thick cylinder where its barrel should have been. Saskia referred to it as a sticky detonator, capable of launching an explosive grenade from a safe distance. Saskia's computer was sealed up in a waterproof pouch and tucked inside the bag slung over her shoulder. And inside that was the virus, the key to their entire plan.

"When I was in training," Owen said, dropping his gaze back down to them, "we did everything in squads. They wanted us to learn how to work as a team."

Green-scented rain tumbled around them. Evie pulled her hand away from the pistol. *A pep talk*, she thought. He was going to give them a pep talk.

"Before a mission, my squad would always try to give us at least one piece of advice we could take with us into the field."

The four of them stood quietly, waiting.

"It helped," he went on. "It helped me. I didn't trust the others at first."

Evie resisted the urge to look over at Saskia.

"I didn't think anyone could have known what I went through, before they found me. But of course they did, in their own way." His voice was quieter, blending in with the rustle of the rain. "Just like the four of you. You're scared for your families, for you friends." He smiled—always a disconcerting sight. "For one another, I hope. That fear is a good thing. It means you're alive. It means there's still a chance you'll survive this. Together."

Something flushed inside Evie. A sudden surge of strength. She looked at Victor, her oldest friend; at Dorian and Saskia, her two newest. All of them were pale and trembling. Dark circles ringed their eyes. The rain plastered their hair to their heads. They were a mess. But they were ready. They had to be.

"I never gave these kinds of talks," Owen said. "Not in training, not in service. I typically wasn't the team leader." He reached up, polarized the visor, concealing his face again. "So I'll just tell you the truth. I know you can do this. All of you."

Maybe it wasn't the kind of stirring speech that filled Victor's holo-films, but Evie still felt her chest swell with pride. With hope. They were going to save the town.

"Let's go," Owen said.

They merged back into their single-file line and wove through the forest. The wet leaves, the squelching mud—it was the same path they had always taken but it felt unfamiliar during the day. Too many details Evie had never noticed before: the shape of tree leaves, the texture of the bark.

And the flooding.

She could see what Owen had described to them only two hours earlier, the glassy stretch of water creeping over the forest floor, strangled trees sticking out of it like wrinkled fingers. The woods tended to flood during the rainy season, everything turning marshy and thick. But she couldn't remember ever seeing a lake spreading out across the undergrowth, swallowing up the land.

The images came to her unbidden: the shelter where she had stood and listened to Dorian's band play a million years ago now full of dark water. Pale, lifeless faces orbiting like planets in the murk. The entire town, drowned in the space that was meant to keep them safe. The place where she would have been if she hadn't snuck out with Victor.

No, she told herself. *I won't fail them.*

And then Owen stopped again. This time, Evie knew, speaking would be too risky. He turned around and gestured: two fingers to the western edge of town, one to the east, one deeper into the woods. They all had their places to go. Their roles to play.

Dorian glanced back at Evie and gave her a small smile. He hoisted up his rifle. "I've got your back," he whispered, his words bleeding into the rain.

Victor nodded in agreement. He punched Evie gently on the arm and gave her a thumbs-up, like they were just about to go in for a calculus test. Owen was already making his way to the west, and Victor and Dorian followed, heads bent down.

"You ready for this?" Saskia whispered.

Evie patted her backup. "I think so."

Saskia smiled. "Me too." She looked shrunken in the rain, wrapped up not in her fashionable clothes but dark pants and a sweatshirt, her hair tied back in a knot on the top of her head. A plasma rifle was strapped to her back, a pistol and spare ammo hung from her belt. They had voted when they left: who would have the most important job. Who would bring the townspeople to safety.

All of them had voted for Saskia.

Without thinking, Evie wrapped her arms around Saskia and drew her into a hug. After a moment's quiet pause, Saskia returned it.

"See you soon," Evie whispered.

Evie cupped her comm pad under her hand, trying to block the light from the holo. Dorian had drawn up a map for her before they left, marking the way to the computer. With the comm systems down, the map couldn't track her location, but at least she knew she was headed vaguely in the right direction—north-northwest.

The path squelched beneath her feet, and mud splashed up around her ankles. Evie switched off the map and held her hands out to the side for balance, moving slowing over the saturated ground. Patches of water glimmered around her, shimmering reminders of her father down in the shelter. Her father, and everyone else.

Something snapped.

Evie froze, listening. Some distant thunder? A tree branch breaking in the wind?

There it was again: *crr-runch*. She whirled around, fumbling for the pistol at her waist. Her comm pad slipped out of her fingers and landed in a patch of tall grass.

"Crap!" She knelt down, felt around in the watery mud. Her breath came tight and short. There—her fingers brushed something smooth and metallic. She wrapped her hand around her comm pad and straightened up—

An Unggoy stared at her from behind a bar of trees.

Evie screeched in panic and scrambled to her feet, slipping backward over the mud. She shoved her comm pad back in her pocket and fired off a round from her plasma pistol.

An echoing blast of energy, an explosion of wet leaves, a puff of smoke. The Unggoy squealed and darted forward, firing off rounds from its own plasma pistol. The bolts streaked overhead, steaming in the rain.

Evie fired from her pistol again. Once. Twice. Missed both times. All the lessons she had gotten from Victor and his sisters had vanished from her memory—all she could think of now was survival.

She turned and ran.

The Unggoy gave chase, although it stopped shooting; she could hear it crashing through the underbrush behind her. She ran wildly, splashing through the puddle, whipping herself around tree trunks. In the back of her mind, she knew she was losing herself in the forest. With all the flooding, she'd never find the path again.

Evie's lungs were burning. Her vision was blurred with rainwater. The Unggoy shrieked behind her.

And then she came across a huge swath of flooding, water stretching off on either side. She whipped off to the left, arms pumping.

A plasma bolt struck a tree in front of her, and she whirled around and fired at the Unggoy, which let out a wail of pain and stumbled backward. Her chest seized. *I hit it*. The realization wasn't as comforting as she would have thought.

Still, she knew she had to get to the computer. Had to unleash the virus. Her feet pounded the mulchy ground, flinging up droplets of mud and old rainwater. The Unggoy shrieked behind her, but the shrieking grew softer the harder she ran.

She wove deeper into the woods, glancing over her shoulder, waiting for the blast from its plasma pistol. Nothing happened.

Eventually, she slowed, wheezing hard. She leaned up against a nearby tree and blinked out at the forest around her, dizzy with that sudden, inescapable feeling of being lost.

She pulled out her comm pad and drew up Dorian's map. Splotches of green, a few crisscrossed paths. She had been on the main path earlier, when she came across the Unggoy. Then she had run left. She squinted down at the map. If she kept going straight forward, she should hit the clearing.

She started walking, glancing over her shoulder to see if the Unggoy was following her. It wasn't. Still, she kept her pistol out.

Eventually, the trees started to thin, and the rain fell heavier, churning up the wet mulch. Evie's heart fluttered, and with a burst of energy, she took up a light jog. Branches lashed at her face. *Please be there, please be there*, she thought, as if she could will the clearing into existence.

She spilled out of the woods.

For a moment, she was stricken, afraid she'd made it to the *wrong* clearing—she saw no sign of the computer. Everything was veiled by the rain. But then a green light flashed in the distance, and she found the lump of greenery that had grown over the computer. She whooped with excitement and raced across the clearing. She knelt in front of the computer and slid her bag off her shoulder. Then she took one last glance around—no sign of the Unggoy. No sign of the Covenant.

Evie entered in the code Dorian had told her. The computer's holo flowered to life, shimmery with the rain.

"Salome," she said. "I need to talk to you."

An unbearable pause, and a million terrors flashed though Evie's head: What if the Covenant had destroyed Salome somehow? What if the emergency power that ran the computer was down?

But then there was a flash of holo-light and Salome materialized in a hazy green outline. "Evelyn Rousseau," she said, frowning deeply. "How many times have I told you? You need to leave the area."

"I still have some work to do." Evie pulled out her laptop. "I just wanted to check to see if you're okay. I know the Covenant has been messing around in town."

"This is why you need to leave." Salome put her hands on her hips and pouted. "I have so much to worry about! Those aliens are destroying my infrastructure!"

Evie flipped open her computer, trying her best to shield it from the rain with her own body. She felt around on the town computer for the wire port and plugged in the connecting wire. No comm channels meant she had to do this the old-fashioned way.

"I know," Evie said. "That's what I'm here to work on."

Salome's projection arced around so a tiny Salome floated on Evie's shoulder. "What are you doing?" she chirped. "It is my job to know. The city engineers always keep me informed."

"It's just a little update." Evie brought up the file and tapped it open. Hit the Transfer icon.

"An update?" Salome sounded suddenly worried. "Am I not good enough anymore?"

Evie could kill whichever maladjusted nerd it was that had tried giving Salome more "natural" emotions. Clearly they had never spoken to a human being before.

"You're fine." Evie sighed, watching as the transfer bar slowly filled. "You probably won't even notice it."

"How did you even get the access to update me anyway?"

"My dad," Evie said promptly.

"Mikal Rousseau?" Salome's projection flitted around again. Now she hovered in the air above Evie's computer. Evie could see the progress bar shining through Salome's stomach. "But he doesn't have access to my files! He's a professor!"

"He must have gotten them from somewhere, then." Evie was surprised by how calm she kept her voice. Inside she was rioting. The progress bar was still only about 75 percent. *Finish, finish!*

An explosion boomed from the direction of the town, louder than thunder. The ground trembled.

"What was that?" Salome head whipped around in a blur. "Oh, it's those aliens again. I bet they're digging up my town square this time."

Black smoke billowed over the trees. Distantly Evie could make out the *zip, zip, zip* of plasma cannons.

"It's not the aliens," she said, and the scent of rain and the scent of fire mingled together over the town.

"Oh?" Salome said. "Then who is it? I can't see *anything* over there, not since they blew up Old Brume. Can you believe it? The oldest neighborhood in town!"

Ninety percent.

"They're monsters," Evie said softly, thinking of the Unggoy she had left in the woods.

Another explosion tore the sky in half. Purple-red light flashed through the rain, staining everything like a bruise.

"Again!'" shrieked Salome, her projection flitting a meter away from Evie. "What are they doing out there? Oh, I wish they hadn't destroyed my cameras."

Ninety-nine percent.

Evie's hand trembled. She held it up to the screen. Waiting—

One hundred percent.

Activate?

Evie hit the icon and held her breath. Salome's hologram flickered twice. She was still looking out at the fire burning beyond the trees.

"My *town*," she wailed.

"Salome," Evie whispered, her voice hoarse in her throat. *Your code's perfect*, Victor had told her. But he'd never been that good at coding.

"Yes, Evelyn Rousseau?" Salome turned back to her. She looked the same as always. But then, the virus wouldn't affect her appearance.

"I need you to open up the shelter," Evie said, in a rush. "Not all of the doors. Just number five. The one near Rue le Verre. It's nowhere near the explosion."

Salome blinked. Evie curled her hands into fists, breath trembling in her throat.

"Ah yes," Salome said. "I can see Rue le Verre quite clearly! No damage there."

Evie wanted to scream at her—*just say yes, say yes, say yes.*

"The threat level is acceptable," Salome said. "I will open the doors immediately."

CHAPTER TWENTY

DORIAN

G o, go, go!" Owen shouted, releasing a stream of blazing cover fire from his rifle. The mayor's office burned with white flames, smoke and steam belching up into the misty sky. The same flying Covenant soldiers that Dorian had escaped the night of the invasion swarmed overhead, sending plasma fire into the rubble below, where Owen, Dorian, and Victor were hiding.

Dorian didn't have to be told twice. He took off at a low crouch, plasma bolts zinging overhead. He doubted the soldiers—Owen called them Drones—could actually see him. Downtown had been shredded, the old brick buildings toppled into piles of stone and glass, meaning there was plenty of cover if you kept yourself low.

A green fireball erupted a few meters in front of him, and Dorian screamed, slammed against the wet ground. He craned his neck up— the Drone? Did they have some kind of grenade launcher?

No. He couldn't be so lucky. A pair of round purple aircraft winged overhead, four streaks of light following behind them.

"Banshees!" Owen yelled—Dorian couldn't see him. "Get the hell out of here *now*."

"I'm trying!" Dorian shouted back. He crawled on his hands and knees around the flaming rubble—they'd hit the old *Welcome to Brume-ser-Mer* sign, of all things, the painted wood charring and smoking in the rain.

Dorian scrambled forward. He could hear the *rat-tat-tat* of Owen's rifle. In the moment, it was as reassuring as a lullaby.

The rubble cleared up ahead. Dorian slowed, looked up into the rain. The Banshees were behind him, firing plasma cannons one after another. The Drones were headed his way. Four of them, plasma pistols at the ready.

He swung his head toward the edge of downtown. Rue le Coquillage was wide open. On the other side of the street was a residential area. Their rendezvous with Victor.

Dorian took a deep breath and flung himself around, firing his rifle up at the Drones. It kicked powerfully with each shot, the Covenant parts sizzling in the rain. One of the Drones exploded into pieces, bug bits spiraling down to the wreckage below. The others squawked as they looked for their comrade; Dorian took that moment to run as fast as he could across the street.

The Drones screamed. A plasma bolt scorched the air a few millimeters from Dorian's face, and he drew its smoke into his lungs as he breathed. The smell reminded him, sharply and suddenly, of the smell on Tomas's boat.

There had been plasma fire from the sky that night too.

Dorian bounded into the front yard of a ramshackle house, flinging himself under the leaves of a big, sprawling banana tree. Not much of a cover, especially since the Drones probably saw him dart under there, but it made him feel safe.

Plasma fire ripped through the leaves.

Dorian fired off his rifle in return. Then he ran toward the house, conjuring up all his speed, all his strength. The Drones shrieked and chattered behind him.

A meter from the house, he leapt, twisted his body, and slid feet-first through the front window.

Glass shattered, and Dorian hit the floor hard, pain reverberating up from the soles of his feet. He moaned. Debris crunched underneath him. Hot wetness smeared across his back.

Plasma fire burned a line in the house's carpet.

Dorian rolled onto his side, pushed himself up to his feet. The Drones were a few meters away. He hobbled sideways away from the window, then moved toward the back of the house. Into the dark hallway, down into the abandoned kitchen, which stank of rotten food.

A crash from the front of the house.

Dorian ducked into the dining room. Where the hell was the back door?

Skittering, inhuman footsteps. Chittering voices. Dorian glanced down and saw drops of his blood shining on the wooden floors.

"Damn," he whispered. He dove through a door in the dining room, into a—thank god!—sunroom, a glass door leading out into the backyard. Dorian eased it open, slid out. Was he still dripping blood? Of course. Why even bother to be quiet?

The backyard smelled like smoke. But it was still raining, and Dorian stepped into the open. The rain stung when it hit the cuts on his skin, but at least it washed away the blood.

He jumped the fence into the neighbor's yard. Did it again, into the next neighbor's yard. Again. He half limped, half jogged his way through the backyards of the neighborhood, weaving closer and closer to the park at the center. The rendezvous.

The Covenant didn't seem to follow.

Occasionally, he heard the whine of the Banshees screaming overhead, but he stayed close to the ground, sticking to fences and trees. The glass cuts still stung, but he kept on.

The rendezvous point was on Rue la Pieuvre, two blocks ahead. He kept to the yards. Easier to stay hidden, away from the steady glow of streetlamps. Through all this destruction, Salome had kept them burning. Uncle Max would certainly be impressed. Dorian couldn't decide if he was. He needed all the darkness he could take right now.

He made it to Rue la Pieuvre safely and jumped fences until he was at the yellow house he had suggested for the rendezvous point. Easy for them to find, without worrying about street numbers.

Dorian slipped in through the back door. Unlocked. Victor must already be here. He stumbled through the dark hallway until he came to the kitchen. Victor was sitting at the table. Owen stood behind him. Neither was speaking.

"How'd you get here so fast?" Dorian asked Owen.

Owen lifted his head, his face hidden behind the visor. "Are you injured?"

Dorian glanced down at himself. Blood was starting to well up through his glass cuts again. "I jumped through a window to get away from the Drones. I'll be fine. I thought you were behind me?"

"Looks like you took a detour," Owen said. Dorian thought he might have heard a hint of humor in his voice. Maybe it was just the helmet.

"I guess." Dorian slumped down into a chair. He hadn't realized until then how exhausted he was, how much every muscle in his body burned. He leaned forward on the table and left blood smears on its surface.

"You think Salome's opened the shelter door yet?" Victor said.

"Assuming Evie got there in time, yes." Owen's visor vanished. "Not sure how long it'll take the Covenant to notice. You chose a good exit location."

Dorian smiled, despite his exhaustion and pain. "I know my way around this cruddy town."

Victor laughed. "You jumped through a window to protect this cruddy town."

Dorian shrugged. He didn't bother to correct him, though: It wasn't the town he cared about—it was the people. His uncle. Remy. He had abandoned his bandmates back on Tomas's boat, and he wasn't doing that to anyone he cared about ever again.

"We need to move forward with the assumption the door is open," Owen said, swapping his rifle for the larger and more imposing railgun. "Which means setting off the next distraction. Five minutes. Then we head out."

Dorian leaned back in his chair and stared up at portraits hanging on the far wall. He thought he recognized the family, although he couldn't quite place them. Probably he and Uncle Max had done work for them at some point. Back when things were normal.

He wondered if they had made it to the shelter in time. If he'd find them at the end of this, huddled and traumatized. If he'd remember them when he saw them in person.

Owen activated his visor. "Okay, rest's over," he said. "Let's move out."

"It's been five minutes already?" Victor rubbed his face. *"How?"*

Dorian pulled himself to his feet, muscles aching in protest. He wiped half-heartedly at the blood on the table and succeeded only in making the smears worse.

Victor grabbed the bag of supplies and hoisted it over his

shoulder, one of Saskia's prototype rifles slung on his back. Silently, they followed Owen out of the house, into the black, smoking night. It had been so quiet in the house that Dorian had almost forgotten the war zone outside.

War zone. He'd managed to follow in his parents' footsteps after all.

They moved single file through the neighborhood: Owen at the front looking down the railgun's sight, Dorian at the back, Victor in the middle with the explosives. They snaked their way west, toward the beach and the edge of the energy shield. Away from the woods. Away from the survivors funneling out of one shelter door and toward safety.

There was another reason too for selecting the beach. It happened to be the place the Covenant had hid their shield generator, something Owen discovered on their last excursion. He had described it as a large Covenant platform embedded in the sand, with four upward-facing prongs that apparently generated, shaped, and projected the dome shield that kept the entire area locked down. Owen said that if they could get close enough with the explosives, it could be neutralized. Dorian wasn't so sure, but their entire plan was riding on it.

The Covenant were still searching over the neighborhood, Banshees and Drones arcing around, their silhouettes illuminated by the fires burning up the mayor's office. Dorian kept glancing backward, afraid they'd swoop close enough to see. But they were concentrating on the far edge, where he and Owen had run in.

Wouldn't stay that way for long, he knew.

They pressed on, slipping out of the neighborhood and onto the quiet, dark road leading down to the beach. Owen stopped them. "Fan out," he said. "Weapons ready."

Dorian hoisted up his rifle, his hands sweaty against the barrel. Wind blew in from the ocean, spraying the rain sideways. It had relented a little, but in the wind, everything shimmered with a gray haze. Good cover.

"Keep alert," Owen said, stalking forward. "Don't forget that aerial surveillance either."

"Don't forget to look up," Victor translated. "Got it."

They glided down the street. Dorian jerked his gaze around, body tense. The wind gusted, and he caught the salty tang of the ocean, a scent he'd grown up with his entire life but which, after the invasion, after waking up on the beach, flung him backward in time. All those people on the boat. The Drones firing plasma bolts across the deck. Screaming at Xavier and Alex and Hugo to run backstage and then never seeing them again.

Focus, he told himself. *Maybe you didn't save them. Maybe you did. But here's a chance to save the entire town.*

Behind them, a siren rose up, long and wailing and definitely not human. Dorian whipped around.

"What the hell is that?" he shouted.

Owen was at his side almost immediately. "The Covenant have probably discovered that the shelter door is open. We need to move fast." He took off running toward the beach. Dorian followed, half-blinded by the rain.

The road sloped down, gritty with wet sand. Dunes rose up ahead, and beyond them, the pale glow of light that seemed to cyclone up into the gray sky and disappear. It had to be the shield generator, on the beach just like Owen had said. As they rounded the corner, they could now see it clearly. Tall, angry waves crashed up against the enormous Covenant platform.

Victor pulled a round metal canister out of his bag. The last of the explosives from Dorian's house. He handed it over to Dorian. There were two more in the bag, including one that was four times as powerful as the canisters. Dorian didn't even know why Uncle Max had it.

"Lay them out!" Owen shouted. "We've got one shot at this. Then take shelter."

Dorian nodded and raced forward, lungs and limbs burning. He set his gaze on the water. Last year during weather like this he had been down on the beach, watching Hugo surfing in the storm waves. It felt as intangible as a dream.

He skittered down through the dunes, stumbled out onto the beach proper. Behind the hum of the energy shield, the waves roared. He slowed to a jog and made his way to the shoreline, where the sand sucked at his boots and erased his footsteps. The shield generator—even larger than he had imagined it—thrummed in front of him, its prongs funneling energy upward into the clouds. He set the canister down at its base and then moved back.

Victor was jogging toward him. He no longer had the backpack. All the bombs had been set.

"We need to get farther down the beach!" Dorian shouted at him. "This is too close!"

He didn't know if Victor could even hear him over the wind and the waves and the rain, but Victor veered off to the left at the last minute, and then Dorian followed. He glanced back, spotted Owen behind them. Owen held up one hand. Five seconds.

Dorian turned forward and pumped his arms, running harder than he thought he could.

Four.

Rain lashed at his face.

Three.

Victor was a dark smear up ahead.

Two.

The siren rose and fell like the rhythm of the ocean.

One.

The entire world shook. A wall of heat slammed into Dorian's back and shoved him off his feet. He hit the sand headfirst and rolled. The pain from the glass cuts awakened, screaming from the sand. He couldn't hear anything. Not the ocean. Not the siren.

He pushed himself up. The beach was on fire.

"Victor?" he shouted, though he couldn't hear his voice. In the orange light, through the mist of thick smoke and burned sand, he saw a dark lump on the beach. He struggled to his feet, dragging his rifle behind him. The dark lump moved. "Victor!"

He knelt down beside him. Victor rolled over, rubbed at his face. Dorian's ears rang—his hearing was coming back. "That was fun."

Dorian grinned. Then he looked up through the haze, his eyes watering. From the distance, the generator initially looked like it might have survived, but then he saw the scorch mark amid the shower of falling sand. A third of the generator had been riven completely off.

The shield flickered.

"I think we got it," he gasped.

Victor lifted his head, tilting his gaze toward the ocean. As they watched, the shield shimmered and flickered and then collapsed entirely, revealing the broad stretch of black sky.

Dorian let out a shout of victory and leapt to his feet. "We did it!" he screamed. "The stupid thing's out."

Victor laughed deliriously beside him.

Dorian turned to the beach and looked back at the fire. Where the hell was Owen? Fear stabbed through his elation. Yeah, he'd been behind him, but his entire body had been programmed to survive worse. And in that suit—

"Owen!" Dorian shouted. He stood up. "Owen, where are you?"

And then something stepped out of the flames. A man made of metal, skin gleaming orange.

Owen held up one hand over his head in a weary hello.

"He's fine," Dorian said. "You hear that, Victor? He's fine."

"Of course he is," Victor mumbled back.

Owen glided toward them, the fire scorching the beach at his back. He stopped a few paces away, bringing the railgun up to his shoulder.

"Get ready," he said.

That was when Dorian heard it, over the muffle of his damaged eardrums. The scream of Covenant propulsion engines.

He looked up.

Beyond the fire, dots of blue light from the Banshees were now headed their way.

CHAPTER TWENTY-ONE

SASKIA

Saskia huddled next to the shelter door, arms wrapped around herself. The rain had turned cold, and a sharp wind blew in from the direction of town, carrying smoke and the occasional burst of gunfire.

Hurry, she thought. *Hurry, hurry, hurry.*

It was torture, waiting without the comm system up. She had no idea if Evie had even made it to the city computer, much less if her virus had worked. She had no idea if Owen and the others had survived their carefully staged distraction, a series of explosions designed to take out the energy shield and lead the Covenant away from the shelter.

All she knew was the rain, the cold, and the locked door.

She tried it again, the way she'd been trying every few minutes. It didn't budge.

Lights flashed in the distance, over the town. Aircraft? They were moving away from her. Toward the beach. Toward Owen and the others.

"Saskia Nazari?"

Saskia jolted at the voice. It was Salome, shining out of a holo-gram projector built into the shelter door's lock. Saskia let out a long sigh of relief. Evie had done it.

"Salome," Saskia said. "Are you here to open the doors?" *Please, please, please—*

"I am." Salome tilted her head. Her projection shimmered. "The threat of the Covenant is at an acceptable level. Evelyn Rousseau told me to open shelter door number five."

"This one?" Saskia said cautiously.

Salome nodded. "It's unlocked, by the way."

Saskia's adrenaline surged. She pushed on the latch and felt it move beneath her touch. The door creaked open.

"The threat from the Covenant is at an acceptable level."

"Thank you." She glanced over her shoulder at Salome. "You've just saved all their lives."

"The threat level from the Covenant is at an acceptable level," Salome said again. A side effect of the virus, Saskia figured.

She slid in through the door, closed it behind her, then tested to make sure it was still unlocked. It was. She took a deep breath and descended the stairs into the shelter proper, following the sound of panicked, babbling voices. Her heart surged, and she doubled her speed, leaping over the last two stairs. She landed in half a meter of water and her heart dropped.

"I'm here to get you—"

She froze.

There was no one in the shelter. The emergency lights glowed a sallow yellow, and the air was thick with humidity. The voices she'd heard rising up along the walls. Not voices.

Water.

The water had swollen above the grating, surging and roiling and splashing up in miniature waves. When she'd come for the concert, it had been a low trickle, barely visible in the darkness. Now it was a white water, surging underneath the town.

Saskia waded out of the stairwell. The water splashed around her thighs, and she had to brace herself against the wall to keep from being swept away.

A voice crackled over some ancient sound system: Salome.

"Attention," she said. "The threat from the Covenant is at an acceptable level."

"No!" screamed Saskia. "No, Salome, that's not—"

"Door number five is open. Please proceed *calmly* to the exit."

Saskia took off, half running, half swimming, water splashing up around her. Salome repeated her message. "The threat from the Covenant is at an acceptable level."

"No, it's *not*," Saskia shrieked. She had to get to everyone and explain. Salome was making it sound like the Covenant had left.

Saskia moved as fast as she could, cold water splashing everywhere. She hoped this corridor was the only way to get to the exit. Dorian had told her the shelter was designed to be easy to navigate, but down here everything looked the same.

Salome's voice droned on in the background.

A triangle of light appeared up ahead, brighter than the dull safety lights casting everything in eerie shadows. Did Saskia hear voices? It was hard to tell, with the river, and with Salome's warning blaring out of the walls. But as she approached, Saskia was sure of it. Definitely voices. Panicked, confused voices.

The corridor ended at the light, a sharp turn veering off to the right. The water level was lower and Saskia picked up speed as she careened around the corner.

She found herself in a massive room, the light so bright it hurt her eyes. For a moment, she blinked, trying to make sense of the chaos. People. Hundreds of people, splashing around in the ankle-high water, shouting, arguing. Half of them were gathering up soaked blankets and supplies, the other half seemed stricken still with fear.

Saskia was pierced with a sudden, paralyzing anxiety. None of these people would listen to her. None of them had even noticed her.

"The threat level is acceptable?" a woman shouted, off to Saskia's right. "What does that even mean?"

"What do you think it means?" said someone else. "The UNSC kicked the Covenant's ass. What are we waiting for?"

"Why is it just one door?"

"The others are flooded!"

"I'm not going out there. Not until we know for sure."

"Me neither! How do we know it's not some Covie trick?"

"Better than drowning!"

The conversations bled together in Saskia's head. She hadn't prepared for this when she and the others had made their plan with Owen. *Saskia will get everyone to the hangar.* That was her job. She thought she might have to fight off the Covenant. Not deal with panicked townspeople.

She moved forward, deeper into the crowd. She splashed through the water as she scanned the faces, looking for some familiar adult.

Except what good would an adult do? They were all as panicked as the kids. Maybe more so. What she needed was a way to get everyone's attention.

"—at an acceptable level. Door number five is open. Please proceed—"

Salome. She needed to get Salome to broadcast a message for her. Saskia darted through the crowd, over to the nearest wall. There had to be some kind of comm station around here somewhere. The place was old enough that they would have built them into the walls.

There. Up ahead. A panel of blinking lights. Everyone was ignoring it while they scurried around. Must have realized the system was down. But she didn't need the system. Not in town. Salome was clearly able to access the shelter's communications.

Saskia shoved her way through the crowd and slapped her palm against the contact button.

"You know it's worthless!" someone shouted. "Comm system's still down."

Saskia ignored her. "Salome," she said into the speaker. "Salome, let me talk."

A hitch in the announcement and suddenly Salome was in two places: reciting her blasted message and speaking softly to Saskia through the comm station.

"What can I help you with, Saskia Nazari?"

"Can you patch this through to the sound system?" Saskia asked. "I have to explain what's going on."

"I've got the matter under control," Salome said.

Saskia gritted her teeth in frustration. What would happen if she told Salome she'd been infected with a virus? She should have paid more attention in computer science. The last thing she wanted was for Salome to lock the door if she found out the Covenant were actually still a threat.

"You don't," Saskia said. "People don't know what's going on. The path outside the door—it's clear. I need to tell them that. Okay?"

A pause.

"Salome?"

"Okay. Patching through now."

Salome's voice vanished from the loudspeaker, and in the silence it was replaced by confused gasps, some shrieked insistences that this all had been a Covenant trick.

"Ready," Salome said in her soft comm station voice.

Saskia took a deep breath. "Hello?" she said, her voice wavering and unclear. "Hello? Attention?"

The panicked hum of voices transformed into confusion. "Who's that?"

"Salome?"

"What's going on?"

"Attention," Saskia said, more firmly now. She braced herself against the wall. "My name is Saskia Nazari."

Her name drew a gasp of shock, the way she expected it to. It was followed by a quiet murmuring.

"Me and a team of—of others, we were trapped outside during the invasion. We're here to get you off the planet. To safety. We have a ship. We were able to open one door, door number five." Voices rose in confusion, and people were turning toward her, gaping at her with wide, desperate eyes. She peered over at them. "I'm here to escort you to the ship. There's a Spartan—"

The voices exploded. Old-timers shouted in distrust; young people whispered in disbelief.

"A Spartan," she said, more firmly, "who was stranded here. He's been helping us. He's leading a distraction against the Covenant—"

"The Covenant are still here?" came a voice from the back.

"Yes." Saskia looked out at the crowd, all those pale, frightened faces staring back at her. "But the shelter is starting to flood—"

"Half of it's flooded out completely," someone shouted.

"We knew we had to act fast," Saskia said. "If you want to fight, to help with the distraction, the Spartan and the others are at Brume Beach. They have weapons." She hoped they had made it, at least. "Everyone else, I can take you to our ship."

Everyone stared at her.

"That's it," she said. "Please, hurry, we don't have much ti—"

It was enough. The crowd erupted into motion, surging toward the exit, churning up the dark water. "Slowly!" Saskia shouted into the intercom. "The water in the corridor came up to my thighs, and it's moving fast. Be careful." She took a deep breath. "And let me get to the front. I know where we're going."

They didn't listen.

Saskia dropped her hand to the pistol. Owen had told her that they might be panicky, that panicked people didn't always listen to reason.

She pulled the pistol off her belt and fired it into the wall. Chunks of stone exploded out into the water.

Someone screamed, and then there was a ripple effect, people slowing, staring at her in horror.

She stepped forward into the crowd, holding the pistol over her head. This time, the crowd parted for her—or maybe they parted for the pistol. She didn't care. Whatever worked.

"Saskia!" A man came pushing through the crowd, his eyes and hair wild, his face haggard. "You said there are others."

She stopped and looked at him.

"Is my daughter one of them?" he gasped. "Evie? Evie Rousseau?"

Saskia nodded. "She's the one who got Salome to open the door," she said softly.

"Oh, thank god." He sagged in place. "My daughter. She's my only daughter."

"She's fine," Saskia said. "You'll see her soon."

This was technically true: Evie was supposed to meet up with Saskia on her way to pick up Victor's car so she could pick up the others from the beach. Assuming Victor's car still worked. They hadn't had a chance to double-check. But Saskia didn't think Evie's father needed to know all of that.

"Thank you," he said. "Thank you."

Saskia wasn't sure what else to say, so she only smiled and pressed onward into the crowd. She wondered where her parents were. If anyone would come to tell them she'd survived. If a light would switch on behind their eyes when they learned she had.

But right now, her parents didn't matter. What mattered were the people in the shelter, almost the entire population of Brume-sur-Mer. And they were looking at her like she was their leader.

"This way," she shouted, gesturing with the pistol. "We're going to be walking a full kilometer through the woods! Don't bring anything you can't carry!"

She led the crowd into the corridor. The water had risen by another several centimeters.

"Hold on to the wall!" she shouted, glancing back at them over her shoulder. "Don't try to move too fast."

She led them down the river that had once been the corridor, up the stairs, into the gray daylight. The rain had slacked off, but the air was thick with smoke from the fires.

"Oh my god," someone gasped behind her. "The town. It's on fire."

"We don't have time," Saskia said. "I told you, the others are keeping the Covenant away from us." She turned around, walked backward toward the woods. "There's a path!" she shouted. "It leads to an old Sundered Legion hangar. That's where we're going. Stay alert! If you can fight, move to the edges. If not, stay in the center!"

People listened to her. They were afraid, that much was clear, but they did as she said, rearranging themselves as they spilled, blinking and gasping, out of the shelter door. Saskia stepped away from the crowd and directed them to a narrow clearing between the trees. "Follow the path," she said. "It's faint, but it's there."

She watched them go, all these people she had lived so close to for the last five years. She didn't know any of them, not really, but it didn't matter. They were shaking and afraid, their eyes darting around like they didn't trust the open air. But she was going to get them to safety.

A woman peeled off from the line of townspeople. "I want to fight," she said.

Saskia blinked.

"You said some people were fighting to keep the Covenant away."

Saskia hesitated. "Yes, but if you can fight, I'd rather you stay here. Help get people to safety." She handed her pistol to the woman. "Here," she said. "Take this. Go to the front of the line while I make sure everyone gets out of the shelter."

The woman studied the gun for a moment before taking it. "What about you?"

"I'll be fine," Saskia said, retrieving the Covenant plasma rifle from her back.

The woman's eyes suddenly went big before returning to the pistol. "Sounds good."

Saskia watched the woman trot toward the narrow clearing. Then she turned to the others. "Keep going!" she said, walking alongside them. "Into the woods." She jogged over to the shelter door. People were still pushing their way out, gasping when they stepped into the open air. Harried parents, wide-eyed children, tired old people. All of them gaping up at the rainy sky like they'd never seen it before. Some of them thanked her as they walked past, and Saskia just offered them a tight smile. *We're not off Meridian yet.*

When it seemed like the last people had left the shelter, Saskia called up Salome to confirm.

"Yes," Salome said. "The shelter is empty."

Saskia let out a long sigh of relief and then ran up the side of the line, weaving through the trees and underbrush, until she got to the front. The woman with her pistol was up there, along with a new trio of adults armed with hunting rifles. They must have brought them down into the shelter during the evacuation.

"We heading in the right direction?" asked one of them, a rangy woman with a hard expression. They all eyed her plasma rifle, not sure what to make of it.

"Yes. Like I said, there's a path, but it's hard to see."

"Especially in this weather," the woman muttered.

Saskia didn't disagree. The rain made everything slick and dark and wild. But the path was there, a faint outline trailing up through the woods. It had probably been created by the Sundered Legion a hundred years ago, the path from the town to the hangar.

The crowd made a lot of noise as they walked through the woods. Owen had warned her it would be like that. He had also told her it would be too difficult to make them stay quiet. It wasn't just from talking—very few were talking, really—but rather the crackling, shredding distraction of a group of people fighting their way through a wet, overgrown forest. It made Saskia realize how adept she and the others had become at creeping silently through the woods, measuring their steps, taking advantage of the ambient noise of the forest.

All that sound made Saskia nervous now.

She hefted the plasma rifle in her hands, checking its energy levels on a holographic readout. The rifle looked like two large violet teardrops connected by a heavy grip clearly made to be used by another species. Rather than taking a weapon from her parents' stash, Saskia ended up selecting one of the Covenant's that Owen had retrieved. She wasn't sure if this was because she'd become strangely accustomed to the Covenant weapons over the past few days, or if it was some kind of act of defiance against her parents. Either way, she felt more comfortable using the plasma rifle at this point than anything else.

As the caravan of people slowly trod down the path, she flicked her eyes around, looking for movement in the leaves. *Just a kilometer*, she told herself. And Owen and the others were drawing the Covenant down to Brume Beach, and—

Someone screamed.

Saskia squeezed her fingers around the plasma rifle's grip and whirled around, holding the weapon up high, tight against her shoulder. Screams rippled down from the crowd, which was scattering into the woods.

"The Covenant!" a voice wailed. "They found us!"

Saskia gestured at her armed guards. "Go," she said. "Fan out along the sides." They did as she asked without question. Saskia bolted forward into the crowd, which parted for her, their eyes on the Covenant rifle, which sparked with an electric charge at its mouth. The screaming pierced at Saskia's ears.

Then she saw it. A Covenant soldier. A Sangheili. Two and a half meters tall, its legs and torso covered in heavy ivory armor and its bare arms fiercely muscled. The UNSC called them Elites and she didn't have to guess why—they were proud, strong creatures that looked like they were born to kill. Its mandibles clacked. One strong hand was wrapped around the neck of a skinny, wild-eyed man, who thrashed and clawed at its arm.

The Sangheili looked up at Saskia, eyes gleaming behind its helmet.

"Let him go," Saskia said, holding up the rifle, in fighting stance, the way Owen had showed her.

The Sangheili spoke in its language, heavy, growling syllables. The man in its grip gasped and kicked.

"Let him *go*," Saskia said. And then, with a flash of white anger behind her eyes, she unloaded a barrage of plasma bolts into the alien, its armor seemingly absorbing the fire. In one fluid motion, the Sangheili dropped the man, reached for something that had been latched to its thigh, and activated it: two white, curved blades of superheated plasma, a Sangheili energy sword. Then without hesitation it bounded for her at an astonishing speed. Saskia dove to the ground and rolled into the underbrush as the sword burned through the greenery after her. She burrowed herself into the growth.

The Sangheili said something again, growling through its mandibles, as it began leveling the brush she'd darted into.

Through the dripping leaves, she watched the man crawl away, into the arms of another terrified-looking man, who dragged him into the trees. The Sangheili ignored him. She knew it was looking for her.

She couldn't fight this thing and win. But she could get it away from the townspeople.

The Sangheili finally stepped into the underbrush, its heavy armored foot a few meters from her position. She sucked in her breath and whipped her rifle around and fired at its massive column of a leg.

An energy shield flared again and the Sangheili's sword came down into the mud right where she'd been, but Saskia was already stowing her rifle on her back and racing deeper into the woods at full speed. She grabbed hold of the first low-hanging tree branch she saw and frantically pulled herself up into its branches. The

Sangheili roared somewhere behind her and must have swung its energy sword close to her leg, because she could feel the heat of it scorch her skin. She continued to scale, trying to get as much distance as she could between her and the alien. The Sangheili's pale, shark-like eyes tracked her movements for a few seconds before it hefted itself up after her. It wasn't going to give up easily and Saskia began to wonder if this might not end the way she wanted. When it came within arm's length, she leapt from the tree, landed hard, and ran, weaving through the vines and crowded trees. She didn't have a plan. All she knew was that she had to draw it away from the townspeople.

In the distance, she heard screams. Plasma fire.

The Sangheili launched from the tree like a panther on the hunt, shouting something in its thorny language. She suspected it was telling her to give up.

A volley of human gunfire. Shouts of triumph. There couldn't be that many Covenant here. Not with their attention focused on the town. But it wouldn't stay that way for long.

Saskia grabbed ahold of a thick, dangling vine and scrambled up into the dark canopy of a banyan tree, roughly fifteen meters aboveground. The Sangheili made a noise that even to her human ears sounded mocking. She found solid footing and reached for her rifle, aiming it down at the alien. According to the energy readout, she had 70 percent left.

Please be enough, she thought. The Sangheili deactivated its sword, returning it to its thigh as it approached the trunk of the tree. It leered up at her with a satisfied gaze and crouched low to the ground. Then it jumped.

It shot straight up into the canopy and landed amid the branches with astonishing power and speed. Saskia screamed and fired off a trio of shots that scattered off the Sangheili's energy shield, burning the leaves around her. It made that mocking sound again, and began to climb upward—

And crashed down through the branches.

Saskia let out a terrified laugh. It was too heavy for the tree. She scrambled forward and peered down at where it lay sprawled on the ground. Its energy shield flickered.

It growled, jerked to its feet. But it was moving slowly.

She pointed her rifle at its chest, using the branches to support her. Just like firing on the Locust. Enough firepower would have to take it down.

She squeezed the trigger.

The Sangheili's shield flared, but she kept unloading into it, realizing that the rifle would eventually need to vent, otherwise it would overheat. It tried to jump again but only made it about halfway up the tree. She glanced at the readout and saw the rifle's heat spiking; the weapon was getter hotter by the second.

The Sangheili roared and lunged at her again. She slid backward on the branches. Kept firing.

Her rifle began to fume acrid plasma.

The shield vanished. Saskia's arms trembled.

Her hands began to burn against the rifle's grip.

The Sangheili screamed. Dark blue blood sprayed across the leaves, and the Sangheili's arm jerked backward, pulling the rest of its body with it. It landed hard on the ground and then scrabbled to its feet, roaring. One arm hung useless and bleeding at its side.

Her rifle finally choked, venting large torrents of gas from its side. Her hands felt like they were on fire.

The Sangheili took advantage of this opportunity and leapt up the side of the tree, grabbing at the vines with its good arm.

The plasma rifle had finished venting and showed that a thirty percent charge remained. Saskia wasn't sure if that'd be enough to finish the job, but it didn't matter—she didn't have any other options. She lifted the rifle and fired as the Sangheili came dangerously close to her position, ripping through the muscles in its other arm. It fell to the ground again, howling, and this time she scrambled down the other side of the tree and ran, its final screams echoing behind her.

CHAPTER TWENTY-TWO

EVIE

vie heard gunfire as she raced through the woods to the rendez-vous point, halfway along the path between shelter door number five and the Sundered Legion hangar. She faltered in her steps, tripping over a tangle of wet vines.

Owen and the others should be at the beach by now. And that last shot sounded much, much closer.

Evie yanked her plasma pistol out of its holster and held it awkwardly in front of her as she resumed running, straining for any sound over the rustle of raindrops.

Was that screaming?

"No," she whispered, and she tore through the underbrush, wet branches slapping at her face. The screaming grew louder. Closer. Through the trees she saw flashes of movement. Human movement. They weren't screaming anymore, but there was a panicked urgency to the voices.

She burst out of the trees, into the wild, overgrown path. Haggard people clumped together. A handful of them were brandishing guns.

"What's going on?" she shouted.

A man looked over at her, confusion crossing his brow. "Weren't you down there with us?"

Evie shook her head.

"She's one of the others," a woman said, pushing through the crowd. "The Nazari girl said there were others."

"I heard gunfire," Evie said.

"We got attacked by the Covenant," the man said. "A couple of Sangheili. The three of us shot one dead. Don't know about the other one—couldn't see."

"She chased it away." A little boy leaned around his mother's legs. "The girl who saved us."

"Her name is Saskia," Evie said, then dashed away from the line before they could ask her any more questions. Fear clawed at her chest. Saskia had chased it away? How was that even possible?

She pushed her way to the front of the line. She let out a sigh of relief when she saw Saskia was there with her plasma rifle, looking weak and exhausted. Leaves and twigs were tangled up in her hair, and her arms were crisscrossed with angry scratches. But she was alive.

"Evie," Saskia gasped. She darted forward and threw her arms around Evie's neck. Evie squeezed her in return.

"Did you really chase that thing away?" Evie asked.

Saskia laughed. "I guess. I drew it out into the woods and shot it." There wasn't much humor in her laughter, though, and she looked out at the crowd. "We need to get them moving again. I'm not sure it's actually dead; I didn't stick around to find out. I think there are going to be more Covenant on the way."

"I didn't see any on my way here."

"Still." Saskia looked over at her. "Can you spread word down the line? That we need to move?"

Evie nodded, then gave Saskia another hug before jogging back down the line.

"We need to keep moving!" she shouted. "Follow the path!"

The startled cries of the crowd started up again.

It was coming from the end of the line. People jumped, shouted, surged forward. "Stay calm!" Evie screamed. "But keep moving!" She took off. In the rain, she heard the pulses of plasma bolts, smelled something burning. A handful of lights shone through the trees and then vanished.

"Go, go, go!" she shouted as she ran.

A squat figure darted in front of her, squealing and shrieking. She yelled in surprise, fired at it. Missed. More plasma fire up ahead. She took off, shoving past frightened townspeople, until she saw a streak of purple light, heard a terrified scream. People were spread out on the ground, their hands covering their heads. Blood splayed across the leaves.

No, she thought. *No no no no no.*

"Sniper," someone shouted. "Up in the trees."

Evie dropped down to the ground, but tilted her gaze up at the canopy. Two could play at that game.

Rain splashed through the leaves and into her eyes. She craned her neck, peering through the web of leaves. It was the opposite of the surveillance work she'd done with Dorian. It was harder.

Then she saw it. A flash of violet in the wash of green.

Evie fired off her pistol just as a beam of light exploded out of the trees. The bolt hit the wet mulchy ground centimeters from Evie's body, leaving a black streak in its wake. She fired again, her hands shaking.

A weight slammed out of the trees.

Evie struggled to her feet, dizzy with adrenaline. She was aware of people shrieking and crying around her, but she just drifted forward until she come to the body of the Kig-Yar. The same species that had tried to pull her from the car the night of the invasion.

It was dead.

She turned back to the townspeople. Two people lay on the ground. Another few were bleeding, although they could stand.

"We have to go," Evie said, her voice hoarse. "Before they send more."

"We can't leave them here!" a woman shrieked, gesturing at the two men. One of them groaned, and fear stabbed at Evie's heart. *Wounded*, she thought.

"No," she said without thinking. "We'll have to carry them. It's not far. Less than a kilometer."

The woman nodded, knelt down between the two bodies. The one who had groaned was a young man, his face waxy and pale. The other was an older woman, blood darkening the side of her stomach. She blinked her eyes, smiled weakly at Evie.

"You got him," she said.

Evie blushed. "I did what I had to."

Someone had gone to fetch a couple of men—fishermen types, from the look of them, tall and broad-shouldered. They picked up the two wounded, cradled them carefully against their chests. One of them looked over at Evie, as if waiting for approval.

"Go as fast as you can," she said, hoping this was the right answer. "We might be able to treat them on the ship."

Slowly, the crowd began to move forward. Evie trailed behind, walking backward, her pistol extended. She was exhausted, and all she wanted was to fight through the crowd until she found her father. But that wasn't part of the plan. Not yet.

Rendezvous with Saskia. Help her if needed.

Get Victor's car. Bring it to the extraction point on the beach. Get Dorian to the ship.

Get the hell off Meridian.

The car was waiting for her halfway between the rendezvous point and the hangar. They should be getting to it soon. Part of her didn't want to leave—what if there was another attack? But she told herself that Saskia could handle it. Saskia and the people of the town. They had handled the two Sangheili. And they only had to go a kilometer.

Plasma fire sliced through the woods, sizzling the tree leaves. Evie fired in the direction of the shot, her gun blasts shattering the forest. She whipped her head around—the last of the crowd were running now, screaming, but it didn't look like anyone had been hurt.

Another shot from the woods. Evie moved forward, fired into the trees. Something cried out, then thudded hard into the ground.

"You need help?"

Evie whirled around. A quartet of townspeople had broken away from the line. All of them were armed.

"I got him," she said, "but there will be more." She paused. "And I'll be splitting off in a minute. To get the rest."

"The people fighting on the beach?" A woman holding a pistol against her chest smiled thinly. One of Saskia's parents' pistols, Evie realized.

"Yes," Evie said. *And the person who can fly that ship out of here.*

"We've got you covered," the woman said, and then, moving with all the grace of a dancer, she steadied her pistol and fired off a round of ammunition. A squawk from the woods.

"Good eye," one of the others said.

Evie took a deep breath. She was too distracted. She had to focus.

"You," the woman said. "Go. Get the others." She steadied her pistol again. "We'll be fine here."

Evie looked from each person to the next. One of them, the other woman, seemed vaguely familiar, and after a moment, Evie realized she was a waitress at the little seaside café where Evie and her father would go eat in the evenings sometimes. When things were normal.

"Thank you," Evie said. Then she jogged away, ducking into the woods. The voices of the townspeople followed her as she wove through the vines and leaves, her eye on the glint of metal up ahead.

Victor's car. Her ride into town.

CHAPTER TWENTY-THREE

VICTOR

Victor pressed his back against the collapsing sand dune, sucking in air, desperate to catch his breath. The round count on his rifle glowed a dull blue. Twenty-three. He fumbled around in his bag, found one other ammunition pack. One hundred twenty-three rounds total.

He had no idea if it would be enough.

The rifle was unique among Saskia's parents' cache. It had been designed with a barrel attachment that glowed orange and charged each armor-piercing round with some kind of explosive energy. The results were effective on vehicles, but even more devastating against Covenant infantry.

A Banshee screamed overhead, and Victor instinctively ducked his head, pressing himself into the sand. It fired green-tinged explosives onto the beach, the scent of melting sand wrapping tight around Victor's throat. He risked peering around the side of the dune, through the web of glossy dune vines. The beach was crisscrossed with lines of glass. Farther down the shore, weapon fire rattled. Victor jerked his head back behind the dune and took a deep breath.

Get back out there, he told himself. *They need your help.*

He'd gotten separated from the others after they'd detonated the explosives. A squad of Unggoy had come spilling onto the stand, firing their needlers and screeching in the Covenant's language. Owen had shouted for them to split up, and he and Dorian had taken off in opposite directions. Victor had fired blindly on the Unggoy as he ran, half in panic and half in anger. It wasn't until he'd gotten away from them that he'd realized how much ammunition he'd wasted.

A familiar whine cut through the air again. The Banshees were coming back. Their lights gleamed low in the sky. A trail of plasma bolts hit the dunes up ahead, igniting them in smoke and ash. Victor scrambled to his feet and ran out into the open beach, jumping over the molten, glassy pathways left by the last Banshee attack. He peered through his rifle, keeping his scope ahead of the Banshee as it roared down over the dunes. Just like Owen had showed him.

Fired.

The Banshee jerked; its right side glowed an angry blue, like the hottest part of a flame. It veered off to the left, screaming in circles over the dunes. Victor didn't wait to see it crash. He took off running toward the firefight happening at the far end of the beach. Plasma light streaked through the misty air. Dark lumps lay on the sand.

He dove back into the dunes and headed toward the sound of weapon fire, skittering and slipping over the wet sand. Covenant voices grew louder. So did the plasma blasts. But he kept his head low, moving in the way his sisters had shown him, on this same beach, in these same dunes. This was his home. He knew it better than any of the Unggoy firing on his friends.

Eventually, he saw the disturbances in the sand that meant Dorian and Owen had been there already. He jumped through the indentations, clutching his gun tight, keeping his head low. The plasma fire wasn't hitting the dunes. Which meant they didn't know he was there.

Eventually, the footsteps veered away from the dunes, toward the beach proper. Victor peered out at the open.

It was impossible to make out anything in the chaos. Smoke and rain billowed across the sand, smudging the Covenant soldiers into shadows. The plasma fire looked like lightning.

A scatter of gunfire erupted out of the smoke, shimmering like stars. Owen's imposing form followed. He fired onto the Unggoy, blasting them backward over the beach. A few seconds later, Dorian appeared, flashes of light erupting from his rifle.

Victor looked through the sight of his rifle and targeted the Unggoy racing toward Owen and Dorian. He squeezed the trigger, sending a trio of shots sailing over the beach. Immediately the Unggoy turned their weapons onto the dunes, and Victor leapt backward and crawled deeper into them. He yanked the new round out of the bag and clicked it into place.

Then he ran straight for the beach.

He had guessed right. Owen and Dorian were only a few paces away.

"Nice work!" Dorian shouted as Victor swung around to flank Owen with the needler in his hands.

"Agreed," Owen said, his voice deceptively calm. "Good job."

The Spartan had been using the railgun, apparently with some efficiency based on the debris field of Covenant armor that covered the beach in front of them. A Jackal with a spherical shield on its arm suddenly darted from behind one of the dunes. Owen stepped away from the dune and immediately tracked the enemy with his weapon, its barrel charging in a coil of energy before firing. The blast and impact were almost instantaneous, and what remained of the Jackal was sent reeling across the beach and into the waves. Then another wave of Covenant appeared around the berm.

All three opened fire again. The Unggoy swirled around in confusion, some of them firing at the dune, others returning their attention to the three of them. One round came extremely close, and Dorian grabbed Victor and dragged him behind Owen.

"He can take the plasma fire, man!" Dorian screamed in Victor's ear.

Owen strolled forward, still firing, as calmly as if it were an ordinary day at the beach. Victor and Dorian huddled behind him, firing off shots when they could.

A telltale whine filled the air.

"Banshee!" Victor shouted.

Just one Banshee this time, the one he hadn't shot. It sailed overhead, wheeling back around for a better shot. It had no doubt spotted them. Owen tilted up his railgun and led the target for a few seconds. Then the weapon heated in coils around its barrel and fired in a burst of white light.

The Banshee exploded. Heat and debris rained down on them.

The Unggoy screamed and hurled something toward the Spartan.

Everything went white with a deafening sound.

And then Owen flew backward.

At first, Victor couldn't place what happened. He'd been crouched in the sand, protecting his head from the burning Banshee, when suddenly he was exposed. No one stood between him and the Unggoy.

"Owen!" Dorian screamed.

Victor fired on the Unggoy. At least two of them collapsed. His round counter blinked. Thirty-five remaining.

"Damn. Victor! Owen's hurt."

It didn't make any sense. How could Owen be hurt? But of course he'd been hurt this entire time. His suit had been damaged.

Victor kept firing into the Unggoy, beating them back. Black smoke billowed across the beach. He whirled around. Dorian was kneeling beside Owen, his hand pressed to Owen's side. His fingers were smeared red.

"He's *hurt*," Dorian said, a vague disbelief in his voice.

Victor's thoughts rattled. For a moment, he was back on the beach during happier times. It was bright and hot and there was no smoke. Camila showed him how to hold a gun. Told him how she never left a fellow soldier behind.

"Get him to safety," Victor shouted.

"He's too heavy!"

The Unggoy had stopped firing. Victor didn't think that could possibly be a good sign. Still, he knew he needed to save his ammunition, and so he scrambled over to Owen's side. He pressed the polarization button on the side of Owen's helmet, and the visor flickered away. Owen blinked at him, his eyes bleary and unfocused.

"Grenade," he said. "Armor's compromised."

Victor looped his arm through Owen's. Dorian nodded and did the same.

"One. Two. *Three*." Victor heaved, his muscles screaming in protest. Owen groaned in pain. He didn't move at all across the sand.

"It's pointless," Dorian gasped, collapsing backward. "He's too heavy."

"Just leave me," Owen rasped. "Get back to the ship."

"No!" Victor shouted.

"Look at me," Dorian said, his voice almost a snarl. "I'm not leaving anybody else behind."

Owen smiled a little. There was blood on his teeth.

"Trained you too well," he said jaggedly.

The beach lit up with a brilliant streak of white light. A fireball plumed out of the sand. The entire world shuddered.

Tall, muscular figures emerged from the smoke. They were clearly the leaders and heavily armed.

"Damn," Dorian said.

Sangheili. An entire squad of them, marching row by row.

"Run!" Owen shouted. "Run! Now!"

"No!" Dorian screamed.

Victor lifted his rifle and fired into the rows of Sangheili until his counter clicked to zero. Then he grabbed a needler from one of the fallen Unggoy and held the trigger down until the weapon was empty. The Sangheili lines broke up, but most continued toward them.

"Leave me!" Owen screamed, flecks of blood scattering across his helmet. "That's an order!"

"I'm not in the UNSC!" Dorian screamed back.

And then a flickering light arced over their heads, slamming into the Sangheili's front line. For a moment, everything seemed to stand still. Then the light exploded and a handful of Sangheili toppled backward, the sand burning white-hot.

Victor scrambled to his feet, whirled around.

His car was barreling toward him across the sand. The driver's window was opened and out of it pointed a one-handed weapon—Saskia's sticky detonator.

"Evie!" he screamed. "Evie's here!"

Plasma fire flickered around them on the dune, sparse and erratic. The remaining Unggoy were still approaching with those Sangheili who hadn't gotten caught in the explosion from Evie's weapon.

The car screeched to a stop, kicking a wall of sand over Victor and Owen and Dorian. Victor sputtered, wiped the sand from his face.

"Get in!" Evie shouted. "The detonator needs to be reloaded!" It was sitting in the passenger seat, a pile of other charges beside it.

"Owen's hurt," Victor shouted. "We can't move him."

Evie's eyes went wide. "He can't even stand?"

Victor whipped around and knelt beside Owen. "You've got to get up," he said. "Dorian's right. We're not leaving you."

"Yeah, just get in the damn car." Dorian reached over and flung open the back door. Immediately it was struck with a plasma bolt and went flying backward five meters over the sand.

"My car!" Victor yelped without thinking.

Dorian wrapped one of Owen's arms around his shoulder. Nodded at Victor, who did the same, the shock of his missing door fading.

"Hurry!" Evie screamed. "They're coming!"

Victor didn't look back. He focused all his strength on pushing *up*. "Come on, man!" he yelled. "You know we can't do this without your help!"

This time, Owen moved. He howled in pain, and blood spilled across the sand. But he moved, his legs trembling. With a shout, Dorian and Victor pushed him into the car, which rocked sideways on its wheels.

Evie stuck the sticky detonator back out the driver's side window.

Another round streamed across the beach, landing in a patch of sand at the heart of the encroaching Covenant soldiers.

A massive fireball plumed up from the sand.

Victor scrambled into the back seat, and Dorian slammed the car into gear, throwing up more sand. Hard wind blew in through the gap of the missing door. Evie whipped the car around, drawing it close to the rushing water of the shore.

Then they were off, plasma fire following thinly in their wake.

CHAPTER TWENTY-FOUR

DORIAN

Turn right!" Dorian shouted. *"Right!"*

The car rocked back and forth as Evie jerked the wheel to the left, then to the right, sending them careening down a muddy dirt road.

"You sure you know where you're going?" Evie said.

"I told you," Dorian said. "Uncle Max and I drove everywhere. I'm getting us as close I can."

He twisted around in the front seat. Owen was still splayed out in the back, hand clamped down on his side, blood gleaming on his armor. Victor crouched over his legs.

"How's he doing?" Dorian asked.

"He keeps passing out." Victor's eyes were wide with fear. "Can Spartans even pass out?"

"If they get hit square in the side with a plasma grenade, they can." Dorian turned back around. He couldn't stand to look at Owen. Yelling at them to just leave him behind on the beach—what the hell? After everything he'd said about *being a team*?

No. Dorian was done leaving people behind.

The car shuddered. Mud splattered up against the windshield.

"Put it in third!" screeched Victor.

"Your car's done for," Dorian shouted back.

"It'll get us through the mud, dumbass."

"Shut up, both of you." Evie slammed her palm against the control panel. The car jerked forward, tires squealing. Dorian almost slammed his head on the dash.

"Okay," he said. "Next road you see, turn left. That should get us there."

Evie nodded. Her fingers were wrapped so tightly around the steering wheel her knuckles had turned white.

"The Covenant had found them," she murmured. "There were soldiers—Sangheili—Elites—"

She'd told him this already. She'd told him this about five times, murmuring it like a prayer.

"I know," he said. "But they've got Saskia to take care of them. And we're almost there."

Tree branches slapped at the car, leaving wet streaks across the windshield. Rocks pinged against the undercarriage. Dorian peered out the window. This road would dead-end in the middle of the woods, and he was almost certain that the hangar was just a few meters from where the road ended. It would explain how he and Uncle Max had ridden all over the forest and never seen it. Probably the Sundered Legion had blocked the road at some point, sealing off that hangar and the ship from Brume-sur-Mer's collective memory.

The car hit a ditch in the road and slammed upward, along with all its passengers. Owen roared, an armored fist hitting the back windshield. The glass shattered.

"Sorry!" Evie said.

Trees blocked the path up ahead. "There," Dorian said. "The hangar should be just through there." He glanced back at Owen, who was clutching at his side, his face contorted in pain. "Sorry, but you're going to have to walk again."

"Great." Owen clenched his teeth.

The car slowed. Evie pulled up right to the trees but left the engine idling. "Are you sure this is it?"

Dorian climbed out. The area was thick with underbrush, and the forest was filled with the sound of rain. He hacked at the brush with his rifle, beating it down, trying to clear a path. The hangar had to be on the other side. He had checked and double-checked the maps before they left. He had been so sure—

Then he heard it, over the rain. Voices. Human voices. He slapped away a low-hanging branch and revealed the clearing, the hangar, and a knot of ragged refugees crowding up to the ship.

"We're here!" he shouted, running back to the car. Evie and Victor had already helped pull Owen out of the car, and he leaned unsteadily against Evie. She strained against him, looking as if she were about to sink into the soil. Dorian rushed over to them, slipped into her place. "Here," he said, "let me." He nodded toward the trees. "We've just got to get through there. You can do it."

Owen nodded. Together, the three of them hobbled toward the path Dorian had cleared. Dorian's chest burned with a brilliant exhilaration—*We can do this. We're almost there.*

Then the screaming started.

Owen stiffened against Dorian's grip, and he nearly fell under the Spartan's weight. Shots rang out. Dorian caught the familiar, toxic whiff of plasma fire.

Evie pulled out her plasma pistol, looked over her shoulder at them. "I'm going to help," she said. "Get him through as fast as you can." She vanished through the trees.

"You can still leave me," Owen said, gasping between each word.

Dorian stared straight ahead, at the flicker of panic through the trees. "I told you," he said. "I'm not doing that again."

They lurched forward. Some of Owen's weight eased off Dorian. "My rifle," he gasped. "One of you—"

"Victor," Dorian said. "You're the marksman."

"Got it." Victor let go of Owen, who managed to stay standing. He pulled the rifle off of Owen's back and ran forward into the clearing, releasing a stream of cover fire. Owen and Dorian followed.

A group of Jackals were shooting at the crowd from the far woods, kept back by Victor, Evie, and a handful of townspeople, who fired off shots from the hangar. A few bodies lay in the grass—Covenant bodies, Dorian saw. But he and Owen were going to have to run straight through the cross fire to get to the ship.

"Get on my other side," Owen said.

"Really?" Dorian shrieked. "You think that's going to be good enough?"

"They need you," Owen said. "To fly them out of here. I'm going to get you to them." He took a deep breath. "Make yourself small."

"Great advice."

The Covenant and the people of Brume-sur-Mer traded fire. Bullets and plasma bolts zipped back and forth. *No-man's-land*, Dorian thought, *like from old Earth*.

"Let's go," Owen said.

He pushed off with a burst of strength Dorian didn't think he'd had left in him. They ran into the cross fire. Distantly, Dorian heard Evie scream, "*Stop!*" and then the plasma bolts were streaming around them. Owen howled, jolted, stumbled. Something hot and stinging brushed against Dorian's leg but he kept going, a tunnel vision closing in around him, with the hangar at the end. The human gunfire started up again. Dorian's leg burned. His feet hit the cement of the airstrip. Closer. Closer.

And then Evie was grabbing him by the wrist, pulling him into the safety of the hangar. Behind him Owen let out a terrible sound and pitched forward, slamming into the side of the ship. For a paralyzing moment, Dorian thought he was dead. But he caught himself, straightened up, looked Dorian straight in the eye.

"Get us out of here," he said.

Dorian grinned and flung open the door to the cockpit. He activated the controls and then opened up the back hatchway. "Everybody get aboard!" he shouted, leaning out of the ship. "We're getting off this rock!"

He activated the engine, hands flying over the holo. The Covenant soldiers raced forward, plasma rifles firing, striking the hangar, the airstrip.

With a grunt and a scream, Owen flung himself into the compartment immediately behind the cockpit, careful this time to stay against the bulkhead. He was followed by Evie and Victor.

"Are we good to go?" Dorian asked, adjusting the controls, accessing the ship's forward weapons. With a quick check, he started aiming the missile with the targeting holo. Plasma fire erupted around them as dozens upon dozens of Elites, Jackals, and Grunts emerged from the tree line. Was this the Covenant's entire occupation force in Brume-sur-Mer? He slammed his fist against the ship's Fire button and a missile screamed out of the top of the ship, barreling straight through the Covenant and then exploding in an orange fireball off in the woods.

Screams echoed back from the body of the ship. Dorian flicked on the intercom. "Nothing to worry about," he said. "That was us."

A confused pause, then an eruption of cheers.

"Saskia," Dorian said into the speaker. "Can we leave? Give me some kind of sign." No one was shooting at them now thanks to the ship's missiles, but he knew it wasn't going to stay that way for long, not with that fire blazing in the woods.

Saskia's head poked through into the cockpit. "We're ready," she said. "Everyone's aboard."

"Great." Dorian closed the hatch, activated the engines, and pushed forward on the throttle. The ship rumbled onto the airstrip. Rain streaked across the windows. Dorian shifted the engines and the ship lifted, cresting on the air. *You've done this before*, he told himself, although that wasn't entirely true—he'd never broken atmosphere.

Light blinked off in the distance—a lone Banshee, shrieking toward them. "Victor, Evie, there's a weapons station off to the right," he said. "I'm going into stealth mode."

Footsteps behind him. He activated stealth mode, hoped it would be enough to get them out of Brume-sur-Mer airspace unscathed. The Banshee kept streaking toward them, and Dorian shot the ship straight up into the air—too fast. He was flung forward onto the dash. Shouts rose up behind him.

"Sorry!" he said, then pulled back on the throttle. The ship tilted upward. They were lifting, sweeping through the rain, into the clouds. The Banshee screamed right past them. Dorian laughed nervously. "I can't believe how well that worked."

They burned through the gray murk of the cloud, then exploded onto the other side, the sun bright and glinting. It was the first light Dorian had seen since before the invasion.

"Are they following us?" Evie slid into the copilot's chair.

"Doesn't look like it." They climbed in altitude, building up speed.

"Be careful," gasped Owen, "when we break atmosphere. It'll be—" He broke into a ragged cough and Evie slid out of her seat, disappearing from Dorian's vision. The hot glow of the atmosphere burned around the edges of the ship. This was officially higher than Dorian had ever gone.

Up. Up. Up. The blue of the sky vanished behind the wall of burning oxygen. The ship rattled. What if the damn thing wasn't even space worthy? What if they burned up before they even got out of Meridian's atmosphere?

Dorian wiped the sweat from his brow. It was too hot in here. The fire seemed to burn through the glass. Did he hear screams coming from the holding bay? He couldn't be sure. The engines were roaring, and sometimes he heard screaming in the back of his thoughts. The screaming from the concert the night of the invasion.

The holo blinked wildly. Dorian kept pushing up—up—

They burst out of the heat and noise and into silence. Dorian's head bowed as the artificial gravity kicked in. It wasn't quite strong enough. Everything seemed suddenly lighter.

And then the holo exploded with a shrieking, insistent chime. Lights fluttered all around the cockpit. Dorian froze, eyes flitting—he didn't know what half of these meant.

"What's going on?" Evie again.

"I see something!" Victor shouted. "On the tracking screen!"

"Warning," said the ship's soft, mechanized voice. "Incoming."

The ship jolted, flinging Dorian up against the far wall.

"Impact," the ship said. "Assessing damage."

Dorian scrambled back into his chair and jerked the ship around.

"Damage minimal. Avoid further impacts."

"Victor!" Dorian screamed. "Did you see who it was?"

"It's a Covenant ship." Victor's voice was clipped and urgent. "Their corvette."

"Is the stealth not working?" Dorian asked.

"I think it's shooting blind. It can't see us, but it knows we're here."

"Can you fire on it?" Dorian pushed the throttle down, built up speed again. He had to get them clear. All their careful planning to get off the colony and none of them had really considered what would happen if the Covenant ship actually spotted them, or even once they breached the atmosphere and found themselves in the middle of a large-scale naval engagement.

"Yeah."

"Then do it!" Off to the side, a new screen flickered onto the holo—the weapons station. Victor processed it quickly, but it seemed to take ages. A pair of missiles visualized on the holo, blinked red, then whooshed off the console.

"A hit!" Victor shouted. "But they're still coming after us."

"Evie," Dorian yelled. "Get over here and help me."

She was in the copilot's seat instantly. "I've never flown before."

"That's fine." He swiped at the holo, brought up the copilot's station. "You're going to help with control. We're going to push this thing as fast as it can go."

On the weapons screen, another pair of missiles vanished.

"Warning," the ship said. "Incoming."

"There's another one!" Victor shouted.

"Brace yourselves," Dorian hollered, just as the ship jolted sideways. Red lights flickered in the walls. This time, Dorian was sure he heard screaming in the holding bay.

"Pull back on your throttle," he told Evie, who slid her hands over into the holo-controls. She yanked back—too fast, but it didn't matter.

They'd been tossed around so much, no one was going to notice. The ship jerked forward, building up speed.

Another pair of missiles vanished from the weapons station holo.

"Good job, Victor," Dorian said.

"I think that did it. They're turning around."

Dorian risked glancing over his shoulder at Owen, who was lying still on the floor. His face was an unnatural gray. Blood mottled his armor. For another panicked moment, Dorian thought he might be dead.

But then he lifted his face. His eyes glittered darkly.

"Punch into the military comm channel," he said roughly. "The one I showed you. And give them this code. Nine. Alpha. Sierra. Three." His words were swallowed up in a fit of coughing. "Tango. Do you have—"

"I got it," Dorian said. He glanced at Evie. She nodded.

"Keep pulling on that throttle," he said. "We need that speed."

He waved his hands over the holo, pulling up the comm system. Punched in the military channel they'd tried to use back on Meridian. This time, it worked. A gruff voice crackled through the speaker: "Identify yourself."

Dorian leaned forward, repeated the code from Owen, his voice trembling. Part of him was afraid it wouldn't work.

But then the voice said, "Welcome back, Spartan. Stand by for assistance."

CHAPTER TWENTY-FIVE

SASKIA

Saskia stood beside the closed hatchway of their starship, her plasma rifle pulled and ready. Behind her, the survivors were crammed into the holding bay of the ship, their voices low and frightened and urgent.

"They're finalizing the air locks." Dorian's voice crackled over the speakers. Saskia took a deep breath. She wasn't sure she quite believed that they had made it through the battle, plasma blasts ricocheting off the outside of the ship, the survivors all jostling together in the panic. For the first time, she'd truly felt like a part of the town, as they'd been flung wildly through the black, uncertain of their fate.

Saskia still wasn't certain of anything. Dorian had come on the speaker and said they'd been picked up by a UNSC cruiser, that they were clear of the fighting, that everything was going to be okay. But she'd carried her rifle anyway. She had brought all these people this far. She wasn't going to let her guard down now.

Harsh grinding noises erupted on the other side of the closed hatch. Alarmed voices rose up behind Saskia. She lifted her rifle, arms trembling. *Please*, she thought. *Let it be safe.*

Yellow light cracked around the edge of the hatch. The air hissed. The hatch pulled away.

A woman in a UNSC officer uniform stood on the other side.

Cheers erupted from the closest survivors and trickled back through the ship. Saskia gasped with relief and dropped the Covenant weapon. It clattered against the ship's metal floor. The UNSC officer glanced over at her. Smiled a little.

"Were you going to shoot me?" she asked.

Saskia shook her head. "I just—I wanted to be sure—"

The officer nodded. "Pick up your weapon. If you want to help them, help me get some order here."

People were already surging toward the hatchway, but the officer stepped in front of them, her hands held up. "Single file!" she shouted, her voice cutting through the roar of hope and excitement. "You will need to sort yourselves out as you board the *Sparrow*! This is for your own safety."

People were shuffling forward, only half listening. The officer glanced at Saskia. "Go on through. Help direct people."

Saskia nodded. She slipped her rifle onto her back and passed through the hatchway, through the airlock, and then onto the deck of the *Sparrow*, a huge, echoing, cavernous space with the same burning engine fuel scent as their own ship. UNSC soldiers were everywhere. One of them stopped her. "Are you a survivor?" he said.

Saskia nodded, dazed. "The officer on the ship—she told me to help direct people."

The soldier grinned. "Fair enough. We're funneling people into two areas. Corridor six for anyone in need of medical treatment." He pointed to the right. "And corridor twelve for everyone else. We're setting up food and supplies for them right now." He pointed toward a brightly lit hallway behind him. "You got that?"

Saskia nodded. She turned around just as the first of the Brume-sur-Mer townspeople were crossing over to the *Sparrow*. It was a young family, two parents, a little boy. The mother blinked up at the ceiling, her face drawn and pale.

"Are you injured?" Saskia asked, stepping forward.

The woman turned toward her. Blinked. "You're the one who saved us," she said. "Who brought us out of the shelter."

Saskia's cheeks flushed hot. "I did what I had to."

"Thank you," the woman whispered, and then she wrapped her arms around Saskia in a quick hug, which Saskia returned, her thoughts fuzzy.

The family was not injured, as it turned out, and so Saskia told them to head toward corridor twelve. She looked at the faces of the survivors, of the people she had saved, as they left the rescue ship. Directing them aboard the *Sparrow* was so much easier than anything she had done since the start of the invasion. She told them they would be safe; she told them food was waiting for them. Some of them blinked dazedly at her. Others, like the young mother, thanked her and embraced her. Almost everyone had tears in their eyes.

"Saskia!"

The voice was a familiar note in the cacophony of the ship deck. Saskia turned around just as Evie flung her arms around her, pulling her into a tight hug.

"We did it," she whispered fiercely. "We got everyone to safety."

Not everyone, Saskia thought, although she pushed it away. Now wasn't the time to dwell on everyone they'd lost.

"Have you seen my dad?" Evie asked.

"Not here," Saskia said. "But I saw him back on Meridian. I'm sure he'll be disembarking soon."

Evie nodded, her expression strained. "The others wanted me to find you. They took Owen away—he'd gotten hit pretty bad, but—" Her voice faltered.

Ice gripped tight around Saskia's heart. "What?" she said. "Is he okay?"

Evie tried to offer a smile. "I think so. I think he'll be fine." She hesitated. "He has to be fine, right?"

But before Saskia could answer, Victor ran up to them, throwing one arm around Evie's shoulder. Dorian strolled up a few moments later.

"Good flying," Saskia told him.

He rolled his eyes. "I hope I never have to do that again."

"You got us through when it counted," Evie said. "That's what's really important."

Dorian nodded and looked out at the crowd, his eyes flicking back and forth. Saskia didn't know how many times she had seen that expression on the faces of the survivors as she guided them away from the rescue ship. That frantic desperation as they tried to find someone they'd been separated from.

The others were doing it too, scanning the crowd, the faces hopeful and afraid. Something shrank up inside Saskia's chest—she had no one to look for. Her parents, if they were still alive, wouldn't be coming off that ship.

Suddenly, Victor let out a shout of excitement and bolted away from the rest of them. He darted across the floor to an older couple with tears streaking down their cheeks. Saskia knew immediately they were his parents. His mother swept him up in an enormous hug and buried her face in his hair while his dad leaned over the both of them, saying something Saskia couldn't hear over the noise of the corridor. Victor pulled away from his mom and started talking, gesturing wildly with his hands, his parents' expressions a blend of awe and pride and terror.

"You see your family?" Saskia asked, trying to mask her own disappointment.

"No, not yet," Evie said, her voice tight.

But Dorian broke into a huge laugh, his whole face lighting up. "Remy, Max!" he cried. "Over here!"

A little boy with the same shiny black hair as Dorian came barreling out of the crowd. Dorian dropped down to one knee and pulled him close, still laughing.

"I'm so glad to see you, buddy," he said, tousling the boy's hair.

"Is this Remy?" Saskia asked. Evie was still scanning for her father.

"Sure is." Dorian straightened up. "Remy, I'd like you to meet my friend Saskia."

"Hey," Remy said, giving a little wave. But then he immediately turned back to Dorian. "We were down in the shelter!" he exclaimed. "It was the first time Dad ever let me see it! And then the water started coming in and *whoosh*!" He turned around like he was caught in a riptide.

A tall, rangy man stepped up to them, put a hand on Dorian's shoulder. "You made it through," he said, his voice quiet. "I can't tell you how happy that makes me."

"Same here," Dorian said. He ducked his head, hair falling into his eyes. "I still don't know what happened to the guys. We were on the boat when the Covenant attacked—"

"Let's not talk about that now." The man—he must be Dorian's uncle Max—pulled Dorian into a half hug. "I hear they're serving food down in corridor twelve. You hungry?"

Dorian nodded and grabbed Remy's hand, and the three of them slid away into the crowd. Saskia watched them go, a tightness coiling in the back of her throat. Tears stung at the sides of her eyes, and she blinked them away before turning back to Evie.

Except Evie wasn't there.

For a moment, Saskia just stood in place, aware of the reunions happening all around her. She felt like a pillar, like part of the ship. Solid and invisible.

"Saskia!"

Evie's voice cut through the noise for the second time. Saskia looked up, and there she was, cutting through the crowd, pulling her dad behind her.

"There she is," he said, wrapping his arms around her. Saskia blinked in surprise. "I hear you saved my daughter's life."

"She saved your life too," Evie said.

"She sure did." He grinned down at her. "You were a vision coming into that shelter. We'd all pretty much given up hope."

Saskia's cheeks flushed hot. "I did what I had to do."

"Saskia's parents were out of town when the invasion started," Evie said.

Mr. Rousseau's expression flickered. "Is that so? Do you have a way of contacting them?"

"Once I get to a working comm system," she said softly. The tears were threatening again.

"Well, I'll make sure that happens," Mr. Rousseau said. "In the meantime, why don't you come with us? We're going to get cleaned up."

Evie grinned, her smile incandescent. "We'll stick together," she said. "It'll be okay."

Saskia nodded. The cold knot in her chest was unraveling. Evie reached out and grabbed her hand and pulled her along toward corridor twelve, and for a moment, Saskia felt a fraction of what it was to find your family waiting for you on the other side of horror.

Saskia sat on her cot in the middle of the refugee barracks, checking her comm pad for the millionth time. She'd sent dozens of messages to her parents since the town had been picked up by the *Sparrow* two days ago. Not a word in response.

She knew there was a chance they were dead. But she knew as well there was a chance they had gone to ground, that they hadn't received her message at all. It was painful, the not knowing, especially since Victor and Evie and Dorian had all found their families.

Saskia tossed the comm pad aside and fell backward on her bed. The noise of the refugee barracks swarmed around her: a hundred familial conversations. Almost the entire population of Brume-sur-Mer, relocated to a UNSC ship in the middle of empty space and spread out over four barracks.

Almost the entire population—but not quite. There had been casualties—the names had been coming in the last two days, and already a memorial was starting to form in the corridor linking the four barracks. A holo flashing images of the dead, their lives caught in a loop of some happier time: celebrating a birthday, dancing at a wedding. Flowers made of scraps of old metal lay in makeshift bouquets on the floor. People scrawled messages on the metal walls: *I love you. I'll miss you. We'll be together again.*

Saskia and Evie had both knotted roses out of old clothes, an old woman two bunks down showing them how to do so. The roses had been for Dorian's bandmates. Their names had come in yesterday morning. Xavier Dupont. Alex Linville. Hugo Chastain. Saskia thought of watching them play as she twisted the fabric around into the approximation of a flower. In some ways, it had seemed like such a pointless gift, but it was also everything she had to offer.

"I've been looking for you."

Saskia blinked at the voice. "Owen?" She lifted her head off the cot.

And gasped. It was Owen, only he wore a crisp UNSC military uniform rather than his heavy, plated armor. He smiled, patted his side.

"They got to me just in time," he said.

Saskia jumped off her cot and hugged him without thinking. She was surprised when he returned it.

"I can't believe you got better so quickly!" She pulled away from him.

"We're designed to." His smile broadened. "I was actually sent to fetch you."

"What?" Saskia's hopes glimmered: Had her parents decided to surprise her? Had they shown up on the *Sparrow* without letting her know first?

Owen smoothed down his coat. "Naval Intelligence wants to see you."

All that hope washed out of Saskia. Goose bumps rippled over her forearms. "ONI? Why?"

"I'm not entirely sure. But they want to see all four of you."

"Now?"

"I'm afraid so."

Saskia looked down at her clothes: a drab cotton shirt, a pair of loose-fitting pants. Everyone in the refugee barracks had been issued the same clothing.

Owen put his hand on her shoulder. "You look fine. They know what you've been through."

"I look like garbage," Saskia said.

Owen laughed. He actually laughed, like a real human being, someone who understood jokes.

"I looked a lot worse during my first meeting with ONI," he said.

Owen guided her forward, toward the exit. Out in the corridor everything was quiet save for the soft hum of the ship's engine and the clicking of Owen's regulation shoes on the tile. The holo-images at the memorial flickered silently as they passed.

Saskia's heart pounded. ONI! What could ONI possibly want with her? With all of them?

Eventually, they came to a narrow door at the end of the corridor. Owen pressed his hand against the identification lock and the door slid open, revealing a conference room lit with garish yellow lights. The others were already there, along with a tall, angular woman dressed in a dark, severe suit set. She smiled thinly at Owen.

"Thank you, Spartan. Saskia Nazari, welcome."

Saskia crept forward and slid into a seat beside Victor. She hadn't seen much of the others since they'd arrived. They'd been caught up in their families, and anyway they'd all been placed in different refugee barracks, spread out across the ship.

Owen sat down at the far end of the table. The woman stayed standing. She held a military-issue black comm pad in the crook of one arm, and she tapped at it, reading the screen.

"Before we begin," she said in a clipped voice, "I must remind you that the conversation we are about to have is highly classified as part of the functional operations of the Office of Naval Intelligence's XEG presence on this ship."

Saskia glanced over at Victor beside her. He just looked dumbfounded.

"Excuse me," Dorian said, leaning forward, folding his hand on the table. "What exactly is XEG?"

The woman stared at him, and for a moment, Saskia was sure she was about to have him shot. But then she said, "The Xeno-Materials Exploitation Group. We'll explain more in due time. Now, as I was saying." She swept her gaze around the table. "What you hear in this room is not to leave this room." She peered at them over the top of the comm pad, her eyes as sharp as a laser. "Do you understand?"

Saskia shifted uneasily.

"Do you?" the woman prompted.

"Yes," Evie said first.

"Yeah," said Dorian.

The woman turned her gaze to Victor and Saskia. "And you two?"

Saskia nodded, whispered a faint yes. Victor gave his assent.

"Very good." The woman tapped on her comm pad. "You may call me Daniella. Spartan-B096 gave me a full report of your activities on Meridian."

A holo flared to life, four figures racing through a hazy gray wood. It took Saskia a moment to realize she was looking at herself, tattered and soaked with rain, clutching a plasma pistol to her chest. It was all of them. Dorian. Victor. Evie. They were marching through the forest on their way to rescue the townspeople from the shelter.

Daniella looked up at the room as the holo played out across the table. "I reviewed the feed recorded by Spartan-B096's armor during your activities. I must say, I was very impressed. We all were."

Saskia shivered. Who was *we*? She wondered suddenly if there were others watching this meeting, behind cameras or trick windows. She forced herself not to glance around.

"We are planning on giving all four of you the UNSC Medal of Honor."

Victor let out a strangled gasp.

Daniella turned to him. "I see at least one of you recognizes it. As for the others . . ." She paused, smiling faintly. "The Medal of Honor is our highest civilian award. You four will be the youngest to ever receive it."

Saskia felt dizzy. She pressed her palms against the top of the table to steady herself.

"We'll be announcing it publicly, as part of an award ceremony. It should boost morale among Meridian's survivors. However"—Daniella flicked her hand dismissively—"that is not why I'm here."

Saskia barely heard her. The UNSC Medal of Honor! She looked across the table at Evie and Dorian, who seemed just as stunned.

"In his report, Spartan-B096 mentioned that you found evidence that the Covenant were attempting to retrieve a Forerunner artifact. That is—concerning to us." The holo froze. It no longer showed the four of them marching through the woods, but rather the Covenant drilling structure in Old Brume, in the moments before the explosions went off.

Daniella set the comm pad down and leaned over the table, her eyes piercing. "We want you to go back."

"What?" squawked Dorian. "After we nearly killed ourselves getting *off* Meridian?"

Evie jabbed her finger in his rib cage, scowling. He glared at her.

Daniella just smiled at this, however. "We'll train you, of course. And equip and compensate you. All four of you were set to graduate this year, so this isn't terribly unconventional, and you will be the appropriate age by the time we're finished. We can conduct a truncated version of our ground operatives training program."

"Truncated?" asked Victor.

"We don't know how much time we have before the Covenant uncover the asset. We've developed a specialized team to secure the artifact before the Covenant do. All four of you have skills that will be immensely beneficial. Besides which, you know the terrain better than anyone we have on our side. You proved extraordinarily adept at avoiding the Covenant. We want to know what that artifact is. We want"—she paused, her eyes glittering—"to potentially retrieve it for ourselves, to aid with the war effort."

Saskia drank this all in, her heart thudding. They wanted to send them back? It seemed cruel, after everything they'd been through. And yet she couldn't deny the thrill Daniella's words had sent down her spine. She would be *immensely beneficial*.

Daniella straightened, smoothed out the harsh lines of her suit. "We won't be sending you off to training tomorrow, of course. You'll have time to rest and recover. To see your families."

"And if we don't want to go get ourselves killed for ONI?" Dorian asked. "I mean, it's always easier sending kids to die, isn't it?"

Daniella smiled. There was something predatory in her smile, Saskia thought. Something dangerous.

"You're not a child, Dorian."

Dorian frowned.

Daniella tilted her head. "I know you aren't the UNSC type," she told him. "But you won't be part of the UNSC. Not officially. You'll be a special . . . militia organization, a subset of Meridian's local defense force that's working directly with ONI. No one's going to make you cut your hair."

Dorian rolled his eyes. Daniella just gave him that harsh smile again.

"Think about it," she said, to all of them. "This week you rescued your town from certain destruction. Now's your chance to rescue your entire colony, and all of humanity."

She didn't give them a chance to respond to that. Just scooped up her comm pad and strolled out of the room, leaving them in the stifling fluorescence.

For a moment, they all sat in silence. Owen was the first to speak.

"I know it seems like too much," he said, very quietly. "But give it time. Civilian life will be hard for you now." He paused. "You'll see."

Saskia looked across the table at Evie and Dorian. She looked at Victor, slumping back in his chair, his expression vaguely stunned. She thought about the four refugee barracks, crammed with the population of a town she had never thought she was a part of. She had brought them here. Her parents had abandoned her to an invasion, and she had fought back instead of hiding.

"I'll do it," she said, so quietly it was almost a whisper.

Evie jerked up her head. "Really?" she said.

Saskia swallowed. "Yeah. I want to do it." She smiled at Evie, at Dorian. At Victor, who smiled awkwardly back. "But I don't want to do it alone."

The room buzzed with silence. Saskia wasn't sure what they would say. She wouldn't blame them if they said no. They had families.

"You won't have to," Evie said.

"Yeah," Victor said. "You won't."

Everyone turned to Dorian. He shook his head, looked at some spot on the wall. "Yeah," he said. "I'm in too."

It felt too enormous a decision for such a small room. But Saskia knew it had really already been made for them, during their week down on war-torn Meridian. Their town had burned, and they had changed.

Somehow, they had become heroes.

ABOUT THE AUTHOR

Lightbox Shop Photography

CASSANDRA ROSE CLARKE's work has been nominated for the Philip K. Dick Award, the *Romantic Times* Reviewer's Choice Award, the Pushcart Prize, and YALSA's Best Fiction for Young Adults. She grew up in south Texas and currently lives in a suburb of Houston, where she writes and serves as the associate director for Writespace, a literary arts nonprofit. She holds an MA in creative writing from The University of Texas at Austin, and in 2010 she attended the Clarion West Writer's Workshop in Seattle.